ALSO BY NEIL CONNELLY

Brawlers (forthcoming novel, fall 2019)
Into the Hurricane (forthcoming novel, fall 2017)
The Pocket Guide to Divorce (A Self-Help Work of Fiction)
The Midlife Crisis of Commander Invincible
The Miracle Stealer
Buddy Cooper Finds a Way
St. Michael's Scales

IN THE WAKE OF OUR VOWS

Stories

Neil Connelly

Fomite

Burlington, VT

ISBN-13:978-1-942515-71-5
Library of Congress Control Number: 2016961038

Fomite
58 Peru Street
Burlington, VT 05401
www.fomitepress.com

Cover art— Meghan Fleming

For Carol and John Wood,
my teachers

Contents

Acknowledgements

Abiding thanks to my wife Beth and our sons, Owen and James.

I'd like to acknowledge all the writers I worked with as a professor at McNeese State, but especially those from fiction workshop, among them Corliss, Michael, Camron, Marymarc, Matt, Judd, Nic, Mike, Billy, Shonell, Megan, Michelle, Casie, Jessica, Carol, C.D., Chris, Charles, Josh, Max, Emily, Dan, Carver, Sarah, Jason, Matt, Elizabeth, Vanni, Brendan, Stacey, J.D, Charley, Scott, and Brittany, as well as Daniel, Bryan, and Summer. When we were meeting in the Mallard Room and I was your teacher, it seemed wrong to share how much I was drawing inspiration from you. But I suspect you knew anyway. In any event, thanks.

I'd also like to gratefully acknowledge the editors of the literary journals which provided a home for the following stories included in this collection:

"Dear Literary Agent, Editor, or Publisher" *Literary Salt*
"Excepts from a Billboard Diary" *Sundog*
"Failure to Thrive" *Life and Legends*
"Pretend This is Your Baby" *Southeast Review*
"The Lost Art of Believable Make Believe" *Pembroke Review*
"People Like That, People Like Them" *Blue Lyra Review*
"The Complete and Illustrated Guide for Meeting Your Most Sacred
    Obligations as an Altar Boy" *Santa Clara Review*
"Henry Wants to Know Your Name" *Grist*

"Holding Your Peace" *Southern Indiana Review*

"What Walter Lost" *Mulberry Fork Review*

"The Dad in Question" *Gulf Stream Literary Magazine*

"The Trials of Isaiah" *Scintilla*

"Nine Times I Failed My Second Wife" *Southern Indiana Review*

"Still" anthologized in *Tartts Six* (Livingston Press)

Dear Literary Agent, Editor, or Publisher,

ENCLOSED PLEASE FIND (PLEASE! PLEASE!) a manuscript you deem completely without merit or potential. I sincerely hope you can reject me as soon as possible as I am faced with a deadline of sorts. Here's my dramatic situation: under the terms of a recent court order signed by the Honorable Judge Francine Kleinschmitt, 2nd District Court, City of Lake Charles, I must "vigorously pursue any and all avenues" which might lead to the publication of my novel, *Stations of Love*. Judge Kleinschmitt defines the progress of this pursuit in terms of rejection. Specifically, in order to avoid being held in contempt of court, fined and jailed, I must submit at least six letters of rejection from literary professionals every thirty days. This is the part where you come in.

Understand that Kleinschmitt isn't some fan trying to prompt me to literary greatness. She's just eager to ship forty percent of any proceeds from my writing straight to Brenda, my recently exed-wife, and her attorney Jeffrey, who's been filing more than legal briefs with Brenda, if you catch the key I'm singing in.

Kleinschmitt thinks I'm stalling, waiting a while before making an honest effort. What she doesn't understand is that rejection's a way of life with me, a hobby like building bird houses or painting by numbers. She doesn't realize I could wallpaper West Texas with all the bad news that's come through my mailbox. To complicate matters, the good judge wasn't at all pleased with how I handled my big "success" a few months back, when the *Under the Rainbow Review* accepted an excerpt that got sent out about a billion years ago. Once I got over the shock, I wasn't too upset. I realized they only paid two contributor's copies; so, via certified mail, I shipped one copy to Brenda's. How the cover got ripped off I'll never know.

Now that my circumstances are clear, I have to ask a special favor. Back in my college days I was assistant editor on *Millipede: The Literary Journal of a Thousand Voices*. Truth be told that's where I met Brenda. (Whatever else I may think of her these days, she's always been a hell of a good reader.) Anyway, I know what it's like to have those towers of manila envelopes cluttering up your office. And like you, I dreaded the times I felt compelled to write a personal note to accompany the standard rejection form letter, struggled to think of something kind to say that was also the truth. I'm mentioning all this because of a troublesome stipulation in that court order. Anything rejected with a form letter doesn't count. So the thing is, I need you to go to bat for me. I require a dated, signed rejection on company letterhead. Two originals would be ideal, as I could then keep one on file. Kleinschmitt needs to confirm these are legitimate rejections. She wants specifics, no doubt eager to read them by the fireplace in that big old house she lives in alone. I understand the gigantic hassle this will be for you, but in an effort to minimize your workload, I thought I'd point out a few things in the manuscript:

Larry, the main character, is weak-minded and unlikely to be sympathetic to many readers. His decision to stay in Kirbyville is clearly motivated not by his love of Laura, as suggested, but by his fear of striking out and making something of himself. He acts out of the belief system that if he does good things, good things will eventually happen to him. That worked fine for Forrest Gump, but readers simply won't buy it from someone who's not a bit off kilter.

Laura's devotion to Larry despite his series of catastrophic failures strains the boundaries of credibility. Perhaps she'd be supportive through his bouts of pseudo-alcoholism and the bankrupting of his landscaping firm, but after his blunder burns down the trailer, does Laura have to actually hold his hand as they stand in the ashes? This reeks of sentimentality. (That's exactly the kind of thing Kleinschmitt would love to see: "This manuscript reeks of sentimentality.")

Two Christmases ago we were visiting my family in Ohio and I accidentally threw away the only draft of chapter four. Brenda spent three hours in the garage plowing through turkey guts and wrapping paper until she found it.

There are eleven misspelled words in the first chapter alone as well as numerous comma splices. Apostrophe usage is spotty at best.

The extended descriptions of the natural world, especially those concerning the park Larry and Laura take walks through and eventually make love in for the first time, are self-indulgent and call attention to the writer. Loaded words like "lush" and "blooming" lose all meaning because of overuse. The reader is likely to cringe when Laura suggests holding the wedding under the weeping willows that line the river. (Actually I'm the one who suggested an outdoor wedding, but Brenda's allergies would have gone haywire.)

3

Similarly poorly conceived and executed is the Easter parade in the penultimate chapter. Larry and Laura's big fight, including her melodramatic declaration "Our love is dead," seems contrived, and is clearly little more than a set up for what follows. While having an Easter float hit a little girl in a bunny costume may be visually intriguing, her miraculous resurrection, complete with concerned members of the Kirbyville High School marching band huddled around her, comes across as uninspired and heavy-handed. Note the following passage:

"Larry and Laura stood side by side, like two dead statues that couldn't move or touch. On the street in front of them, the bunny girl gazed longingly into the clear spring sky, as if she knew she might never see clouds again. Then her eyes closed peacefully. A bloated tuba player started to cry. Somewhere a lost dog began to bark. A lonely church bell chimed. Laura's hand slid into Larry's and he folded his fingers around hers. The bunny girl blinked and one of her fuzzy white paws twitched twice and the air filled with life and possibility."

In court Brenda testified that this scene was based on a childhood experience of hers involving a mockingbird that seemed dead until she warmed it between her cupped hands. Then it fluttered to life and flew off. Though this was a total lie, I found her tale strangely moving.

In addition to the overall saccharine tone of the novel, the point of view switches several times, freely entering Laura's mind in some instances while in others inexplicably avoiding her thoughts. This is especially true in moments of intimacy. For example, when Laura's high school love reappears in chapter five and offers to steal her away to Hollywood, her rejection of him is a forgone conclusion, yet the reader has no idea why she is so dismissive of the offer. Why so quickly refuse the chance at her childhood dreams of acting? Laura's loyalty to Larry seems insufficient rationale.

It's kind of ironic, but that Easter parade scene was once Brenda's favorite. I read her the whole chapter in bed the night I finished it, and I remember how her eyes softened and her breath went light, as though she was being . . . I don't know, transported? Like my words had lifted her above the weight of our crappy cars and our 18.9% Visa bills and the lady downstairs who beat her kid. That's one hell of a feeling. Maybe it was all just in my head, but it seems like nights I read to her our love making was different somehow, sharper. Nights like that you're plugged into something primal and pure, something essential. Something you miss.

Brenda writes too—poetry. And before we got married she used to read it to me some nights. Her inner landscape was populated by deadbeat dads and latchkey kids, lovers lying back to back with their eyes wide open. As her work grew darker, she became protective of her rough drafts. If I wandered into the back room while she was writing, she'd dial down the computer screen, and she started keeping her poems on a disc she buried in her sock drawer. That disc was something I should've subpoenaed. Who knows how much evidence I've missed.

I can't be sure Brenda's mockingbird story was a lie. Maybe she told me and I forgot it.

I should mention the considerable support I've received from many in the publishing industry. Only a few have sent just form letters, and some have misguidedly included encouragement, even praise. I trashed the letter from White Pine Press because the editor went into the manuscript's "barely submerged potential" and claimed the second half "crackled with energy." He apologized for not having space for it in his spring line-up. That guy just didn't see the bush for the berries.

Much more on board were the enthusiastically negative responses that came in from certain New York agencies. Not to be too pushy, but the following are near perfect examples of the kind of rejection I'm hoping for:

"Unremittingly optimistic. Almost fairy tale-like in its simplicity and naivete."

—Carl Thayer, Stanford Wilson Artists United

" . . . hard to imagine any mature adult reading this with any degree of believability."

—Amanda Dmuchovsky, Pearson and Associates

"All foreplay and no sex."

—Celeste Donahue, Carson Literary Alliance

"Perhaps you should consider turning this into a screenplay for *The Fmily Channel* or *Disney*."

—Gene Williams, Williams & Williams

(Thank you Mr. Williams! Kleinschmitt ordered me to send a copy to both, so soon I'll have rejections from Pat Robertson and Mickey Mouse.)

In fairness to the manuscript, I suppose overall it may be a little on the upbeat side. But in my own defense I must point out that the work underwent a major revision during the first year of our marriage, the happiest time of my life. I was graduated and feeling lucky to be assistant managing at the Books-A-Million. Brenda was starting her last year of undergrad at USL, talking about Ph.D. programs in Poetry. Things weren't perfect or anything, but we had it better than a lot of couples.

I suppose the first signs of trouble appeared after we moved into the house on Sixth Street. This was after the novel had been out to maybe a dozen places and back again. Despite these failures, Brenda convinced me to keep trying and even got me to work up some of the better passages as excerpts. She put all her energy into getting me published. In hindsight her enthusiasm seems even stranger because she had begun to lose faith in herself about this time. Only three of the seven grad programs she applied to had accepted her, and none had offered an assistantship. I remember the Saturday that she got her rejection notice from LSU, her first choice. Right after she read the letter, she stormed Office Depot with the Visa, mailed out fifty copies of a ten-page excerpt I didn't even like.

The worst memories, the flashbacks I'd pay cash to have burned from my brain, involve coming home from the bookstore after Brenda was already back from school. Days she'd already gotten the mail and seen those self-addressed stamped envelopes returned home like beaten carrier pigeons. She'd leave them unopened on the kitchen table, pretending she didn't recognize her own handwriting. And when I'd come in she'd always greet me at the door, always hug me and ask how the bookstore was. Always with that smile.

It got so bad that I took to driving home on my lunch break just so I could intercept the postman and steal my own mail. I'd sneak my stash back behind the mall, park behind Sears, and read my rejections with the engine running. Then I'd pitch them into the open mouth of the industrial size dumpster as if I was getting rid of evidence the FBI might be after.

Now this went on for quite a while, and you might wonder if that kind of constant bombardment had an effect on my confidence. I will admit those days brought a certain reduction in the faith I had in my writing. After all, my hopes had been high. Some very good readers had thought well of early drafts of this piece. Brenda in particular had felt publication was a strong possibility. This was years ago, just before we'd started dating. She was the first reader I gave a "completed" draft to. We met at O'Toole's and went through her reactions over a pitcher of beer. I remember she told me she found it "uplifting and inspirational." When she went to the bathroom, I scribbled those words on a bar napkin and saved it, tucked it away in the pages of the manuscript. After we got married, I used to imagine showing the napkin to her on some distant wedding anniversary, the two of us laughing at how far we'd come together.

Under oath, Brenda testified that the manuscript had "significant literary value" and that her professional opinion was that "publication is a high likelihood with the proper commitment of time and resources." Those weren't her words. Jeffrey the lawyer told her to say those things. But it was nice to hear her say them, nice to think again that she believed in me. It'd been nine months since I heard her say anything about my fiction, and that had hardly been under the best circumstances. It was the Sunday we fought in the Lake Charles Municipal Animal Shelter parking lot. The fight disintegrated like these things do, and before long I was mocking her "martyr poetry," saying she'd probably wear a hair shirt if she ever gave a reading. I'd only said that after she told me I was wasting my time writing "Santa Claus fiction." But she regretted that, I think. That day in court, after she'd spoken Jeffrey's carefully scripted dialogue, her eyes found mine and she leaned into the microphone and said, "Really. It is a good book. A very good book. One of the best things I read in a long time." I saved that page of the trial transcript.

The pound parking lot. Our last scene. As an editor/publisher/agent, you'll appreciate this. We'd gotten up early like we did any Sunday we weren't hung over. I'd made French toast while Brenda went and got a paper. In the "Life" section was this "Pet Corner" feature. Some pure-bred collie named "Shadow" was due to be gassed first thing Monday morning if nobody came for it, and Brenda wanted to go down and save it. I remember thinking about the poor guy who had to start every Monday morning off by gassing dogs. Things between me and Brenda were going sour by then; I'd spent more than a few nights on the couch and such, so even though I hate dogs I said sure. Besides, Shadow was kind of cute, even by my dog-hating standards. On the drive over I acted all cheery, like this was the best idea since multiple submissions. But by the time we got to the pound, some other couple had brought Shadow home, or so we were told by the chunky blonde in charge.

The kennel was oddly full of sleepy-eyed couples whose breakfasts had clearly been similarly disrupted, and I had a pretty strong suspicion that this "Shadow" had simply never been. Brenda figured the same thing. She was pissed in a major way, on the verge of making a scene like only she can. I could really imagine her going after that blonde. There'd be pulled hair and cracked nails. But instead Brenda huffed off, and just as I was about to follow her, I heard this crazy barking that made me stop.

I can't explain it, but that barking called me back into the crowd, through all these people eyeing up the dogs that were working the system. Dogs that sat and wagged their tails and longed for love like lined up orphans, eyes wide with the mad notion that somebody might actually want them. Brenda followed.

My barker was housed in the cell at the end of the hall, next to a steel door painted sky blue. He was some kind of mongrel mutt, marked by a dark patch under his chin and a tail that had seen better days. Brenda and I watched him. He'd hunch curled up in the corner for a minute, then spring and charge the cyclone fence, foaming and snarling, retreating only after he'd backed off whoever was looking. Here was one dog who knew why he was in the kennel at the end of the hall. A dog that knew what Monday mornings meant. But despite that, he was changing the script. He was never going to give another snot-nosed brat the chance to slide behind Mommy's leg and say, "But he's so ugly."

I said to Brenda, "Let's take this one home."

She wanted nothing to do with this dog and thought I was being sarcastic. But I was dead serious. I'd had a vision of Larry and Laura saving this dog, turning its whole life around, bringing it on trips to their special park where it would snap frisbees from the air and chase children squealing with delight. I wanted that dog to be in our lives. When I told Brenda this, she shook her head and bolted. By the time I caught up with her we were in the parking lot, which became the setting for our final fight. We went at it and eventually she dropped that line about my "Santa Claus fiction." There was a long silence. A couple came out with a puppy straining against a red leash. Brenda said, "Look. I'm sorry. But I just can't do this with you anymore." Then she got in the car and drove away. Just to show what a sick twist my mind can take, I stood in the center of that parking lot thinking, "This is when I get my epiphany."

I waited for half an hour, then called a taxi.

It's not hard to imagine how things went from there, a montage of the worst kind of clichéd scenes: The awkward meeting at the grocery store. The terrible hour with the counselor. The Wednesday night that went too far. The series of drunken phone calls. The morning she showed up crying in my doorway. And finally, the lunch where she told me she had "seen somebody about filing the paperwork."

But somehow Brenda and I skipped the scene where we talked about what had gone wrong. That's the one question I wanted to ask her on the witness stand, the one question that keeps me staring at the still ceiling fan at 3 a.m. Because in all this time, Brenda's never really told me why.

This is crazy, but last week a manila envelope was forwarded to my apartment. I pulled it free of the mailbox and saw my name in Brenda's handwriting. Almost immediately it registered that this was simply one of the long lost rejections coming back from the Office Depot batch, much like the one I need from you. But I couldn't keep from fantasizing that it contained a message from Brenda herself, and I settled onto the steps with all my midnight wonderings and I imagined what she might write:

Dear Aspiring Husband,

Thank you for submitting yourself for inclusion in my life. I understand the time and effort you put into your life and appreciate the opportunity to consider it. To begin with, let me point out the many favorable qualities I do see. You have an optimistic tone and a crisp style, along with a fine instinct for light-hearted humor. However, you remain surface level and seem unaware of your own emotional center. What really matters to you? Ultimately, I just don't believe in you as a character.

Because of this I'm going to take a pass here. But please don't feel bad. This is not to say someone else might not find many appealing qualities about you and your life. It's just not for me.

Fondest wishes,

Brenda

I've got that manila envelope, still sealed, in a box in the back of my closet. It keeps company with the official letters Jeffrey sends over and the page I saved from the transcript and Kleinscmitt court order and copies of my rejections and yes so help me God even that stupid tattered napkin from O'Toole's. I have poured over those pages absolutely certain that waiting somewhere is a theme, a moral, an answer. But none of this matters. That story is over.

Before I close I want to thank you for the time you spend with my manuscript. And although I'm confident you'll have no problems finding ample evidence for rejection, I hope some passages are somewhat appealing. As hokey as that little girl miraculously coming to life at the Easter Parade may seem, I'm not ashamed of the section. And I don't think my handling of Larry and Laura's first night alone is all that sentimental. After all, people still make love in parks; they have to.

Though I know I've already asked you for a lot, could I trouble you with one more favor? If maybe you like one of the scenes, or find something engaging in the text, could you jot out a quick letter, separate from Kleinschmitt's of course, mentioning what you liked and why? I'd really appreciate any positive comments, even the briefest of notes.

Who knows, maybe in the midst of all these legal shufflings, I might accidentally paperclip such a note to some court document that Brenda's eyes might fall across. Despite all that's happened, I know she still cares for me. Deep down. (What I said before about Brenda and Jeffrey, I made that up. Brenda's not like that). I can imagine Brenda smiling when she sees the note, when she wraps herself in a quilt on our old pullout sofa bed and warms with the memory of what it was like to believe in the book and believe in me. And who knows, maybe she'll find herself wondering about the need some people have for rough drafts, and the way stories can transform with revision.

Many thanks for all your time and consideration. Looking forward to hearing from you very much.

Excerpts from a Billboard Diary

DAY ONE, JULY 1ST

I didn't agree to live on a billboard for the chance to win a Winnebago. Chris and Paul did though, that's clear enough. It's all the two of them talked about once we were alone, the "Winny" and the ten grand. Chris plans to "See America," from Niagara Falls to the Golden Gate, visiting every crappy tourist trap in between with his wife and their two kids. And Paul, he fantasizes about tailgating the Penn State games, home and away, drinking and playing poker with a legion of old dorm buddies. Paul's the type who pictures God to be a lot like Joe Paterno in the old days. Kind, benevolent and wise. And always following an obvious game plan.

When they asked me about myself, what I'll do if I win, I fed them the same cover story I concocted for my official entry: I'm a freelance copywriter from Gettysburg, a town I drove through for the first time two days ago. I remembered that PBS special, and Miranda being disturbed by the association of those bright open meadows with bayonets and amputations. My R.V. fantasy involves reckless driving, rock concerts, and "babes," the kind of crap I figured the management at a classic rock station would eat up. And, of course, they did. So nobody knows the truth, that I'm living on this billboard for a higher purpose.

DAY FOUR

Our first big fight. Middle of morning rush hour Chris decides this should be a non-smoking billboard. Gives Paul a lecture on second-hand smoke. I thought the exhaust from Route 22 made Chris' argument a little weak. So when they turned to me for the deciding vote, I orchestrated what I consider a solid compromise. Paul can smoke in his tent and behind the billboard by the Port-O-John, but not on the platform out front.

We watched the fireworks from a distance tonight, trading my telescope back and forth. Chris said they were coming from some place called Dorney Park, where he goes twice a summer with the kids. Between beers Paul would comment. "Wow." "Nice one." "Look at that."

DAY SEVEN

Buddy Shifter, of Buddy Shifter's Recreational Vehicle Paradise, appeared in person today. He seemed small. Though after a week beneath his fifteen foot smiling face, I guess that perception is inevitable. Using the supply basket, he sent up a gift, a bullhorn like police use to talk down suicides. We've been having a hard time communicating with people down below.

Paul, whose lobster skin sunburn has not improved, came out of the shade to test the bullhorn. He leaned over the railing and asked Buddy how many Winnebagos he's sold like the one on the board.

Buddy held up four fingers and smiled and suddenly seemed just like his picture.

DAY TWELVE

People continue to congregate at the base of the board, bearing offerings like pilgrims. Today's haul included a bottle of Jack Daniels, some sunglasses, a bra and three Bibles. Paul claimed the bra. Most folks wander over from the mall parking lot, where my Honda still sits, what's left of all my worldly possessions crammed inside. Our visitors have no trouble crossing the four lanes of traffic, as rubbernecking continues at an alarming rate. We stopped waving so as not to encourage gawkers.

Reluctantly, I packed up the telescope early tonight. The lights from the billboard completely kill the stars, so I can't even make out Venus, though I know it's there.

It's been fifteen years since I read anything from "The Book of the Apocalypse." I wonder how St. John felt, receiving all those images of the future in a single flash.

DAY FIFTEEN

Same old routine. Chris' wife and kids stopped by around sundown, waving from the overpass with the same "We Miss You Daddy" sign. After they drove off, we all huddled around the radio in front of my tent. Chris told us that Christine asks the craziest questions. "Why are you my Mommy and Daddy?" "Why wasn't I born a hundred years ago?" "Does Jesus know what I'm going to have for breakfast tomorrow?" "What if I want to be an astronaut but Jesus wants me to be a secretary?" These, I agreed, were hard questions.

Tonight, Paul told us another story about his college days while downing seven or eight Rolling Rocks. Chris drank a couple to be sociable. Again, I abstained. I have to be focused and sharp when the revelation comes. I have to understand the rest of the plan.

DAY EIGHTEEN

Here is a copy of the last list we sent down to Webster:

Sun block, maximum SPF

Some fresh decks of cards

Books (Stephen King, Tom Clancy, John Grisham)

Some Playboys, maybe a Penthouse (Chris objected, Paul insisted.)

A beach ball

Softer toilet paper

Cigarettes—preferably Camels (We need more because Chris has taken up smoking.)

DAY TWENTY

Cops finally towed the Honda today. I wonder if they'll trace the serial number. I can picture Miranda, standing in the kitchen with that orange and nectarine wallpaper I hated forever, picking up the phone and saying, "Pennsylvania?"

And then, I suppose, she'll put the phone down.

DAY TWENTY-THREE

The police have posted a car to enforce a minimum 45 mph speed limit on 22. After last weekend's bottleneck, people are getting pissed.

The *Morning Call* article ran to three columns. Front page of the local section. They used only one statement I made, and misquoted me, claiming I saw life on top as a "freak opportunity." What I said was "unique." A unique opportunity.

Much to Paul's disappointment, we've abandoned the notion of three man poker. Simply not workable. Chris suggested we ask Webster for some board games, said Nancy makes quite a hobby of puzzles.

I haven't shaved in eight days.

DAY TWENTY-SIX

Marco, a worker from Adams Advertising, came up to change the billboard today. New one again features a giant-faced Buddy beaming over a Winnebago, though the slogan's been changed from "The Road to Freedom" to "Freedom Wheels!" Another addition is a blonde directly over Chris' tent, smiling in front of the Winny with her arms thrown over her head and her chest straining against a red, white and blue t-shirt. Paul claims he can make out her nipples in the field of stars and has named her "Betsy."

Marco gave us the news on down below. Most betting pools say we'll all crack by the end of August, but Shifter is hoping we make it to October, a slow month for R.V. sales. As he was packing his gear, Marco asked us if we had any "special needs" and pinched an imaginary joint to his lips.

Just before he descended, he wished us all luck and we shook hands. I realized he was the first human being I had touched in twenty-six days. I didn't want to let go.

Day Twenty-eight

Paul's mother came by and sent up some fried chicken and a blueberry pie. She reminds me of Aunt Bea, and I see where Paul gets the extra weight from.

Again we all slept most of the day, gathering to monitor the afternoon traffic jams. Paul added Louisiana and Oregon to his license plate list. When he asked how I knew the state mottos, I told him I guessed.

Around 8 we had the fried chicken, then sampled a.m. radio shows all night while attempting Yahtzee, a game I didn't care for. Something about all those dice disturbs me.

Day Thirty-one

Trouble tonight. Chris frisbeed the Risk board into the forest behind us when Paul captured Greenland, a strategic keystone.

That broke things up, and I settled alone in my tent and got to thinking. It's been over a month but I'm not getting impatient. I'm in no rush here. Still, it couldn't hurt to meet things halfway. So I eased onto my cot and closed my eyes and listened and waited. There was the whine of the billboard lights outside my tent. The drone of dull traffic, single buzzes spiking and shrinking. A plane pulling free of the airport. A car kicking to stubborn life by the overpass. For a moment, I thought I heard waves. But nothing else. Not yet.

Day Thirty-five

Paul's best story tonight involved his sophomore year road trip to Daytona Beach, where some schmuck had a drunken run in with a transvestite/hooker. "Poor guy got a handful, if you know what I mean." In the story the schmuck was some unsuspecting friend of a friend, but I think it was Paul. Most nights he talks for at least an hour and a half, though after a month I've never heard one detail about his life since he graduated. That was two years ago.

Day Thirty-eight

Nancy and the kids waved a fresh sign from the overpass tonight: "Hang in There Dad!" Then they slipped into the Perkins Cake & Steak as the sun disappeared. Chris borrowed the telescope to watch his family eat dinner. Nancy had some kind of chicken pasta. Chris told us she's a great cook. Gourmet leftovers. Best mother in the world. He'll make it all up to her. Buy her a diamond necklace with the prize money. Nobody deserves it more.

Here is the schedule of the talk shows we've settled on: 4-7 *Sportsflash!* 7-10 *Rush Limbaugh*. 10-1 *Learning to Help Yourself*. 1-3 *The Loveline*.

Day Forty-one

WPVI sent a news crew up from Philly, a camera man and a redhead reporter raised up to interview us from an electric-company basket. Even across the six feet of open air between us, I breathed in the scent of her shampoo. Oranges.

At one point in the interview, she asked, "Do you have any message for your friends and loved ones?"

The camera turned to Paul. "To all the guys from Packer Hall, have one for me!"

Chris smiled and stood very still. "Hi Nancy. Hi Jennifer. Hi Christine. Daddy loves you all. I'll be home soon. I love you Nance."

I was preparing some funny white lie like, "Honey, I think I left the iron plugged in," but when the camera man aimed the lens at me, the redhead raised her microphone and asked, "What brought you up here?"

Miranda flashed in my mind, somehow seeing this from two time zones away, and my tongue turned to stone. Why am I up here? I thought about the wrong turn. But it wasn't a wrong turn.

Finally Paul stepped in. "He's here for the same reason we are." He pointed to the billboard. "Freedom Wheels!"

I am not up here because of a wrong turn.

Day Forty-seven

Today was Chris' anniversary. Eight years. Nancy and the kids came by just before rush hour, and Chris lowered the roses he had Marco pick up for him. "Something nice," he'd told him, "but don't make it look too expensive."

He explained to me later that Nancy doesn't like it when he spends a lot of money on non-necessities.

Paul stayed in his tent today. This heat is just too much for his body.

Day Fifty

The station threw a party for our fiftieth day on top. Webster announced that our billboard is the most viewed advertisement in the Lehigh Valley. Buddy Shifter said he's sold nineteen Winnebagos since this party got started. He likes to spread his good fortune. The prize money's been doubled to $20,000.

Day Fifty-one

Yesterday's party made CNN. Just a thirty second spot before a commercial break. I thought those cameras were local. I wonder why Webster didn't have them interview us.

Chris is up to two packs a day. He taps his ashes on the railing and watches them drift down to nothing. Paul's decided to try and quit altogether, a good choice considering his health.

DAY FIFTY-FIVE

Marco brought up a paper with him today. Some council woman, Amelia Baxter, wrote a letter to the editor saying we were "The biggest disgrace to hit Allentown since that Billy Joel song." She went on to say that "the nationwide CNN audience witnessed the dehumanizing depths to which big business will sink in search of a buck." She also said we looked like bums.

In the basket today was some soap, shampoo, a few razors, and a clipper. Paul and I took turns cutting each other's hair. Chris cut his own.

DAY SIXTY-FOUR

The deal with "The Geraldo Show" fell through at the last minute. Buddy Shifter refuses to pay Geraldo for on-air advertising. Webster won't cover the board.

Paul's parents came by and his mother pleaded with him again through the bullhorn. Same story. Come home. We're sorry we yelled about the DUI. His father simply stands there with his arms crossed.

I asked Webster for a CB radio so I can listen with the truckers at night. I watch them go by with the huge antennas mounted on their cabs and I wonder how much they can pick up, what kind of messages they can pluck from the air.

DAY SIXTY-NINE

Nancy and the kids stopped by today. Haven't seen them in a while.

And they didn't really stop by. They pulled onto the shoulder on 22 and waved. No sign. The kids were wearing school clothes so it must be September. September?

Paul was reeling up the bullhorn, but by the time he had it, Nancy was sliding back behind the wheel. She honked the horn twice, then laid tracks into rapid traffic.

Paul held the bullhorn and asked, "You must miss her awful, huh?"

"I miss her," Chris said. "Of course I miss her. She's my wife."

DAY SEVENTY-TWO

Bitch Queen Supreme Baxter won't let up. Her new angle is that the billboard is zoned for business, not housing. A court date is set for next week. She can't pull us down yet. I have to be here when the time is right.

Paul and Chris played Battleship tonight. I stared into the bright haze the billboard lights throw off and tried to remember the constellations.

"A-17."

"Miss."

"B-21."

"Miss."

"A-18."

"Miss."

"D-33."

"Miss."

"A-19."

DAY EIGHTY-TWO

We all listened to the Penn State-Pitt game on a.m. radio today.

It felt like old times, all three of us laughing together. We made hot chocolate and did the wave. Paul seemed very happy. The final score was Nittany Lions 34, Pitt Panthers 22.

Day Eighty-nine

Paul's mom brought a quilt out today. She made it herself. Along the rim is a chain of stick people holding hands.

Marco told us he'd have to raise his prices. Nothing personal. Market forces.

Day Ninety-four

As soon as I saw the Aerostar coming down that off ramp, I knew it was going to hit the guy in the Jeep. He was changing lanes so he could get off, but the Aerostar didn't see him. The Jeep slammed into the rear corner of the Aerostar and cartwheeled back into the passing lane. The Aerostar jolted up and over the guardrail, then nosedived into a ditch. This was maybe two hundred yards from the board.

Paul and Chris turned to me, like one of us should run down. I trained my telescope on the Aerostar and saw an arm hanging out the driver side window. The arm was wearing a wedding ring.

But I didn't do anything. Looking back on it now, there were a good dozen motorists already at both vehicles, far faster than I could have gotten there. But I didn't even try. The thought of leaving the billboard never even occurred to me.

Day One Hundred

Our big party got canceled. Probably all the ruckus lately. Today there were protestors out here, led of course by Bitch Queen Supreme

Baxter, who made a speech. Inhumane she calls this. Says we're all going crazy. Dehydrated and malnourished. She's drafting a letter to Amnesty International. Paul wanted to piss on her head, swore he could douse her good, but I talked him out of it.

Chris finished off the last of the weed tonight.

DAY 113

That court-appointed doctor showed up today. Said we all needed to bathe more and handed over some antiseptic soap. He also said we needed to get more exercise, especially Paul.

I heard Chris ask the doctor for sleeping pills.

DAY 122

Nancy's sister brought the kids by yesterday. They were dressed in their Halloween costumes. One was a cheerleader and the other was Cinderella or something. Chris couldn't tell which one was Jennifer and which one was Christine.

Paul's cough is getting worse.

DAY 132

The nights are too cold to sit outside and talk like we used to. Paul sat in my tent this evening in silence. He looked at my books and flipped through *Making Sense of the Stars: A Beginner's Guide to Astronomy*. He recognized the term *alignment* from when his car didn't pass inspection.

Chris continues to mostly keep to himself. I heard him shuffling cards tonight and slapping them down. We asked Webster for some kerosene heaters, but he told us anything like that would be a fire hazard. Insurance. You understand.

They want us down. We've become a liability. Screw them man. That's what Paul says. Screw them.

DAY 138

Thanks to the kindness of Councilwoman Baxter, we all three now have electric blankets. Together with the double thermals, it's not so bad.

DAY 142

Chris is gone. Gone gone. No note to us or anybody. He didn't take anything we could tell, but according to the cops who came up here to question us, there's no trace of him.

I didn't like it when the police were up here. They frightened Paul.

DAY 148

I tried for almost five hours straight but still couldn't relocate her signal. I inched up and down and back and forth along the a.m. range, and even though I couldn't tune her in again, I know it was Miranda. She spoke in another language, some tongue I've never known, but the ebb and flow of her voice, even for those few seconds, was enough for me. If only I could've secured the right frequency, if only I'd have been blessed with perfect reception.

DAY 152

Thanksgiving on top. Turkey and such from Paul's mom. As we ate he said, "The holidays must be rough for you."

When I asked him why, he answered, "Well, you know, with what happened to your folks and all."

I'd forgotten that particular lie and regretted it. It was wrong of me to lie to Paul.

Day 161

If Marco set this up, I'll jam my thumbs through his eyes. It's one thing to smuggle up a few joints and some porno mags, but this was bad. I mean, those noises Paul made. When I woke up, I thought somebody was hurting him. And then afterwards, the way she opened my tent flap and smiled at me. Like we were old friends.

Poor Paul. I had to plead with him to untie his tent flaps. He cried for two solid hours, apologized for inviting a stranger up top, and finally confessed that he flunked out of Penn State his junior year. I cradled his head and said, "It's okay. I forgive you. We'll just put this behind us. I forgive you." And I pretended Miranda was saying these words to me and it felt like a dream, like the kind of thing a man wishes for in his last moments before dying.

I wanted Paul to know the truth. And I was ready to tell him about how and why I left Miranda, and the seven weeks I drove every day, south out of Oregon, then east and north again, those nights spent in rest stops and McDonald's parking lots. And how I felt drawn here into Pennsylvania and the glorious wrong turn off 78. How can I describe the sight of the sunbeams flaring out from behind this billboard as I neared? How can I explain seeing the construction workers preparing this platform and the words arching across the Winnebago, "What Would You Do To Be Free?" That was my sign. That was how I knew that in all the universe, this was exactly the place I was meant to be. So I came up here and waited for my message, waited for word on what to do next.

But by the time I finally started talking, Paul was fast asleep.

Day 167

We listened to Penn State lose to Notre Dame today. Paul seemed to take it in stride. He's quiet a lot, but that's okay. I sent a note down in the basket for his mother requesting some more chicken with rice soup, which seems to be his favorite.

Day 173

Webster wrote us a nasty letter demanding we put Paul's tent back up. We rolled the note up with some weed and smoked it. Screw them. That's what I told Paul. Screw them. After all it's simply a matter of practicality. Even with both cots there's plenty of space inside. And with Paul's tent down now as well as Chris', we finally have a bit of elbow room up here.

Day 181

Heavy snow today. I sat Paul outside and made a snowman in our yard, sticking a joint in its mouth to make Paul laugh.

We tried some Christmas carols to lighten our spirits, but the only one we knew all the words to was "Rudolph the Red-Nosed Reindeer." There's only so many times a man can sing a song like that.

Day 190

Tuned in to "Dick Clark's Rockin' New Year." Paul tried to stay awake, but drifted in and out of sleep. Sometime after the ball dropped, he woke with a shout. He'd had a dream that I'd left him alone on top. That I'd just crammed all my things into my duffel bag and left in the middle of the night without any explanation. I shuddered, remembered the chill of the early Oregon morning, and told him I'd never do that kind of thing. Never.

Day 197

I fear the worst. Paul's illness seems to have entered a new stage of some kind. Again last night he shivered so much it kept me awake, and again this morning our sleeping bag was wet with sweat. When I mention a doctor he almost weeps. He thinks they'll make him come down. He's right, I'm sure. I'll give it two more days.

Day 210

The doctor they sent up was a quack. I didn't trust him with Paul, but he'll be better off in a warm hospital for a few days. I have to do what's right.

Day 211

Webster visited first thing this morning. Through the bullhorn he congratulated me. Plans for party tomorrow to welcome me down, present me with the keys to the Winnebago. Got angry when I told him Paul was coming back. Illness like this clearly an exception to the rules of the contest. Webster said his goddamn contest, his goddamn rules and I was damn sure gonna get off the goddamn billboard. That's what he called my home. The goddamn billboard.

221

The siege escalates. No food again in supply basket, just a certified letter stating I was being charged with destruction of private property. Scraps of Buddy's fifteen foot face still cling to the bare tree branches beneath me.

Somebody cut the bullhorn chain during the night. Sometime soon, they'll be coming for me. Let them try. Just let them try.

224

I don't know how she got past Webster's fence, or how she found me, but it was so good to see Miranda again. I woke in the dead of night, freezing between electric blankets, and there she was, right inside my tent, wearing those same green flips-flops and cut off jeans that she wore that first day on Peppercorn Street. Her half top showed off her pale belly, peach fuzz and all. Even her hair was somehow long again, spilling gold across her shoulders. She didn't say anything, but her smile and her eyes told me I should leave this place. No messages will come to me here.

227

Paul, I hope this diary gets to your hands. I want you to have it. Forgive the things I wrote in the early days.

I'm not sure when Webster cut the power, somewhere during the night so no one would notice. My blankets went dead and I woke up stone cold. From inside the tent I noticed the glow of the billboard lights was gone, and I went outside to investigate, wrapped in your mother's quilt.

And oh, Paul, how I wish you could've been here. How I wish you could've stepped with me into the early morning darkness and seen the heavens restored. All the sharp stars above me again.

But when I looked for the Big Dipper, it wasn't there. Orion, Cassiopeia, Taurus, all absent. I scanned the sky for some familiar marker and found none. And when the highway began to hum with traffic below me, I looked down at the thickening stream of cars, at those people, thousands of people hurling ahead, and I wondered how they all knew, how they'd become certain of their destinations.

Failure to Thrive

I WAS THE FIRST OF THE moms in playgroup to notice the man on the bench. He sat in the shadow of a live oak on the far side of the walking trail that circles Drew Park, about a hundred feet away from the picnic table that we gathered around every Wednesday afternoon. He wasn't doing a crossword puzzle or reading a paperback or eating a late lunch. But he also wasn't leering, taking photos, or offering candy. He was merely sitting, staring in the general direction of the huge pirate ship on which all the children played. Anyone occupying that bench would automatically face the kids. The thirty-something man was dressed in Dockers and a dress shirt, the kind of outfit I'd likely pick out for my husband, Brad. That first day, he seemed more mysterious than threatening. So when one of the other moms asked me what I was looking at, I kept him to myself and told her I thought I recognized an old friend. The lie came easily.

The following Wednesday, the second in October, while Marlene and Kristi spiked straws into juice boxes, I saw the man stroll into the park from the entryway down by the lake. He followed the walking trail until he reached his bench. Angela, who never brings her own juice boxes, asked once again if she could borrow one for Frankie Jr. I caught Marlene's eye roll, intended only for Kristi. Marlene said, "Of course. I always pack extra. Just in case."

The roar of a Medivac helicopter from St. Jude's drowned out any other snide remarks. It zoomed just above the pines, racing toward some distant crisis.

The sound didn't wake my ten-month-old, Thomas (always Tommy to Brad), who was sleeping by my side in his blue stroller. About twenty feet away, still dressed in their private school uniforms, Lou, Ashtonia, Blake, Miles, Crawford, and Frankie Jr. clambered over the rope ladders and slides of the pirate ship. They ignored Kristi's juice box invitation and kept playing. Angela's daughter LeeAnn worked a purple crayon over her coloring book at the edge of the picnic table. As a general rule, LeeAnn preferred the company of adults.

The other moms settled into familiar conversation: accomplishments of their children, the plans for the upcoming Halloween party, and the relative flaws of their husbands, all of whom work at ChemCo, one of the chemical processing plants across the lake. Kristi filled us in on Hank's newest home renovation disaster. Frank Sr. hunted every weekend, worked long hours, and always hired sexy receptionists. "Do they always come ditzy and blonde?" Angela asked, apparently oblivious to the fact that she fit the description. Marlene's husband Todd had recently installed an HDTV in their bedroom. "The other night he was watching one of those shows on HBO," she said. "I come out of the bathroom ready for bed and strangers are screwing on my wall. In high def."

They munched on pretzels shaped like tools.

"What about you?" Kristi asked me. "How's that Brad?"

I looked down at Thomas, hoping he'd wake.

"C'mon girl," Angela pressed. "Dish a bit." All three of them stared at me. I thought of Brad's moustache, meticulously trimmed just above his lip.

At the pirate ship, Ashtonia and Lou shoved each other on the plank and screamed. It's a ten foot drop. The other moms stayed focused on me, waiting like a jury.

"Have you noticed that guy on the bench?" I finally said.

Following my eyes, the other moms turned. I went on. "Kind of creepy, don't you think?" I did not, in fact, think he was creepy.

"Maybe he's waiting for someone," Marlene offered.

"No," I told them. "He was there last week too."

"I didn't see him," Kristi said.

"He was there."

"Somebody should call *Dateline*," Angela said. "We have a possible perv sighting."

"He's too cute to be a pedophile," Kristi said.

"What's a pedophile?" LeeAnn asked, and we all looked at her holding her purple crayon.

At that awkward moment, cries rose from the pirate ship. Ashtonia and Crawford wailed from the plank. Below them, Lou lay face down in the mulch, weeping. It took the moms a few minutes to dry tears and sort out who needed to be placed in time out for how long. All the racket woke Thomas, and he wouldn't settle till I pulled him from the stroller. He blinked, cried, and raked a fingernail across my face, as if in retaliation for waking him up. LeeAnn shook her head and continued coloring.

When I looked back at the bench, it was empty.

*   *   *

THE THIRD WEDNESDAY IN OCTOBER, the man was there when I arrived. Usually I steer Thomas' stroller straight across the lawn and duck through the swings, but I gave in to the urge to get a closer look. So after I gathered up the diaper bag and strapped Thomas in, I followed the gravel walking trail. At the picnic table, I saw Kristi and Marlene turn and notice me. They watched to see what exactly I would do. I felt important and interesting.

As I neared the man on the bench, his gaze stayed fixed ahead of him. It seemed undeniable that he was, indeed, watching the children play. The gravel's crunch turned his face and for a moment our eyes came together. "Hello," he said. His hands remained on his legs, but he fluttered his fingers in greeting, like he was playing the piano. He had strong hands. I flirted with the idea that he was a musician, composing in his head.

I said "Hi" and kept moving.

He glanced at Thomas and smiled. It was genuine but reserved.

The dominant impression I gathered from the encounter was that the man was tired. Although he was clean shaven, his eyes looked weary and his shoulders sagged. There was an aura of heaviness about him. Death in the family? I wondered. Lost dream? Broken heart?

I had not told Brad about the man on the bench, though he asked on a regular basis how my day went as soon as he arrived home. He was always careful to get a full report on what Thomas had eaten and when, how long he had slept, the nature of his bowel movements, etc. By October, it had reached the point where what I wanted most to say was, "Why do you need to know any of this? Don't you trust me to take care of our son?" Even taking into account Thomas' "diagnosis," Brad's questioning was extreme. The whole thing had the tone of a returning parent's interrogation of a suspect babysitter.

For my part, I offered no more information than was asked of me. I did not tell him that Thomas played in his crib after his naps and I would, from time to time, leave him there while I watched the end of an afternoon movie or emailed my old friends at the firm or called my mother. I even stashed his favorite truck in the corner, hoping for ten extra minutes. He was happy to play. It was Brad's idea that I stay home with Thomas, and I enjoyed taking care of our son. But it was lonelier than I thought it would be. Every now and then, I'd even take a phone call from a telemarketer and listen to his pitch, just to hear a grown up's voice. If Brad noticed I was lonely, he did not mention it.

Kristi's husband worked in the same lab as Brad, and when the suggestion came in mid July that I join the playgroup, it felt more like a summons than an invitation. Brad thought it would be good for Thomas, even though the kids were much older. He had to learn to socialize. This all closely followed Brad's sister's conclusion that Thomas was sick. *Failure to thrive* was the term she'd found on the internet. The condition covered a variety of symptoms: below-average growth, absence of sustained eye-contact, disinterest in play, irritability, a general withdrawal. Though I thought it silly, Brad took off work to accompany me to the doctor's office.

Sitting on a stool in a bright room the size of an elevator, Dr. Bennet said we shouldn't be too worried about Thomas' fluctuating weight. He'd lost a half pound in the eight weeks since his previous visit. This was atypical but not alarming. He said we should wait and see how some other indicators developed. Brad, who not only held Thomas the entire time but also answered all the doctor's questions, wasn't comforted by Bennet. In the clinic parking lot, he strapped our baby into his car seat and told me about the playgroup. It was just a good idea for all involved, something he'd been meaning to suggest. But I knew Brad was holding back. I knew that he blamed me. He had found me wanting as a mother just as he'd found me wanting as a wife.

Back in August, when he began trimming his moustache, I did not ask him about it. He did not ask me about the second glass of wine I began having at night. And this is how our marriage had settled in the year since our son's birth.

When I reached the picnic table after my reconnaissance mission that third Wednesday in October, Marlene greeted me wide-eyed. "So what did he say?"

I considered lying, then told them, "Just *hi*."

LeeAnn climbed down and waved at Thomas. "Can I push him on the swing?"

I shook my head and Thomas reached for her crayon. She let him have it.

Kristi said, "He's looking at us right now. He's looking at you still."

Angela took out her cell phone and said she was going to call the cops.

"Don't be silly," Marlene said. "He hasn't done anything. Yet."

Thomas sucked on LeeAnn's crayon. I took it away and gave it back to her. "I don't think he's going to do anything."

"Did he have a ring?" Kristi wanted to know.

"Didn't notice."

"What kind of guy just hangs out in the park?" Angela asked.

While the older kids played, I propped Thomas in a swing and pushed him gently. He seemed interested in the movement and the trees. Behind me, the other moms engaged in wild high school specu-lation. The man on the bench was an undercover cop; a park design-er studying how kids played; a participant in the witness protection program; a doctor from St. Jude's taking a break; a recovering addict from Holman House who walked all the way from Broad Street. LeeAnn stopped coloring long enough to propose that he might be an alien studying our primitive culture. She asked again if she could push Thomas and I relented.

As for myself, I decided that the man on the bench was indeed from the hospital, but he was no doctor. His little girl was sick, I was certain, cancer perhaps, and she was in mortal danger and her mother was dead or uncaring, so only her dad could love her, and he did it all day and night, he never left her side, except for half an hour when she took an afternoon nap. He left behind the sterility and walls so white they hurt your eyes, strolled down by the lake and then here to the park, and he breathed the rich air and watched the healthy children and prayed for the day when his baby girl could join the other kids.

As we were leaving that day, cutting under the swings on the way to the parking lot, I lingered in the back of the pack and let my eyes wander over to the man on the bench. He was watching. I left one hand on the stroller, but lifted the other slightly and stretched my fingers toward him as if casting a tiny spell. And he nodded, just a dip of his chin really, then went back to looking at the children. I admired him for his love and devotion. I knew he could use a friend in hard times like these. I thought about his strong hands and determined to tell no one our secret.

That night I woke from a dream. The kind I hadn't really had since early in college, before Stephen, and long before Brad. The man on the bench was there and we were alone, together. After I woke, there was a moment when I was surprised to find Brad next to me, turned on his side and snoring softly. One night in my second trimester, I woke with the craving that sometimes grips pregnant women, and I stirred Brad by nibbling on his ear, caressing his chest. But once he came awake, his hand settled over mine. He held it still. The silence in the room was crushing. I felt underwater, the pitch black bottom of the ocean. Brad whispered, "The baby. I don't want to hurt it." In all the months since Thomas has been born, I haven't disturbed my husband's peaceful dreams.

So that night when the man on the bench visited me in my sleep, I accepted his embrace without shame or guilt. He gripped my hair and looked me in the eye. And when my waking interrupted us, I finished the dream by myself, with my sleeping husband beside me.

THAT SATURDAY, BRAD TOOK THOMAS over to visit with his Mawmaw and Pawpaw. I begged off, claiming I had a list of errands to take care of. Laundry. Walmart. That kind of thing. Brad didn't seem to mind that I wasn't joining them, and I thought again of checking his cell phone for recent calls. I imagined him complaining to whoever she was about how little I was involved in Thomas' life. Early on in our courtship, I realized that Brad had a habit of trimming his moustache when he planned on kissing me and making love. I found it endearing and cute and never told him I noticed. As the pregnancy wore on, the wiry hairs grew bushy and thick, all but covering his upper lip. Then this past August, with Thomas eight months old and asleep in the crib, I heard the snipping of the scissors in the bathroom one night. At first I was elated—misguided fool—and I quickly changed into one of the slick nightgowns Brad once found enticing. I slid under the covers and pulled the sheets up to my chin, waiting to reveal that I was equally eager to renew our love. He brushed his teeth, stepped into our bedroom and kissed me on the cheek, rolled on his side and faced the wall, same as he'd done every night. Staring in the dark at the ceiling fan, I came to the obvious conclusion. Given my experience, I had no right to be surprised. I wondered who she was, fleetingly, and I determined then and there to say nothing, ever.

So on that Saturday, while my husband and child played at his parents', I felt no particular guilt when I drove past Drew Park on my way to Walmart, even though it's on the other end of town. From the parking lot, I saw that the bench in question was occupied by two middle aged women, and an unexpected sense of relief came over me. In the pharmacy at Walmart, when I was picking up ointment for diaper rash, I did not buy condoms.

On the way home, my mind refused to settle. I told myself to be practical. I had milk in the back, ice cream. But when I passed my exit on the loop, I knew where I was going. Pulling into the parking lot, I felt silly and childish. Then I saw him on his bench and there was only the allure of something dangerous.

He didn't see me get out, and without thinking much about an alibi for my appearance, I approached undetected. At the last few feet, he turned. Recognition was instant. "Well hello," he said. "You don't usually come here on Saturdays."

"Why do you even know that?" I asked.

He shrugged. "People tell me I'm observant."

I stood there and he studied me. I thought of what I was wearing, sweat pants and a t-shirt. I noticed he wore no ring. He caught me looking. At the pirate ship, children yelled and laughed. Finally he asked me, "Where's your little one?"

"With his father," I said, feeling like this might keep me safe from myself.

A strange smile formed on the man's lips, one I couldn't read. "That's nice. It's important for a boy to be with his daddy."

Together, we watched some kids shooting baskets.

"You know," I said, "two of my friends think you're dangerous."

"That means one of them doesn't."

"Yeah. She figures you're just weird."

He laughed. "Weird and dangerous. I've been accused of worse. What about you?"

For a few seconds, I thought he wanted to know what I'd been accused of. Then I realized what he was asking. "I'm not quite sure what to make of you."

"A guy can't sit on a bench," he said without hostility, "not if there are kids around."

I looked at him. A jogger passed behind me on the gravel path. The man on the bench looked at the pirate ship then back at me. I said, "You have kids of your own?"

He sighed, then stood. From his back pocket, he pulled out a laminated name tag on a white rope necklace. It read *Lionel: Assistant Kitchen Manager.* "I'm here on my break from St. Jude's. I work in the cafeteria. This time of day, nobody's eating anything but lunch leftovers."

"I'm sorry," I said. "I didn't mean to make you explain yourself. It's just, it's clear that you're watching the kids play."

"This is a relaxing place," he said. "But if it makes you and your friends uncomfortable, I'll sit down by the lake when you're here. Really, that would be okay. I'm a white guy. This is the only stereotype I can complain about."

"Don't be silly, Lionel," I told him. I waited for him to ask my name.

Instead, he glanced at his watch. "I need to get back. Enjoy your exercise."

My confusion must've shown on my face.

"Your walk, whatever it is you came here for."

I couldn't tell if he was being coy, but he held eye contact with me until I looked away. We didn't exchange goodbyes when he left. But I watched him walk down the trail to the lake and turn towards the hospital. Just before he disappeared from view, he glanced back to see if I was looking.

Just outside my house, I thumbed the button to raise the door on the double wide garage and saw Brad's truck. I parked and began bringing in the groceries. He met me in the living room and lifted the packages from my hands. "Thomas played so hard he exhausted himself, so I bailed," he explained. "He's passed out in his crib."

I went out for more bags. While we were unpacking in the kitchen, Brad told me his mom asked about me. "She says she calls here during the week and you never answer."

"I'm fine with Thomas," I told him, thankful for caller I.D. "We have plenty of fun."

"I know that," Brad said. "It's just . . . Thomas really likes being over there. Mom's got nothing to fill her days, and it might be a nice break for you. She's always been good with kids."

"Yeah. She's good with kids." Inside the opened door of the fridge, I bent down and shoved a head of lettuce into the crisper. My caring husband thought I needed a break. When I stood and turned, Brad was right there. He took my two wrists inside his hands. His eyes were soft. One of his thumbs caressed my palm. "Listen," he said. "I'm worried about you."

I knew that concern like this, coming from nowhere, was a certain sign of his outright guilt. Brad may as well have confessed to an affair right there, with the cool air from the fridge rolling past us. I stared at that perfect moustache and said, "No need to worry," then pulled my arms free and went back to unpacking. We worked in silence for a few minutes, then Brad asked, "How come this Rocky Road is so soft?"

STEPHEN, MY FIRST HUSBAND, DID not give such overt signs of his betrayal. Or perhaps, more likely, I simply hadn't learned what to look for. I married him my senior year at Tulane and for three years thought I was the luckiest girl in the world. We laughed and made love and I felt special, protected. We told each other the secret things you never tell anyone else. Then over the course of a winter, things soured between us. Stephen began to insist we attend mass. On a Sunday in February after the 12:30 service, I found myself having tea with my husband and Father Vincent, who explained that he'd been counseling Stephen for some time. He coaxed my trembling husband to confess his infidelity. Stephen cried. Father Vincent passed him Kleenex and suggested we pray. I dumped my tea on the Oriental carpet and went home to pack.

THE FINAL WEDNESDAY IN OCTOBER, I was running late thanks to a longer than usual nap from Thomas. Eventually, I just woke him up. When I got to the park, I was surprised and upset to see the bench empty. But then I found Lionel at the picnic table, his broad shoulders facing me. He was sitting with Kristi, Marlene and Angie. The other moms leaned in, listening intensely. As I neared, it almost felt like I was disturbing something. LeeAnn saw me and waved, which made them all turn. Angie was wiping tears from her face. Marlene and Kristi were somber-faced, pale. Lionel looked over his shoulder, then stood and offered his hand. "Hello," he said. "My name is Lionel."

We shook, and I understood that he hadn't mentioned our Saturday meeting. It was our secret. In the center of the picnic table was a large plastic tray of quartered sandwiches and chocolate chip cookies.

"Who's this little fellow?" he asked as he bent and poked a finger under Thomas' chin.

"My son, Thomas," I explained. Thomas pushed Lionel's hand away. Angie sniffled and covered her mouth.

"It's all right," Lionel assured her. "I'm fine."

"What's going on?" I asked.

"Lionel brought us some food," Marlene said, clearly changing the subject. "He had the crazy idea that we might think he was some kind of dangerous character."

LeeAnn looked over with a raised eyebrow.

"Perfectly understandable," Lionel said. "Nobody could miss me staring. Frankly, in today's day and age, I'm surprised no one's called the police. Really, I'm terribly sorry if I caused you any concern."

"None at all," Kristi told him.

Marlene reached out and touched his arm. "We didn't even know you were there."

Lionel tapped Marlene's hand, as if consoling her. Then he said he had to be going and stepped away. "Lunch hour's never an hour. I really just wanted to meet you and your kids. They're all great." He turned to the pirate ship, where the children hung with chocolate chip smiles.

Angie sobbed and wiped at her nose with a tissue.

"Good meeting you all," Lionel said. As soon as he turned his back, the moms all fixed me with teary eyes. When he paused and returned, they brightened falsely. "Look," he said. "I feel like a total ass that I was freaking you out. The hospital is having a Trunk or Treat on the top deck of the parking garage on Friday. Six o'clock. I wasn't here last year, but everybody tells me it's a real hoot. It's open to the public." Then he turned his face to mine. "You all should really come."

After he was finally gone, they filled me in, practically cutting each other's throats to relay Lionel's story. His wife and child had been killed last September in a car wreck in Houston. Since then, he can't help but see kids and wonder about his daughter—what she'd look like, the kinds of things she'd be doing—if only she hadn't died. So he finds himself haunting parks, school yards, always because it helps him imagine her alive and happy. Marlene and Angie sobbed as Kristi finished the recounting. LeeAnn didn't lift her head from her coloring book when she said, "His cookies don't taste nice."

"Don't be rude," Kristi snapped. "Mr. Lionel is a nice man and his cookies are good."

Angie dabbed at the corners of her eyes. "Next week, we should invite him to come sit with us. It's so lonely, him sitting off by himself like that. It's terrible."

"I know we can't," Marlene said, "but we should blow off that damn plant party."

I was already thinking something along the same lines.

     *   *   *

TWO DAYS LATER, I DRESSED Thomas in a tiger outfit his Mawmaw made from scratch, complete with a hood with pointy ears and a striped tail on the seat of his pants. I strapped him into the car seat and we headed for the interstate that leads to the bridge that leads to the plant. Thomas' costume looked uncomfortable, but he didn't complain. He never complained, really. He might cry when he was hungry, but then he ate. And he cried when he was tired, but he fell asleep after a few minutes of rocking. Sometimes, when he was lying in the crook of my arm as we rocked, he'd suddenly look directly into my eyes, and I'd become certain my infant son could read my mind. He knew I married his father even though I wasn't sure I loved him. He knew that I agreed to Brad's request for a child because I thought perhaps that too might bring joy back to my life. Sometimes it occurred to me that all the bitterness I felt after Stephen had penetrated my very genetic material, that this was the reason my son was stoic and distant.

I drove over the bridge into Sulphur and only vaguely thought of St. Jude's. ChemCo's facilities are huge and overwhelming, something out of a science fiction movie. I circled the parking lot for ten minutes till I found Brad's truck and parked two spots away.

Human Resources holds social events to keep people from feeling insignificant in the global industry. They rent busses to bring families to the Houston Zoo. They have Two-For-One day at the rodeo. They invite parents to bring kids in to trick or treat at the offices near closing time and transform the cafeteria into a haunted mansion. I ran into Marlene near the front gate. Ashtonia was dressed like a witch, and she flipped her wand in my direction. Together, the four of us passed through security, where a football player and an astronaut stood guard.

Thomas seemed uninterested in the various ghosts, cowboys, and cartoon stars. As Marlene and I went from office to office, I stared down every receptionist, wondering if she was the one sleeping with my husband. One wore a tiara. Another was dressed in a striped prison uniform. None avoided eye contact. Finally I reached Brad's office and he pulled Thomas from the stroller and pecked me on the cheek. "Where's your costume?" Brad asked.

In my closet at home hung my nurse's uniform, something that in years past Brad found mildly titillating. And there was a moment right then—I remember it—when Brad's eyes showed desire and disappointment, that I wondered whether he was unfaithful at all, or whether I was simply being paranoid. But before the thought could lodge itself, I answered his question. "I'm not feeling well," I told my husband. "In fact, if it's all the same, I'd like to just head home."

Brad looked worried. "Okay, okay. Want me to stop at the Walgreens?"

"You don't have to leave. I know you wanted to show Thomas off. Go do the haunted house thing. There's two jars and some crackers in the bag."

Brad glanced under the stroller and stared at me. He didn't believe that I was sick, but didn't want to accuse me of lying.

"I'll be fine," I told him. "I just want to go home and lie down in the quiet."

"I don't have a car seat for Thomas."

"I'm parked right next to you. Take the van."

He nodded, realizing I couldn't be persuaded. "Be careful," he said.

Driving back over the bridge, now in my husband's truck, I didn't think to look for evidence of his betrayal. I didn't think about where I was going and what I was planning. I just drove.

Rising up the corkscrew ramp to the top floor of the St. Jude's parking garage, I anticipated a parade of costumed kids and loving parents, families making memories. So when I reached the top, I was surprised to find no more than a half dozen scattered cars, and no children in sight. While I tried to figure out what went wrong, one of the cars left its spot. It looped slowly around the perimeter, circling closer to me. When it came alongside me, I rolled down my window. Lionel rolled down his. "Did I say Friday? I meant Saturday. The Trunk or Treat is Saturday. My mistake."

I didn't smile at his little joke, but I also didn't look away.

"Okay then," he said. "You want to just follow me?"

His apartment was ten blocks south. The paintings on his wall were like the ones from a hotel. On his balcony, he showed me some plants he was nursing back to health and his view of the back of the mall. He offered red wine and played a jazz CD.

The sex was like sex. I turned away when we were done and he spooned up against me, pressing his nose into my hair. I slid from the embrace and got dressed facing the wall. But then, realizing that I was about to head back to Brad and Thomas, that I had nowhere else to go, I hesitated and faced Lionel. Still naked under the sheets, he said, "There's no need for you to run off."

"The wife and daughter in Houston," I said. "Total bullshit, right?"

He tilted his head, considering how to answer. "Only the part about the wreck."

"You're married," I said. For balance, I leaned into the door frame.

"If you want to get technical."

"You have a daughter."

"Haley's about seven now. She's a spunky kid."

"Don't tell me about her."

"I left them," Lionel explained. "I drove off when she was five and there's no good reason and no going back. I screwed that life up. There's my confession. But I like going to the park and pretending I'm a good dad. I pick one of those kids and imagine she's my happy daughter and every now and then I forget what an asshole I really am."

"That's pretty goddamn fucked up."

He sat up a little in the bed. "I'm sure I don't need you to tell me that." He flipped the sheet down next to him and patted the mattress. "Come on. How about you come back for round two? Then you can tell me your story."

I thought about my story. It occurred to me that Brad hadn't been cheating on me at all, that I'd simply concocted his infidelity. I had no desire to tell Lionel anything, but I couldn't bring myself to leave. "When you were on the bench and watching us, what did you think about me? How did you know I might do this?"

"I'm not sure what you're asking."

"I'm asking if I seem lonely."

Lionel seemed to think about my question and reached for his shirt on the floor. He tugged it over his head and sat half naked on the side of the bed. "I don't know. I guess maybe." He pulled his boxers on.

"Do you think I'm cold?"

Now he stood and faced me. "You're comfortable with a secret. That's all."

I wanted to ask him what it was like, leaving his family. It was the kind of thing that had crossed through my mind, now and then. I imagined a distant city, an anonymous job, an apartment with dying plants, a park bench of my own. Without speaking, I turned and let myself out.

I took the long way back to the house, driving slowly and watching the road. The sidewalks were crowded with angels and monsters. By now, Brad would be done bathing Thomas. When I got back, he'd already be in the bedroom with him, rocking him to sleep, worried about where I was, worried because he loved me. Afterwards, he'd come out and find me alone on the couch. I would have a glass of wine. I could picture all this clearly, as if it were a memory. What I wasn't sure of was how my confession would take shape. Navigating those darkening streets on the way home, I was searching for the words that would help me start, for the right place to begin.

Pretend This Is Your Baby

A T FIRST, ANDY DOESN'T RECOGNIZE the box. For the last week, he's been packing and de-junking, emptying the attic, cleaning out under the beds, preparing for the big move this weekend. Late Wednesday afternoon, he's worked his way to the closets of the rented house that he—and then later his wife—gradually filled to capacity over the last five years. It's because the house is so cramped that they decided, or rather Heather decided and Andy agreed, to buy a home of their own now that she was expecting. Halfway through the pregnancy, she's eager to arrange the new nest, a fine 3/2 with a porch and a fenced yard. They needed some help with the down payment, but Heather's father, a widowed contractor, stepped in. Three years ago at the wedding, mildly drunk on rum and Cokes, Mr. Gruzinski pulled Andy aside and said, "I like you fine. But the truth is you're just a boy and you don't know shit about shit. Not till you have kids."

None of this is on Andy's mind right now. He's on a stepladder eying up the box, which had been hidden away on the highest shelf of the utility closet, back behind Little League trophies, roller blades, and a dusty stack of high school notebooks. Even on the top shelf of the ladder, he still needs to get on his tiptoes to reach the cardboard box, and he inches it towards the edge of the shelf, then grabs it with both hands. It's a Crown Royal box—the size of a milk carton—that he picked up at the liquor store over on Broad when he was buying booze for his own bachelor party. Duct tape loops tightly around it.

Andy knows he is alone in the house, but even so he listens for a moment before descending the stepladder, holding the box gingerly. He pokes his head out into the hallway, scans it, makes his way to the living room. There he double checks that the blinds are shut, then sets the box on a coffee table covered in newspapers. He moves a bag of old clothes destined for Goodwill and sits on the couch. He feels a bit like an archaeologist who has uncovered an artifact from a lost civilization.

In the weeks before the wedding, Andy tried to spruce up the rented house, make space for Heather and her things. With a little guidance from Mr. Gruzinksi, he painted the bedroom and even installed two new ceiling fans. As part of his preparations for married life, he recalled packing this box, shoving it up where he doubted Heather could even see it, let alone reach it.

The easiest thing would be to just take the box and leave it out for the garbage crew. But Andy's already noticed one rattling pickup truck slow rolling past the pile of debris, and he knows from experience that the less fortunate folks in this part of Lake Charles have a habit of rifling through anything left on the curb. A box promising alcohol, one sealed with tape, would be difficult to resist. No, he can't just leave it out front.

Andy checks his watch. He has just about two hours before he has to meet Heather at the hospital. He looks at the duct tape and his eyes roam the room. There are stacks of boxes everywhere, newspapers, a broom tilted in the corner, an emptied-out entertainment center, but he can't locate the exacto knife. Viewing this as a minor sign of sorts, Andy decides to leave the box sealed. He takes a quick shower.

When he's getting dressed, he picks out a nice collared shirt, like the ones he wore on early dates with Heather. The hospital is where she works, and he should look his best. The first night, he wore a t-shirt he bought at a Metallica concert in Houston, and only when he arrived did he realize it was a little out of place. Andy buttons the shirt as he navigates the maze of moved furniture and finds himself again in the living room, where the box has been waiting.

He steps to the front window and splits the mini-blinds, scoping out the yard and the tree-lined street. None of his neighbors are out. He carries the box to the rear of his red Mustang, a car that looks good but runs terribly. He balances the box on the bumper, opens the trunk, tosses it inside. He can't help glancing over his shoulder. Relieved by the empty street, he gets behind the wheel and starts the engine. The loud roar used to give him a charge back in high school, when he bought the Mustang. He wonders now, with the engine idling, where the best place might be to go get rid of this box.

He drives first to the Prien Lake Mall. He works as an Assistant Manager at The Crooked Joystick, a small chain store that rents and sells video games. Distractions at LSU caused Andy's grades to slump, and he "took a semester off" to re-prioritize. The job was to keep him busy, get a few bucks in his pocket. That was seven years ago. But he still enjoys working at the mall, thrives on the energy of the young crowd and the easy stimulation of the video games. Sometimes Heather mentions on-line universities, leaves the Sunday classifieds out on the table. At twenty-seven, he is the oldest worker in the store aside from the manager, Albert. The younger employees don't know quite what to make of Andy, though they don't mind letting him buy six packs for them now and then.

He pulls the Mustang alongside the massive dumpster back behind the Sears. There are only a handful of cars in this isolated corner of the parking lot, mostly employees', and he cranes his neck all around, but he is alone. Confronted with the imminent loss of the box, he wishes now that he'd have sliced open the duct tape, poked around inside even if just for nostalgia's sake. He's mildly shamed by this desire and by his reluctance to part with the box. A lady with blonde hair pedals past the Mustang on a bike.

Andy pictures himself getting out, going around to the trunk, throwing the box through the slid-back gate of the dumpster. But the Cineplex is right there, and the rear doors could open at any second, spilling squinting moviegoers into the parking lot. He also sees a white golf cart puttering around the parking lot down by JC Penney. Between over-eager security and nosy teens, there's no end to how this could go wrong.

Andy shifts into first and drives off. He has an hour and a half till he has to meet Heather.

He loops around Lake Charles, over the 2-10 bridge, through the chemical plants in Westlake, then over the 1-10 bridge with the crossed buccaneer pistols adorning the railing. By the lake, where the huge barrel trash cans could easily swallow this relic, a family is having a birthday party. There are balloons and a piñata. He drives to the practice field of his high school, where he was second string quarterback his senior year but did indeed run for a single touchdown on a busted play against the DeRidder Bandits. There are garbage cans and a small dumpster, but the marching band is practicing on the field, and proud parents mill about the parking lot. He steers into the upper deck of the parking garage of the casino, where he once made seven hundred dollars playing blackjack before losing it all, and considers simply leaving the box on the ground. But then he recalls the tales about the hidden video surveillance.

When Andy pulls into the hospital parking lot at 7:05, the box is still in his trunk.

Andy hustles inside and finds his way to the conference room on the second floor. He's greeted by a polite smile from Nurse Nancy, the lady running the class of about a dozen expectant mothers and their birth coaches, almost all dads except for one grey-haired grandma and an older sister. Heather, in the same purple scrubs as Nancy, catches Andy's eyes with her own and guides him to the empty chair at her side. At the front of the room next to a large white screen, Nurse Nancy clears her throat and continues reading from a laptop flipped open on a lectern. "In the first week at home, the newborn faces several distinct challenges. Don't forget, all the child has known so far is the womb. The transition to this new world can be difficult indeed."

Nurse Nancy taps a few keys and the white screen illuminates with a cartoon baby face and the list *Week One Imperatives:* Proper Temperature Regulation; Adequate Nutrition; Sleeping Habits; Basic Hygiene; Parental Bonding. As Nancy begins lecturing on the concepts, Heather copies the list into a notebook. She puts a star next to bonding.

Andy has no notebook. In front of him on the table is only his sticky nametag, which Heather has filled out. "Hi! My Name is: Andrew!"

He peels the paper off the back and obediently presses it over his shirt pocket. The first night of class, six weeks ago, Andy wrote "Yoda" and everyone, including Heather, chuckled. The second week, he wrote "Bart Simpson." After that, Heather filled out Andy's for him.

Last week, after they practiced breathing exercises and discussed other techniques to help ease labor, Nancy asked Heather to demonstrate the birthing ball. With the class gathered around his wife, Andy watched her straddle the oversized beach ball and rock softly, undulating her hips. Andy said, perhaps a bit too loudly, "Isn't this how we got into this mess in the first place?" Some of the other dads grinned, but most rolled their eyes. The grandma shook her head.

Nurse Nancy finishes the introductory lecture and shuts off the power point. Heather sets down her pen. Andy picks it up and writes in her margin: *Packing. Sorry.* Heather shrugs and says, "No big deal."

Nurse Nancy begins passing out baby dolls, receiving blankets, and diapers.

Heather writes in the margins of her notebook: *Abigail Norene? Lucinda Marie?* She raises curious eyes to Andy.

He glances at what she wrote and asks, "How's your shift going?"

"Busy," Heather says after a moment. She inches the notebook away from Andy, as if withdrawing her question. "Barb called in sick again. My back is killing me."

Andy slides one hand inside the chair's back, finds the base of his wife's spine, and presses in with his thumb and forefinger. He massages, tiny swirls pressing into the knotted flesh, and Heather sighs. "Right there," she says, with her eyes closed and her open mouth tilted up. Her head rolls loosely on her neck. She is lovely, and Andy again feels the unbelievable rush of luck that often possesses him in her presence. On the page before her, Andy sees the names and the meticulous notes. She will be an incredibly good mother. He thinks of the paycheck she brings home as an LN, twice the amount of his, and with better benefits. When such thoughts come to Andy, he pushes them aside. He focuses on the pride he takes in doing small services—packing boxes, rubbing her back, making her smile with bad jokes. In the conference room, he wants to kiss her on the neck, just below her ear where she is sensitive. He wants to be worthy of his wife.

Nurse Nancy deposits a naked plastic doll on the table. "Here's your baby, Yoda."

The class laughs.

"More hair, I thought he'd have," Andy says.

Heather forces a tight smile. Andy pulls his hand from her back. "I'll be up when you get home," he whispers. "In case you want the full treatment."

Heather turns to focus on Nurse Nancy, demonstrating now the proper technique for swaddling a newborn. When she's finished, she tells everyone to practice. Andy, who has never quite been able to get the knot on a tie straight, is confused by all the folding and refolding. Next they move on to basic diapering, which Andy does slightly better, thanks in large part to the tape. Still, his effort is obviously amateurish. Nurse Nancy easily works two fingers inside the waist band and says, "You don't want it too tight, but it has to be snug. Keep trying." Nancy and Heather share a look, then the nurse moves on to the next couple.

Andy knows that Heather will get 10 weeks' maternity leave. After this, they will try to coordinate their schedules, with Heather taking three late night shifts a week. Andy will be alone in the house with the baby. He picks up the plastic doll, with its creepy, always open eyes and its odd proportions, and he imagines waking alone in the dark to screams, fumbling to defrost frozen breast milk, the child wailing because she is too cold or too hot, wetting right through her clothes because the diaper is backwards, screaming and wriggling endlessly, wanting only her mother. Andy struggles to push this image from his mind, and when he finally does, it is replaced by the box in his trunk. He wonders why he has to dispose of it altogether. It hasn't hurt anyone, up in the closet these last three years. Perhaps the thing to do is simply sneak it into the new house and find a similar hiding place for safekeeping.

During the fifteen minute discussion on breastfeeding, Andy resists the urge to make a crack about "nipple confusion." Nurse Nancy coaches each mom on proper positioning, using the dolls. Once she's satisfied, she returns to her lectern and activates the power point once more. "The last two things we need to discuss are SIDS and CPR."

Heather passes the doll to Andy and grabs her pen, flips to a new page. Andy has heard of SIDS before, but as Nancy describes it, he begins to feel warmth at the base of his neck, then heat. "Never lay a new baby face down," Nurse Nancy says. "It lacks the strength to lift its head and may suffocate." Andy glances over to see that Heather has written this down, though he doubts he could forget it. "Never bring a new baby into your bed with you," Nurse Nancy says. "Last year there were seventeen documented cases in Louisiana alone of a child being smothered by a loving parent in their sleep." Andy doesn't notice his arms tightening softly on the doll as he pictures their bed and tries to imagine the grim reality of waking with a lifeless baby. Those seventeen moms or dads (surely they were all dads), how could they go on? How could he call Heather and tell her what he'd done? He imagines himself standing next to their bed in the pitch black.

"And number six, never place stuffed animals in the crib of a new baby." Andy, catching his breath, realizes he's missed several of the crucial steps to avoiding SIDS, but thankfully Heather's taking notes.

Nurse Nancy clicks off the power point, which had been displaying a photo of a neat, teddy-bear-free crib. "Lastly, we're required to discuss what is statistically highly unlikely." Now she scoots around the lectern, clasps her hands together. "Though a remote possibility, it may come to pass that you will be required to perform CPR on your child. Are any of you certified in CPR?"

Heather raises her hand, as do six other people in the class, including the grandma. Andy wonders when one would have time to get trained in such a thing. Nurse Nancy tells them that CPR on an infant is slightly different than on an adult, but the principles are identical. She explains that you must softly press two fingers into the chest plate and cover the infant's mouth and nose with your lips when blowing. She demonstrates on one of the dolls, then tells everyone to practice.

Heather lifts the doll from Andy and sets it delicately on the table. She falls into her nurse persona, professional and efficient, cupping the crown of the head with one hand, giving mouth-to-mouth and gently massaging the tiny chest with metronome-like precision. Andy takes a step back, away from the table. Heather's technique is flawless, but she keeps practicing until Nancy walks by and says, "Good, good. Dad, why don't you give it a shot?" Her hand on Andy's shoulder encourages him forward.

Heather slides the baby over in front of Andy. He stares down at it, and it stares back at him. It is wearing his crooked diaper, one with flowers and rabbits. The plastic smile on its face is pleasant and un-perturbed. This baby doesn't seem to need CPR. All the other fathers are now puffing and pushing away. They are bringing their babies back to life.

"Use your pointer and middle finger," Heather reminds him. She reaches for Andy's hand and tries to guide it to the doll, but Andy keeps his arm stiff, his hand posted on the table. He stares straight ahead at the empty white screen and feels the floor tilt beneath him. Heather says something he doesn't understand.

Nancy asks, "Everything okay, Andrew?"

"What exactly am I supposed to be learning right now?"

"It's called cardio-pulmonary resuscitation."

"I understand what the letters stand for. And I'm not trying to be difficult. But why do I have to know this?"

"Because, even though it's statistically improbable, your baby may stop breathing."

"Why would my baby stop breathing?"

Nancy looks at Heather, who is now stroking Andy's arm. Sweat has appeared on the sides of his forehead. "Andrew, this is just a precau-tion, you understand. But it's better to be safe than sorry. Really, it isn't especially difficult with the doll. Just imagine that you got up and went to check on your baby in the middle of the night, that you came in and found her lying in the crib and not breathing. What would you do?"

Andy thinks of the cherry wood grain of the crib they've ordered, of the parade of beaming animal faces on what Heather called a bumper pad. He picks up the doll and tries to imagine it as his living daughter with her eyes closed and her chest still. He imagines the weight of such a thing in his hands.

HALF AN HOUR LATER, AS he drives away from the hospital with his certificate signed and dated, he still feels mildly dizzy and nauseous. Though he fled from the conference room and burst into the men's room, he did not vomit. He knows he embarrassed Heather, in front of one of her colleagues no less, but she won't give him a hard time. She won't even mention it later. And somehow, this makes it all the worse, her acceptance of his weaknesses and flaws.

Instead of turning north on Common Street, he heads south and cruises past the coliseum, where the electronic billboard announces the upcoming high school graduation ceremonies. He passes cows with cattle egrets on their backs and the local airport and a Baptist church with a playground in the treeless side yard. Andy has decided to bring the box to the new house, dump it in some corner of the attic, and return to the issue at a later date. After that, he thinks he may go to a pool hall, maybe run into some old friend, have a few drinks. He feels now no desire to open the box and doubts he ever will in the future, but surrendering this last memento of the life he used to lead seems impossible, like leaping a canyon. It will feel fine, perhaps, to know that it's up there in the new house, a harmless secret only he knows.

But as he approaches the house, he finds his father-in-law's white pickup in the driveway. He considers driving by, but instead parks next to the truck. When he gets out, he can't help but eye the tools littering the bed, sharp-clawed things with ribbed handles, devices he knows nothing about. No one has ever directly suggested that Andy quit his job in the mall and go to work for Mr. Gruzinski, but the possibility has crossed Andy's mind. The advantages for his family are undeniable.

Inside the house, the sound of drilling draws Andy to the kitchen, and he finds Mr. Gruzinski kneeling inside the open door of a cabinet.

He sees Andy and lifts a battered hand. "What do you know?"

Andy says, "Not much. Something broken?"

Mr. Gruzinski shakes his head. "Safety latches. I already put them in both bathrooms. Doesn't take but a minute to install these do-dads. They make things a pain in the ass to open, but you don't need little ones crawling around where they shouldn't be. Cleaners and what not."

Andy walks over to one of the closed cabinets and tries to open it. A white plastic hook catches on something inside and the door refuses to budge.

Mr. Gruzinski gets to his feet and pokes his hand inside. "You got to pop it with your finger." The door swings open.

Andy wants to ask Mr. Gruzinski how he felt when he became a father. He wants to know if it will change, or if he will simply feel this way for the rest of his life from here on out. That doesn't quite seem possible.

Mr. Gruzinski reaches for a beer on the counter. "All set for Saturday?"

Andy nods his head. "Just about. Boxes are packed up."

"We'll be by with the truck 7 a.m. I promised the boys donuts and coffee."

"You bet."

Mr. Gruzinski takes a long drink and seems to be deciding something. Andy says, "I was driving by and saw your truck. You know Heather and me appreciate everything you're doing."

Mr. Gruzinski sets the empty bottle back on the counter top. "Come on." He leads Andy down the hallway, past the bathroom, to the rear bedroom, the one that will be the nursery. He flips on the light and illuminates the empty cube of a room. The walls are a dingy brown, the color of cardboard. Andy again smells the faintest hint of incense, masked now by a soapy odor. Mr. Gruzinski crosses to a pile of plastic bags in the corner. "Tell Heather I got that paint done up like she wanted. I was going to try and get in here tomorrow, take care of this before the move, but two of my guys screwed up a sill beam job in Moss Bluff. I'll get to it this weekend."

Andy remembers Heather showing him the color cards she ordered through the mail. He doesn't recall if she finally picked *April Hay* or *Daisy Petal*.

Mr. Gruzinski runs his hands along the wall. "This must've been a teenager's room. All these damn nail holes can only mean posters."

When the real estate agent first showed them the house, she had the window in this room wide open, trying to air it out. Andy recognized the lingering incense and, though he could not smell the marijuana beneath it, he remembered the dizzy lightness of being high.

Mr. Gruzinski is on his knees, pulling a screwdriver from his back pocket. He pops the top off one of the cans and Andy leans down. The pool of yellow is bright and inviting. This paint is the yellow of Big Bird, the yellow of a smiley face, the yellow of a cartoon sunrise. "These walls'll take two coats, even after the primer," Mr. Gruzinski announces. "But afterward, you'll have yourself a whole new room."

Andy feels the strange urge to dip a finger into the paint. "It's a beautiful color," he says.

Mr. Gruzinski nods. "Heather's got an eye for these things. Just like her mother did."

Mr. Gruzinski has never mentioned his wife to Andy before, and Andy suddenly finds himself wondering what that transition was like, going from a life with a woman you loved to a life without her. And now, of course, as this man is about to become a grandfather, surely he has thought often of the joy his wife would have found in these times. Andy tries to think of a question he could ask in case Mr. Gruzinski wants to talk, but he can't think of anything. Andy wonders how many drinks the man has had. Finally, he simply says, "Heather's the best."

Mr. Gruzinski eyes him. "I know." Then his face softens a bit. He replaces the lid, pounds it lightly with the handle of the screwdriver, and says, "Well, it's quitting time for me. You sticking around?"

Andy tells him he is.

Instead of leaving though, Mr. Gruzinski stands very still and stares at the blank wall for a time. Finally he turns to Andy. "It's a fine house," he says. "A fine place to raise a family."

Andy nods in agreement and is about to again offer thanks for the help with the down payment. Before he can speak though, Mr. Gruzinski hands him the screwdriver. Andy doesn't know why, but he takes it. "Thanks," he says, still confused. "For everything."

"Least I can do for the father of my grandchildren," Mr. Gruzinski says.

After his father-in-law leaves, Andy slides the screwdriver into his back pocket and goes through the plastic bags. There is a tube of caulk, a can of primer, two trays, rollers, a set of brushes. Andy knows that Mr. Gruzinski owns such things and realizes that he's purchased these for the new house. Through the window, he hears the white pickup truck heading north, back toward the city.

He looks down at the cream-colored carpet, the one Heather insisted the real estate lady have professionally shampooed. There are still stains, a burn hole in the corner, and the whole thing looks worn and tired. Andy gets on his hands and knees, lowers his face, and inhales. There, beneath the soap and incense, he can detect it clearly, the smell of burning rope. His mind floats back to the conference room at the hospital, and he thinks of the nights ahead of him here in this room.

Andy doesn't dwell on the future, and he can't know that he'll never have to perform CPR. He can't know that these walls will see fevers, rashes, countless diaper changes. He can't imagine the knot he'll get in his back from rocking his daughter to sleep. He can't imagine the improvised lullabies he'll concoct, or the times when he'll lose his patience just trying to snap the tiny buttons on her outfits. He can't imagine the dread he'll feel when he accidentally draws blood while trying to trim her toenails, and the way her lips and tongue will shiver as she screams, and how tightly he'll hold her as he whispers apologies. He can't imagine leaning over her crib after she's fallen asleep one night, listening to the soft hush of her rapid breathing, and his hand on her back feeling that hummingbird heart settling.

Andy is no prophet, so he cannot know these things are in his future. But he tries to see them nonetheless. And when he's done, Andy takes the screwdriver to the door and unscrews the threshold capping the carpet. He slides his fingers beneath the carpet and peeks under, to the hardwood. Without thinking too much, he yanks on the carpet and it pops free of the nails along the wall. The hardwood underneath is a shade lighter than that in the hallway. It's been preserved. Inspired, Andy stands, still holding the fringe. He rips and tugs. The carpet surrenders without much of a fight, and Andy rolls it into itself, then drags it out into the night. He dumps it near the curb.

When he returns to the room, he sees the thin wooden strips of carpet nails lining the walls. On his knees, he pries at them with the screwdriver, popping some free, splintering others. He picks the pieces with his fingernails.

After that, he turns back to the plastic bags and finds the tube of caulk. He steps to a wall and locates a nail hole. He squeezes a tiny bead of white goop on his finger and smears it into the hole. When he realizes he has no rag or cloth, he unbuttons his dress shirt and rips it in half. He wipes away at the excess caulk carefully, as if he were drying a tear. The patch job looks like a healing wound, and Andy knows that a couple coats of paint will completely mask the damage. He finds a second hole, then a third, and before he knows it, he's patched one entire wall. The white dots spread across the brown wall like stars in the night sky, and he thinks of the day when he'll bring his daughter outside, let her stand barefoot in the dewy grass. He'll show her the constellations and explain. Andy turns to the second wall.

Many hours from now, driving home with his forearms splattered with primer and bright yellow paint, Andy will pass an all night carwash, pull in, and drop the box in a garbage can. He will drive away without glancing in the rearview mirror, feeling a bit lighter, focused on the road ahead. But a strange anxiety will grip him too, a dread creeping in from beyond his headlight's illumination. At home he'll shower before slipping silently into bed. Heather will be on her side, and he will spoon against her under the sheets, and he'll ease one hand around her belly and settle his palm against that ripening flesh. He may feel the child kick and he may not, but as he transitions from waking to sleeping, his mind will roll from one choice to the next, wondering about the best name for their daughter.

The Lost Art of Believable Make Believe

I

ACCORDING TO THE THOMAS THE Tank Engine digital clock on my son's dresser, it's just after two a.m. At the other end of the long hallway, my wife lies in our bed, and the side I'm meant to occupy is vacant yet again. I've been cramped up on this thin mattress for just about two hours, since a couple cats mating under the house pulled Brendan from what I fear are troubled dreams. My fretful son will surely interpret this disturbance as further evidence of the existence of monsters. Even now, though I know he is finally asleep, every few minutes he moans and rolls, twisting his tiny body in the knotted sheets. God only knows what he's imagining. And while my own tired mind turns from one topic to another—the kids at the casino, Lance's red pickup truck, that empty space in my bedroom—I wonder what more I could do for my son if only I were a capable father.

A few Sundays back while my wife made pancakes, me yawning and trying to get the crink out of my back, Brendan explained to us that he needs company to stay asleep because monsters live in his wall. I asked him which wall, certain he meant the closet. This is always the source of monsters for kids on TV. My wife stopped whisking and raised an eyebrow at me over her shoulder, and I wondered how precisely I'd gone wrong. Later I would learn that I'd re-enforced his fears instead of assuaging them. She dog-eared the page for me in *Knowing Your Three-Year Old,* a paperback tome thick as a phone book. But before that, my pajamaed son led me back to his room by the hand, and I made ready my paternal advice. I was fully prepared to empty the closet to show him he was safe and, as a result, assure him he could spend the night on his own. Instead though, Brendan moved to the foot of his bed and raised an accusing finger at the empty wall above his scattered pillows. I was confounded, struck dumb. Finally, I offered, "There are no monsters."

He looked up at me, disappointed, released my hand, and went back to his mother. I stared at the wall for a while, thinking of a time at Rutgers two decades ago when I punched a hole in the drywall of my girlfriend's dorm.

Earlier tonight, I traced circles on Brendan's bare back in an attempt to sooth him to sleep. This, of course, is my wife's technique, and her longer fingernails give her a distinct advantage. So when he didn't seem to be settling, I thought of what a better dad might do. My own father had an endless supply of fantastic tales, each of which began the same: *When I was a little boy, I lived on a farm, and my best friend was Gibberish Duck.* He never told the same story twice, and his descriptions were so vivid that when I learned that he'd grown up in Philadelphia, I felt both shocked and betrayed. If I'd only inherited more of my father, I could tell a story that would lull my son to sleep.

I whispered, "Once upon a time there was a girl named Little Red Riding Hood." Brendan shifted, released the pacifier from his mouth, and mumbled, "Sparkle." He was referring to Sparkle Sunshine, the lead character in the series of books my wife reads to him. The resource-ful Sparkle has a habit of coming across lost babies of all variety (baby turtles, baby squirrels, baby penguins), all of whom need help getting reunited with their animal mommies. I have tried reading these books, attempting different silly voices for Sparkle, her parrot friend, the lost and sad baby mongoose, etc. Always I fail, as Brendan grows quickly disinterested. He corrects my impressions, asks unrelated questions, or worst of all, simply picks up a second book and begins pretending to read it himself. Frustrated and jealous, I have spied on my wife during bedtime, listening to her rendition through the monitor, hoping to pick up pointers on the fine art of believable make believe.

Tonight, despite Brendan's request, I pressed on with Little Red. I knew my wife, an insomniac of the first order, was likely wide-awake and listening through the same monitor, and I didn't want her to hear me give up. I rubbed Brendan's back more forcefully and tried in vain to vividly describe Red's mother, her mission, the dark forest. When I re-alized I was on the verge of planting the image of a menacing wolf into my son's troubled mind as he neared dreams, I paused in mid-sentence. Then I said, "But even though the forest seemed spooky, she bravely skipped through and brought her Grandma the basket of treats. Then everybody was happy." Brendan didn't even bother to spit out his pacifier when he spoke, and it took me a second to realize he'd said, "That's not how it goes." On the nightstand, the red light atop the monitor glowed.

It's rare that I actually sleep when I'm in my son's bed, which is shaped like a race car. My legs stretch over the hood though my feet don't quite reach the floor. Brendan's elbows dig into my back and/or ribs like blunt daggers. So I lie awake and listen to the sound machine that sits next to the monitor on the nightstand. Every night at bedtime, after his Sparkle books, my wife lets him pick a different setting. I prefer "Summer Rainstorm," as close to raw white noise as you can get. And I don't so much mind "Forest Serenade," though the crickets and owls do sound menacing sometimes. One of the ones I simply can't stand is "Womb Song," an ominous pounding human heart. I realize this is meant to be calming, that we're all supposed to be genetically pre-programmed from before birth to find this rhythm soothing. But those nights, the pounding drives into my temples and I think of the insane murderer from that Poe story. I catch myself clenching my fists.

Tonight, I'm stuck with "Ocean's Delight," a thirty-second loop of waves and seagulls. At this point, with him asleep but tumbling still, I stand a 40% chance of getting out of Brendan's room without waking him. It would involve slipping over the side of the race car and then army-crawling to the door. After a successful escape, I could head for the couch in the living room, where the four-hour marathon of *Law and Order* is just getting started on TNT. I think again of the cool stretch of bed next to my wakeful wife. We conceived Brendan at a time just like this, the hazy void between night and morning. I was fast asleep and woke to one of her hands roaming unexpectedly across my chest. She settled on me and I thought it was a dream, this return of my wife, and things moved so quickly that we did not take the usual precautions. Nine months later, Brendan.

After considering my other options, I remain in the race car bed. I tell myself it's because the bars have just closed. Soon enough, Lance will drive past.

The home we purchased three years ago, when we moved to Lake

Charles, Louisiana, is on a sleepy, picturesque street, one lined by live oak trees. Some of my coworkers at the casino, where I'm assistant director of public relations, call the area "Paw-Pawville" because of all the elderly people who live here. One notably exception is Lance, whose age I would put between eighteen and twenty-one. I have never spoken directly with Lance, never been introduced, but his name is emblazoned in black cursive on the side of his red pickup truck, which he drives down our peaceful street at unsafe speeds morning, noon, and night. My wife dismisses my speculation that he is dealing drugs. But when I drive past the house where the red truck sits in the driveway, just three blocks up the road, I slow as if I'm a cop on stakeout. There is no sign of adult supervision: the azaleas are overgrown, the grass is knee high. On the roof, shingles are missing.

Predictably, Lance blasts his radio so loud that the bass rattles the windows. Brendan's room is situated in the front of the house, and I have come to suspect that much of his difficulty staying asleep may be caused by Lance. His red pickup truck, with this attitude and blaring music I thought we left behind in New Jersey, may indeed be the origin of those monsters in the wall.

As loving husband and caring father, what actions have I taken to address this threat to my family's happiness and security? Once, when Lance drove by while I was mowing the lawn, I paused and removed my sunglasses so he could see my disapproving scowl. One rainy midnight when I was out front smoking a cigarette in the covered entryway, I gave him the finger, though it was just after he'd driven past, and it was dark. And last Friday, just a week ago, while my wife and I were sitting on the couch in awkward silence trying to get through the fourth videotape in the *Intimate Reconnections* series, when Lance made his third pass by the house in half an hour, I stomped to the door and yanked it open, even took a single step outside. "Jim," my wife said. "Don't do something stupid."

Something stupid was, in fact, exactly what I had in mind. Our brick walkway is coming apart thanks to the root system of the massive live oak that dominates the front yard. Fragments of broken brick sit in the grass. But that night, I did nothing.

So I have been inadequate thus far in how I've handled the situation with Lance. And laying beside my sleeping son these nights, I have fantasized about how I would deal with this young punk if I weren't 41, if my back didn't hurt for two days after I play golf, if I didn't worry that my insurance probably won't cover any injuries I sustain in a physical altercation which I instigate. Like my lame bedtime stories, none of my fantasies are especially creative. I smash his windshield with one of those bricks. I bang his head in the door. I rip the wiry guts of the stereo from under the dashboard. I am in no way a violent man, and frankly all this shames me.

Brendan, I know, will never be a menace to polite society like Lance. I concede, of course, that this is not something for which I will be taking credit. While pregnant, my wife transformed into a new being, a kind of small scale evolution. Despite racking waves of nausea, she read constantly, scoured the internet for baby clothes, car seats, cribs, hypoallergenic sheets. Our medicine cabinet filled with precautionary medications, and every day when she came home from the bank, she'd have three more ideas on how to better "baby-proof" our home. Having children was a discussion we kept postponing, largely because of my ambivalence and some of the typical problems she and I were encountering after seven years of marriage. My wife was not unaware of my anxiety, and from time to time during the pregnancy, after an ultrasound or driving home from the hospital's free parenting class, she would tell me that everything would change when I held our child in my arms. She'd pat my leg and tell me that at the moment of physical contact, I would be overwhelmed with paternal instincts. That's what she told me would happen.

I love Brendan, care for him deeply. But when my wife goes to the gym for an hour, or stops by the bank at lunch to visit her old friends, or makes the weekly trip to Walmart, I do not know how to fill that space. When Brendan and I are alone in the house, he spends much of his time in his room, making parades of trucks or creating a zoo with his stuffed animals. Trying to get his attention, I stack boxes, roll cars across the hardwood floor, imitate the roar of a lion, even offer him Oreos. He regards me with suspicion and, I think, pity, taking the cookie from my hand before retreating to his play. Quite clearly, he senses that I am uncomfortable around him, though this awareness does not seem to bother him. Now and then, he timidly hands me a toy, as if to calm my anxiety. Once while he was in his room playing, I fell asleep with the Yankees game on. When I woke, he was next to me, watching golf. He said, "You're a good big brother, Jim."

Above the peaceful waves of "Ocean's Delight," I hear rock music outside, maybe a block away but drawing near, and I'm on my feet and crossing the room. The bedroom door smacks the wall and I'm down the hallway, into the living room, out the front door. The air outside is hot and still and vibrating with a distorted guitar solo. Lance's headlights swing wildly as he turns off Jefferson and accelerates my way, and I jump down the steps, stooping in the half-dark for a brick, then cut across the lawn, hoping to get to the streetlight so when he passes he'll see me and know I'm a man who means business. I want him to know that I have my limits.

To gauge my speed, I glance over my shoulder, just in time to see Lance's red truck swerve, sliding on the road as if it were iced. At high speed it sideswipes the Ledbetter's new minivan, careens across the street, jumps the curb, and rams into my live oak. My arms cross over my face and I fall backwards.

When I open my eyes, leaves are shivering from the branches overhead. One headlight is shining around the side of the oak. I stagger to my feet, leaving the brick on the ground, and start towards the truck. Barefoot, I step gingerly on the bits of windshield scattered in the lawn, and as I round the oak, I see the crumbled hood, littered with sparkling squares of glass. The driver's door hangs open, and an ominous crackling spider spreads across its window, as if struck by a stray baseball. There is no driver, and for an instant, I am relieved. The truck was empty, I think stupidly. But when I clear the door, I find him sideways across the front seat. I lean in and say his name, only then realizing that somehow his stereo is still blaring. I snap it off and shout, "Lance!" but he does not respond. On the left side of his head, blood escapes from a gash. A tall can of Budweiser sits crooked in the cup holder. Without thinking about it, I settle a palm on the boy's chest and it is still. I yank my hand away, retreat from the cab, and my naked foot catches on something in the grass. I reach down and my fingers find a set of wire rim glasses. It seems impossible that they belong to Lance. For an instant, I am possessed by a strange impulse. I should sit Lance up, buckle his seatbelt, return the glasses to his face, remove the beer can. But instead I turn to the house, thinking now of 911. When I turn though, there is my wife, sheltered in the alcove of the doorway. In one hand she holds the phone to her head. Her other arm holds Brendan, diapered and blinking. She is speaking to someone, calmly, but her eyes fix squarely on me, as if somehow I brought about this catastrophe.

II

FIRST THING SATURDAY MORNING, DESPITE the pre-dawn light and temptation of television, Brendan insists we go outside and inspect the oak. He's bothered by the tire tracks in the grass, and when I set him down on the oak's roots, he runs a hand tenderly along the scarred bark. He asks if I can get a Band-aid. I tell him the tree will be fine, though he suggests we call Dr. Sanders. To reassure him, I strap him in the blue swing that hangs from one of the branches, push him back and forth enough to demonstrate that the oak's essential function is unaltered. In between pushes, I feel the wire rim glasses in my pocket. In all the parade of strobing lights last night, between the paramedics and the police and the tow truck, I forgot to pass them along to the authorities.

"That car had a big crasheroo," Brendan says. "It spooked me."

"It spooked me too," I tell him. I'd rather wait for my wife before engaging this conversation. I feel like a blind man in a minefield. Already, I doubt that I should have confessed my own fear. Perhaps in the chaos of an uncertain world where pickup trucks collide with trees, a child needs unqualified confidence from a father, even if it has to be fabricated. I'm sure it's in that book.

"The monsters made that car crasheroo," Brendan tells me as he swoops closer and farther away.

"No," I say back. "There are no monsters."

74

He's quiet, but I'm not foolish enough to interpret his silence as agreement. After a few more arcs, he says, "Know what Jim? There are monsters in my wall."

I stop pushing my son, drop my hands and let him float. I strain my brain for a way to assuage his fears without re-enforcing them or in-validating or doing the thing that will forever screw up his life. Finally, I catch the swing and start unbuckling the straps. "Let's go inside," I say. "Daddy needs coffee."

There's no mention of the accident in the morning paper. I even scan the obituaries. Then I flip to the editorial. The casino is hoping to expand and not all the locals are supportive.

That my wife is not up yet gives me hope that she has actually gotten some sleep. After Brendan's birth, she developed real prob-lems. This is why, though our son would prefer her, I am the one who goes to him when he wakes at night. I remember the days when, after I'd settle Brendan and come back to our bed, my wife would sleepily rub my shoulder and whisper, "Thanks for jumping on the grenade."

When my wife enters the kitchen this morning and sees me with the paper spread across the dining room table, she says, "They wouldn't have time to get anything in." These are her first words to me. She did not sleep.

"I know that," I tell her.

"Then what are you looking for?" she asks.

Behind us in the living room, Brendan holds a Magna Doodle on his lap and watches a soft–spoken man paint a landscape. Through the doorway, I hear the man explain, "In crowd scenes, the secret to making good people is using just the tip of the brush."

My wife lifts her chin towards our son, speaks in a low tone. "He say anything about the accident?"

I contemplate this for a moment and then lie. "Not a word," I say. "He did call me Jim again, though."

My wife shrugs at this, one more habit she assures me is a phase. She slides past me, heading for Brendan, who leaps off the couch to deliver the morning hug. After that, they will discuss each other's dreams, then make something together for breakfast. I turn back to the paper and sip my coffee, which has turned cool.

In the afternoon, when my wife takes Brendan to a birthday party, I do my best to remove the glass from the lawn. First I scrape at the ground with a metal rake, then I mow the whole area with the bag attachment. Still, tiny fragments litter the lawn like gems. While I'm mowing, I try to see if anything is going on at Lance's house, three blocks west, but nothing seems different. I take a long shower and have a Heineken with my lunch. I sit in front of the TV with a sandwich but can muster neither hunger nor interest in the college football game that is on. I drink a second beer, then retrieve Lance's glasses from atop my dresser.

Standing in front of Lance's house, it's hard not to conclude the home is abandoned. The St. Augustine is encroaching on either side of the sidewalk, with shoots nearly touching in a few places. A fault line splits the concrete driveway, a tilted section of which has also sunken down six inches into the earth. Lime-tinted mold discolors the home's sideboards. A tattered blue tarp, probably the last one in the city, clings desperately to the roof. FEMA installed these free of charge in the weeks after Rita came through two years back. Before Brendan could even crawl, we had to evacuate.

When I thumb the doorbell, I hear no sound inside. I lay my ear against the wooden door and try the bell again, then I knock gingerly. Though I suspect the house is empty, I am also picturing bereaved parents huddled inside. They've unplugged the phones and closed the curtains against the outside world that took their baby. But I know that they'll want these glasses, and I hold them in my hand like a passport, ready to offer them as immediate explanation for my intrusion on their mourning. When my knocking produces no results, I lean up on my tiptoes and peer in through a filmed window. The living room is nondescript. Square couches. A coffee table with magazines. I wonder if these belong to Lance's father. I wonder what kind of magazines he reads and what clothes hang in his closet and what pictures he keeps in his wallet. I wonder what storybooks he read to Lance as a child. And before I know what I'm doing, my hand is twisting the doorknob. It is locked.

Still holding the glasses, I walk back to my house.

Saturday night, while my wife flips the pages of a magazine called *World of Mothers*, I check the late local news. I sit through stories about new insurance rates, plans to develop the lake front, weather, and highlights of a jambalaya cook off in Hackberry. There is nothing about the crash.

Sunday morning, I wake up stretched out on the floor next to Brendan's race car bed, with my head propped on an oversized hippopotamus. Brendan is standing at the window, splitting two slats of the mini-blinds. "Hey Jim," he says. "No crash."

"No," I say. "That just happened that one time."

He looks down at me. "There won't be no more crashes?"

"That's right," I tell him. "Just that one."

He seems satisfied and, without asking permission or waiting for me, heads out into the house. While the coffee brews, I get the paper from the driveway. Brendan scans the circulars and carefully rips out coupons or photographs of items he thinks we need. Mostly it's bread and juice and cereal, but every now and then he'll want a fax machine. My wife paperclips these snippets together and brings them along to the store. She's giving him a feeling of empowerment.

From the obituary, I finally learn Lance's last name: Fontenot. He was 23, and he graduated from Jeff Davis High. He is survived only by his parents, Cindy and Charles. I'm surprised to read that they reside in DeQuincy, a town about thirty miles to the north. The funeral is tomorrow morning and the wake is this afternoon, 3:00.

Brendan holds up a slip of ripped paper with a coffee-maker on sale for $49. "Is this a good one?" he asks.

I take it from his hands. "That one's the best," I tell him. I am alone in the kitchen with my son. It is morning. "Are you hungry?" I ask. "Would you like some pancakes?"

"Momma makes pancakes," he says.

"I could give it a shot," I offer. "I know the ingredients."

Brendan stares at me with a wrinkled, pained expression. To be polite, he changes topics and turns back to the coffeemaker in his hands. "What makes it the best?" he wants to know.

"It just is," I say.

Later, holding her coffee mug in both hands, my wife says, "You're going where?" Brendan is in the living room, where plumbers on PBS are hard at work installing French drains on a Colonial home in Vermont.

I repeat my intentions.

She sips at the coffee and says, "Why?"

"I want to give them his glasses," I say. I even thought of calling the funeral director in case they wanted the glasses for the viewing. But I know there is more to my desire to go to this wake.

My wife says, "That's a bit of a drive. And it strikes me as a tad voyeuristic, but suit yourself. Be home in time for dinner. I'm making that turkey meatloaf." She puts down her coffee and reaches for the pancake mix in the cupboard.

"Hey," she says. "You okay?"

I tell her I'm good. I tell my wife not to worry.

In the parking lot at the Distefano Funeral Home, which is next door to Mason's Hardware and Rent-All Supply Center, I let the engine run and angle the AC vent so the cool air crosses my face. Cars and trucks fill half the lot, and mourners stream inside at a steady rate. They can largely be stereotyped into two groups: the young and the old. The kids wear jeans with tattered cuffs, but most tuck their shirts in. A few wear baseball caps, even as they enter the funeral home. The elders, of course, are dressed in more dignified clothes, tasteful dresses, suits and ties. These are the aunts and uncles, grade school teachers and coaches of this small town boy who moved south and turned bad.

On Brendan's floor last night, I thought for a long while about Lance's parents. I wondered if they too were awake. They must be castigating themselves for how they raised him. Perhaps each secretly blames the other for failing Lance. They must be recalling key events in his life: the first time he ran away, the time he was caught smoking in the bathroom, the time they found him throwing rocks at a treed kitten. I expect that they must be replaying these scenes and revising their own actions, doing the right thing so that their son would not turn out as he did.

From behind my steering wheel, I watch a group of teens tipping beer cans to their lips in the bed of a white Ford parked in the far corner of the lot. Closer to me, a middle-aged woman walks in circles around a grassy island with one hand cupping a cell phone to her ear. And there's a steady rotation of smokers maintaining the gauntlet outside the main entrance. Though I've been here for half an hour, I can't bring myself to try and pass through them. I imagine the smokers' hard eye contact, someone inside demanding ID. I've come to decide, I suppose, that my wife is right, and I have no place here. Delivering the glasses, sitting now on my dashboard, is an excuse, a ploy through which I hoped to get close to Lance's father. I want to see this man who failed his son. I want to see that he is entirely different than me.

A side door splits open and into the brightness steps a man grey and bent. He is on the other side of the building from the smokers and teen drinkers. I decide that this is Mr. Fontenot. He loosens his tie and lights a cigarette. After a minute, he leans against the building and stares blankly into the pine trees.

I should walk over to him, offer condolences, hand him the glasses, and leave. But something about Lance's father seems all wrong from what I expected, and this unsettles me. I had imagined him somehow alien—a drunken hick, an angry trucker, a Bible thumper thrilled that his boy was finally safe in the arms of Jesus. But this man, the way his shoulders hang with the weight of what could have been, the way he lets the smoke drift from his mouth instead of blowing, the way he studies the forest for something like an answer, this man is much too familiar.

I put the car in drive and head back for the highway.

III

I'M UP AGAINST A PRINTER'S deadline all day Monday, so only occasionally does my mind turn to Lance's funeral. I'm putting the finishing touches on a brochure we're going to distribute at the hotel's front desk. We've had a rash of abandoned children the last few months, and management has decided to take action. Basically, gamblers drive in from Baton Rouge or Texas, get a nice room, plop their 6-year-old in front of the TV, and head for the blackjack tables. The kids learn quick how to order movies, get room service, sneak into the pool. I've seen packs of them running together, because of course they get to know one another one weekend to the next. But these are unsupervised minors. The liability issue alone makes corporate cringe. So the brochure I'm working on outlines our new zero tolerance policy. *We have no choice but to contact protective services,* one sentence reads, *in the event that we encounter unattended children.*

After the threat of police action, there is a note regarding childcare services that the casino is now offering at $15 an hour. Soon, I fear, we'll have a nursery and a playground.

I do take some slim consolation knowing that on the spectrum of parents, I am not in the category of those who would choose slot machines over my child.

Back at the house, Monday's dinner is leftover turkey meatloaf. As I'm changing out of my work clothes, I hear the microwave's impatient beeping, and I get to the dining room just as Brendan and my wife sit. Having a regular family meal is number two on the list of

Eight Ways to Have a Happy Family, and we've eaten at 5:30 almost every night for six weeks. As a result, I have gained four pounds, but feel no closer to my child or wife. She has set a glass of milk out for me, in theory to encourage Brendan to drink his. But he doesn't model his actions after mine. I get a Heineken from the refrigerator and take my place at the table.

I tassel Brendan's hair and ask, "So what did you do today, Buckaroo?" She glances my way.

"There was rain but no rainbow," he tells me. "And the dirt turned to mud and I could splash in the puddles on the sidewalk but not in the street."

"Sounds like fun," I say. I tell my wife the meatloaf is good, though I forget if I complimented her yesterday, when the meal was fresh.

I wipe my mouth with a napkin, take a swig of beer. "After dinner, we'll help Mom with the dishes and then go to the park," I declare. "Just Dad and Brendan."

From either side of me, Brendan and my wife cast suspicious looks. Because my wife is still chewing, Brendan speaks first. "The biting bugs are out."

She nods, swallows. "The mosquitoes will eat him alive."

"We'll stop at Rite Aid and get spray," I announce.

"The slides will be wet from the rain," Brendan says. "My bipper-oo will get soaking wet."

"We'll bring a towel," I say. "I can wipe it down."

My wife excuses herself, and when she returns from the living room she's holding Brendan's Magna Doodle. She holds it up and I read, "Don't try so hard." She has drawn a smiley face. Brendan scoots off his chair and grabs the Magna Doodle, rumbles off into the living room and leaves me alone with my wife. In silence, we go back to our meal.

Somewhere after Brendan's birth—when I gave him a tablespoon of cough medicine instead of a teaspoon, when I applied cream before he'd dried and made his diaper rash even worse, when I forgot to buckle the safety strap and he tumbled from the grocery cart in the Kroger parking lot, when I couldn't walk him to sleep at 3 a.m. and my back was killing me and I knew she was awake and tired and desperate for help and I got so mad I punted a toy school bus down the hallway—somewhere, my wife rightly began to suspect my abilities as a father. And this undermined her sense of me as a husband.

As much as I've become a brother to my son, I have become one to my wife as well.

"Listen," my wife says. I don't look up from the meatloaf. "I think it's great that you're making an effort. But he can tell when it's not real."

I bring my fork down on my plate, and I'm taking a calming breath before asking her what the hell she's talking about, but then Brendan shouts from the living room, "The tree doctor is here."

I'm so glad for the interruption that I'm instantly on my feet, leaving my wife behind. I find my son standing on the couch, splitting the front curtains. Balancing on the oak's gnarled roots, the man from the funeral home parking lot runs a hand along the scarred bark. Behind him, parked along the curb, is a late model Buick. I grab Lance's glasses from my bedroom dresser and slide them in my pocket.

"What does he want?" my wife asks. She's brought the curtains together and is seated next to our son.

"He's going to fix the tree," Brendan explains.

I say, "I'll go find out."

Outside, Mr. Fontenot is bending into the open mouth of the Buick's trunk. He sees me and straightens. I cross the lawn, all the while his eyes on me. As I near, he extends a hand and says, "Charlie Fontenot. It was my boy that—"

"Of course," I say as we shake.

Mr. Fontenot lets go of my hand and steps away. "I was looking at your tree," he says. "I think she'll be just fine."

"I'm so sorry for your loss," I say, despising the cliché.

But he makes no sign that he heard me. "Wife and me, we used to live up the street a bit. I remember when these branches here didn't hardly reach the house. Back then, the Van Normans lived in this place. He was a lawyer."

We are silent together, contemplating the thick branches that now stretch over the roof, shading our home. I wonder why he is here, if he somehow saw me in the parking lot yesterday. I want to know how the funeral went. "Would you care for some coffee?" I ask. "Maybe a beer?"

His eyes stay fixed on the sprawling branches.

I reach into my pocket. "Mr. Fontenot. These are your son's. I found them the night of the accident."

He glances down at my extended hand. "God, he hated those things. Never wore them when he was supposed to."

"That might explain a lot," I say.

This brings his eyes hard into mine, and I wish I had the words back. He winces, studies my face. Finally, he lifts the glasses from my hand and speaks. "I need to be getting back. I come here to put something up, providing you don't object, of course." He returns to the trunk and removes a mallet and a white wooden cross, two feet tall. A necklace of red plastic flowers loops around the stakes. I have seen these before, here in the south, especially along the highway. I've never understood their significance.

"Of course," I say. "Whatever you'd like to do."

Holding the cross and the mallet, Mr. Fontenot walks in small circles on the grass between the sidewalk and the curb, searching I suppose for the right place. When he genuflects and stabs the cross into the earth, I feel the urge to offer my help, to hold it while he hammers. But he seems intent on doing this thing alone. It takes five whacks with the mallet. Each one makes me cringe. He stands and is silent for a time. Then he turns back to me. "I'll be down at the old house, picking up things, tidying the yard and such before we sell it. No point keeping it now. Anyhow, I'll come by and pick this up. A couple, three weeks maybe. My wife'll decide that."

"Leave it as long as you'd like."

"It's a stupid thing," he says. "Damn ugly if you ask me."

Neither of us laughs. A cat crawls out from under the house and watches us from the azaleas. Mr. Fontenot nods at the blue swing. "I saw your boy in the window. How old?"

"Three."

Mr. Fontenot grins, and I can tell he's remembering. "Three's a good age," he says.

The cat darts back under the house, and a moment later the municipal mosquito truck rounds the corner. When it drives past, the hissing mist of pesticides sprays out behind it. Mr. Fontenot doesn't seem to notice. The truck disappears down the street.

He moves away from me, tosses the mallet in his trunk before closing it, and gets back into his car. He settles behind the wheel, starts the engine.

I step to the car and lean in the open passenger window. "When you come down to work on the yard, I could help out. I've got a wheelbarrow, a couple shovels, a good chainsaw. No sense in you hauling all that gear when I've got it right here."

He eyes me for a couple seconds, searching my face again. "That's kind," he says.

"Whatever you need, Mr. Fontenot."

"Everybody calls me Charlie," he says. Then he nods once, and I nod back and step away so he can drive off. But he doesn't. For a full minute, he sits with his hands on the wheel and the engine running, and I do not move for fear of ruining something. Finally, still looking through the windshield, he speaks. "My boy had that wreck cause he was drunk. It had nothing to do with his glasses, and there's no point anybody pretending otherwise."

A few heartbeats later, he pulls away slowly, and I am left alone with the wreath. Lance's name has been burned in cursive across the white wood.

While I give Brendan his bath, my wife sits on the closed toilet and supervises. I tell her about my encounter with Mr. Fontenot and the memorial on our lawn. She can't decide if it's creepy or beautiful. I manage to get shampoo in Brendan's eyes, and when I brush his teeth, he begs me, "Not so tough." But overall the bath is not a disaster.

At bedtime, my wife reads Brendan three Sparkles stories and I once again secretly eavesdrop from our bedroom, listening to every word through the monitor. When she's finished, she tucks him in, tells him to have happy dreams and gives him a kiss. Then she whispers, "I love you," and it sickens me, how I imagine she's talking to me.

Uncharacteristically, I suggest we play Scrabble instead of stiffly viewing another episode of *Intimate Reconnections.* My wife agrees and even sets up the game on the dining room table. For half an hour, things go just fine. She gets the q; I get the z. She asks about the casino and I tell her about the pamphlet, all those terrible parents. Our scores are close, and we take turns in the lead. After my wife gets a glass of wine and plays "sweat," I grab a beer and try to counter with something suggestive, but the best I can do is "thigh." Still, we're pleasant and alone and not tense. Just when she's pouring a second glass of wine though, the phone rings in the kitchen. I nearly tell her to let it go. By the way she starts talking, I know it's her aunt, a sweet but rambling woman who will keep her on the phone for a full hour minimum. From the dining room, I listen to my wife's voice, hoping I guess to hear her true thoughts on me, on my attempts to be a better husband and father. But the update focuses on Brendan, as it should, and I quietly retreat to the bedroom with a fresh beer. I try not to be angry.

Through the monitor, I hear seagulls caw and waves sloshing into the beach. I pick up *Knowing Your Three Year Old* and scan the index, trying to grasp all I don't know, wondering where to start. I think about Mr. Fontenot.

Just before midnight, I wake suddenly and don't know why. My wife is beside me, snoring softly. The ceiling fan spins overhead. Then I look over at the monitor and recognize the odd silence in the air. Brendan has shut off his sound machine. In the darkness, I stumble up the hallway, vaguely aware of the dizzying effects of the tail end of my two beer buzz. Crossing his room, I step squarely on a Lego and almost go down. When I reach his bed, it is empty. This causes no immediate panic, because I've found him out in the house a couple times before—once trying to turn on the TV, once playing with cars in the kitchen. But as I turn to leave and begin my search, I notice a crooked mini-blind in the dark. I step to the window and see my tiny son outside, standing on the curb before Lance's wreath.

I'm running before I'm thinking, through the wide open front door and into the darkness in my boxers. Brendan's facing the house so he sees me charging at him, but makes no move. I kneel in the wet grass, grab him by both shoulders hard enough to hurt and spin him toward me. "What are you doing out here? You don't go outside by yourself." I shake him. With fear and frustration, I shake my son. "You don't go outside."

When I stop, Brendan looks confused. "I woke up and wanted to see it."

"Well," I say, and I dust off his shoulders, "you could have seen it in the morning. It's not safe to be out here now."

"It's safe," he tells me. "The tree doctor knew just what to do. They made that truck crash and now this will scare them all away."

I know I should tell him that there is no such thing as monsters, but when I look at the wreath, sacred and tacky and strange, I try to see it through Brendan's eyes. I try to imagine that all our troubles have somehow been banished. "Monsters don't like pretty things," I tell him.

Brendan nods. "They can't stand flowers."

I pick him up and his head is heavy on my shoulder. I lock the door behind us, and without thinking about it, carry him down the hallway. Miraculously, my wife does not wake when I lower him into the middle of our mattress. I crawl in beside him. He rolls and I'm worried he'll wake my wife, so I reach for his back, rub it, and whisper, "Tomorrow after breakfast, I'll call in sick to work. We'll drive to the store, the three of us, and Mom will pick out the very best flowers, big pretty white ones, and we'll come back home and dig holes beneath your bedroom window. You can use your shovel and I will use mine. We'll water the flowers with the hose and they'll be happy here and grow taller and brighter. Would you like to do that?"

"I don't have a shovel," he says.

I tell him we'll buy him one. And then we lay there in silence, the three of us, and the bedroom is still. My son breathes calmly beside me and we're each picturing the same thing, the white flowers and the rich dirt and the cool water, and I know he wants it to happen as much as I do. And it's true, I'm not sure we'll actually do these things, but for now, in the dark, I decide it's enough to pretend.

People Like That, People Like Them

BECAUSE OF A TRAFFIC JAM caused by a nasty accident involving a jackknifed tractor-trailer, the Franklin family returned to Camp Hill late that Monday night, bleary-eyed and road weary from the turnpike. Over the long August weekend they'd spent at Andrea's in-laws in Pittsburgh, a trip on which Cassie had refused to eat anything but pancakes and Ellie had relapsed in her potty training, something in the guts of the upstairs toilet back home had sprung a leak. So when Andrea flipped on the kitchen light, it shone down on a good-sized puddle pooling on the linoleum. Immediately, she yelled for Mike, who was diligently unloading the minivan. Both the girls ran with him to the kitchen, and they found Andrea with her hands on her hips, staring up at the sagging ceiling. It looked bloated, ready to burst.

"Perfect," Mike said, stepping gingerly into the kitchen to better inspect the damage.

Ellie, always fearless, bolted out onto the slick floor and promptly slipped, whacking her head with a reverberating whomp. For a moment, it seemed to Andrea like the ceiling above her daughter might collapse.

The next morning, while the girls were watching cartoons and eating fruit bars on the couch, Mike called from the bank and told Andrea he'd contacted Krupka Brothers, a firm he'd helped with several loans. Tony Krupka would be sending over somebody before lunch, and they'd get started right away. Andrea, on her second cup of half-decaf, recognized this was great news, but she felt a faint but familiar tightness in her stomach. Before her husband hung up, he said, "Tony and his guys, they're good people."

"No doubt," she said. "I'll get ready for them. Thanks for taking care of this."

When the battered pickup truck pulled into her driveway two hours later, Andrea watched the thick man in the red t-shirt emerge from the driver's side. Middle-aged with a deep tan and huge boots, he was exactly what she anticipated in a handy man. She was surprised however by the second worker. She would place him in his late teens, and he was scrawny and chestnut-skinned, like the boys she saw on the TV in all those protests in the Middle East, the ones where one side had tear gas and the other had rocks, where flags were always burning.

In her youth, Andrea was shy, even mousy. She wouldn't qualify her feelings about strangers as an anxiety, but others had. As she pulled back the front door, she forced a smile, and the older man touched the brim of his baseball cap. "Mrs. Franklin? Got yourself a bit of a problem I hear."

"Yes," she said, and she stepped back to let them in.

The driver strolled inside, pausing to wipe his boots on the welcome mat. The dark-skinned boy followed. The girls, still in their flowing pajamas, came cascading down the stairs. "Who are they?" Cassie shouted, pointing a finger from the first step.

"Cassandra Lee!" Andrea said.

But the driver just grinned at the bad manners. He knelt and said, "I'm Mr. Jim. And this here is my helper, Steve."

Steve, who didn't make eye contact with anyone, dipped his head and shoulders in a sort of half bow acknowledgement, and Andrea wondered what his real name was. In an instant, she conjured a rich history for this teen, who'd surely fled ethnic conflict, been adopted perhaps, and now endured the stares of ugly Americans here in Central Pennsylvania. But when Steve said to the girls, "You two look like princesses," she was surprised to hear no trace of an accent.

Six steps up the staircase, Ellie pulled out her pacifier, beamed a toothy smile, and said, "Pin-cess."

Jim nodded politely and rubbed his hands together. "So where's the patient?"

The two workers began by addressing first the simple origin of the problem, nothing more than a fractured connector valve in the toilet, then began removing the saturated ceiling. In great armloads, Steve carried the soggy chunks out to the bed of the pickup truck, heavy work that Andrea noticed Jim avoided. She spent the morning going about the standard chores that followed a trip, running the dust buster in the van, getting the laundry going, basic clean up. At one point, she remembered the turnpike accident and retrieved the laptop. She learned that the driver of the truck and four others, including an infant, were killed. When Mike slow rolled passed the scene, there was a minivan like theirs on its side in a ditch, the front end smashed in. Andrea had turned away, then checked to see if the girls were belted in properly. Skimming the article, she saw that police suspected road rage as a central factor in the accident.

This unsettled Andrea, even as she worked on a dinosaur puzzle with Ellie and made a Play Doh zoo with Cassie. On the living room floor, she played a game of Candy Land with both girls, carefully winding her way through the ominous Peppermint Forest and past the treacherous Gumdrop Falls.

She wanted to go out to run a couple errands, but she had mixed feelings about leaving the house unguarded. Sylvia from her book club had told her about workers "casing" a home for valuables, or pulling obscene pranks in the absence of owners.

In addition to the occasional chatter of the two men talking, Andrea heard another sound from the kitchen, what seemed to be a third voice. Jim and Steve had hung canvas tarps at both doorways to the kitchen, so she couldn't see what they were doing, and she couldn't be certain about this other person.

Around 1:00, just after Ellie complained of being "hun-gee," Andrea knocked on the doorframe and said, "Pardon me?" Almost immediately, as if he'd been waiting for her, Jim pulled back the tarp. He smiled warmly.

"Can I sneak in there, get to the fridge? I need to feed my daughters."

Jim glanced behind him, as if confirming a fridge was in fact in the room. "Sure, sure," he said. "Mind your footing."

Jim opened the tarp like a huge curtain and she crossed the threshold. Clear plastic was draped over the countertops and another thick tarp covered the floor. Every surface seemed dusted with powdery debris. When the job was finished, she'd need to scrub down the whole room.

Steve was at the peak of a V-shaped ladder next to the fridge, picking away at the edges of the gaping hole left by their demolition.

She smiled at him, but her eyes shifted quickly to the underbelly of the second floor. Beams crisscrossed the opening, and pipes zigzagged along like a highway system. She could see part of the underbelly of the tub, and it was easy to figure out what corner the toilet was in. Unexpectedly, Andrea wasn't rattled by this. Rather, she liked seeing the sturdy inner workings of her home.

"Ain't nearly so bad as it could be," Jim told her. "It was a slow leak that mostly dripped straight down. Didn't do no real damage up above."

"Good," Andrea said, because she felt Jim wanted a response.

"I seen worse for sure. We got in before any mold took hold, and don't get me started on what Formosa termites'll do with wet wood."

Jim kept talking, but Andrea's focus shifted to the source of the third voice she'd heard earlier. It was her under-the-countertop radio, the one she used to listen to NPR sometimes when she was making dinner. Jim had clearly felt the right to not only turn on the radio, but to change the station. Coming through the speaker was the ranting and angry voice of an a.m. talk radio personality, one Andrea reviled for his mean-spiritedness and bigotry. He was talking now about a new immigration policy in Arizona and a union protest against Walmart outside Tucson that had erupted into violence. He said, "Only an idiot wouldn't see that these things are all connected."

Jim said, "We're just about done what we can do today. It needs to air out, dry some, and we'll be back tomorrow to patch up."

Andrea opened the fridge and pulled out two cartons of fruit yogurt. "Fine," she said. As she turned and passed Steve's ladder, something light glanced off her shoulder and fell onto the floor. Startled, Andrea dropped one of the yogurts, which exploded on impact.

"Hey jackhole!" Jim yelled. "Watch the lady!"

Andrea turned up to see Steve, staring down at her apologetically. He said, "I didn't know you was there."

"You alright?" Jim asked her.

She wiped her shoulder. "I'm fine," she told him. "Just caught me by surprise."

Jim glared up at Steve. "How many times I freakin' tell you—"

Andrea thought, *There's no need for that,* but said nothing. This rehearsal of dialogue was a longstanding habit. Instead of speaking, she retrieved another yogurt.

Jim grabbed a rag and began wiping up the mess. From his knees, shaking his head, he said to her, "Kids like this. You can't teach them a damn thing."

Kids like this, Andrea thought. She paused at the doorframe and looked back at Steve in the corner, expecting perhaps to share an awkward moment. But the boy had already gone back to work, hacking away at the ceiling above him with a saw-toothed knife.

That night, when Mike was inspecting the ceiling with some satisfaction, Andrea told him about the encounter.

"So what?" he said. "You've decided our drywaller is a racist?"

Mike had a habit of minimizing, even ignoring his wife's concerns, something that often made her wonder if they were valid in the first place. But here, she stood her ground. "I didn't call him that," she said. "It's just, I have a bad feeling about that guy."

Now Mike turned to her and cupped her shoulders. "Most of the work is done now. Tomorrow they'll hang the new ceiling, probably need to come back Wednesday for touch up. I'll paint it over the weekend and this little adventure will be in the books."

Andrea did take some comfort in the certainty in Mike's voice.

They'd decided to eat out instead of dealing with the kitchen, and together they gathered their daughters for a trip to McDonald's.

Jim and Steve arrived the next morning just as Mike was leaving. From the bay window in the front of the house, Andrea watched the two older men talking animatedly, like they were old high school chums. Next to them, Steve hefted a large white bucket that looked heavy. He seemed uncertain if he should set it down. Andrea held her coffee mug with two hands, warming her palms. Behind her on the TV, Dora the Explorer shouted something in Spanish, and Ellie repeated, "ga-to!"

After greeting the workers she left them alone, again tending to her daughters and some household chores. Following a rousing game of Chutes and Ladders, Andrea decided a second morning show didn't make her a terrible mother, and she sat the girls down in front of *Word Girl* on PBS. *It's educational,* she thought. *It doesn't even count as TV.*

In the small study/guest room, she hopped online and paid a few bills, checked her email and Facebook account. There were photos posted by her sister-in-law from the weekend trip. Andrea didn't think she looked good, but she wrote "Great pictures!" in the comment.

One of her college friends had posted an article about a gay high school boy in Montana who'd been taunted to the point that he killed himself, right in the school cafeteria. No one knew how he'd snuck the rifle past the metal detectors. Therapists and sensitivity trainers were being called in. Andrea saw that the story had over a thousand "likes".

By the time she emerged from the study, Cassie was staring blankly at *Martha Speaks*, a show about a talking dog with an impressive vocabulary. The space where Ellie had been curled on the couch was empty. "Where's your sister?" Andrea asked. Cassie shrugged.

Unwilling to broadcast her negligence as a mother, Andrea didn't want to yell her daughter's name with the workers in the house, so she quickly went upstairs to the unmade beds and crayoned walls, then down to the basement, with castle parts strewn all over the floor. Before they left on the trip, she and the girls had spent hours setting up the castle's four impressive spires surrounding the central tower. Fleetingly, Andrea wondered when it had been destroyed.

Finally, with her heart racing just a bit, Andrea approached the heavy grey tarp that covered the doorway to the kitchen. She stretched out a hand, then when she heard Ellie giggle, she held it frozen in the air. Leaning in, she listened.

Jim said, "The important thing when you're painting is nice steady strokes, up and down. Just let that brush do the work."

Andrea tugged back the tarp and stuck her face through the opening, and she saw Ellie standing in front of the fridge, stroking it with a paint brush. Jim was on a short ladder, applying a white compound to the ceiling with a silver bladed tool. Eyes on the ceiling, he said, "Slow and easy. If you rush the job, you'll have to come back later. So slow and easy. Way better off doing it right the first time. Ain't that right, Steve?"

On another ladder, Steve was sticking thick white tape over what she saw as a fault line where a new piece of drywall met an old one. Andrea recalled a *60 Minutes* story about the boom in fracking for natural gas in Pennsylvania. Several studies suggested that out west, the industry's growth had led to an increase in seismic activity. One expert from Berkeley predicted a major earthquake.

Jim said to Ellie, "Don't let your brush go dry. Get you some more magic paint."

Ellie dipped her brush into a Tupperware container filled with water. "Ma-gic."

"Sweet girl," Jim said, trailing his eyes to Andrea.

She returned Jim's smile. "I'm so sorry she wandered in here. Kids can be a handful."

"Don't I know it," Jim said. "Got four myself. Two and two. We'll be finished up here right about lunch, then back tomorrow to sand this mud and put on a finishing coat. We hit a road bump or two. Genius-boy over there screwed up his cut line. But all in all the job's coming along just great. Just great."

"It looks so good," Andrea told them. "Thank you. Thank you both."

She put extra emphasis on this, focusing on Steve, who hadn't paused in his work with the tape. Andrea admired how he'd ignored Jim's insult.

"Hey Skippy!" Jim snapped, and Steve turned. "The lady's talking to you."

Steve looked tired, tuned out. Andrea said, "I was only saying your work looked good. Come on Ellie, let's let the gentlemen finish." She held out a hand and her daughter followed her.

With lunch coming up, Andrea didn't want to interrupt the workers again, but she also didn't want to leave the house to bring the girls out. Sitting with the two of them at the dining room table, a whole buffet of Play Doh food spread out before them, Andrea thought of another idea. She reached for the laptop.

Just under thirty minutes later, the delivery boy knocked on the door. Andrea carried the steaming boxes to the dining room and went to the kitchen, where Jim and Steve were cleaning up. "I bought some pizza," she said. "Would you care to join us?"

"Ma'am?" Jim asked.

"In the dining room," Andrea explained. "For lunch."

Jim still looked perplexed.

"Free pizza," Steve said, wide-eyed.

But Jim hesitated. "That's very kind. Way we're all covered up though, we'd only make your nice dining room all dirty. No point in that. No point at all."

"Fine then," Andrea told him. "The table on the deck. We'll tell the girls it's a picnic."

The men stared at each other, and Andrea smiled. "I insist."

The impromptu meal was a great success. Jim told the girls a series of knock-knock jokes while Steve devoured slice after slice. Andrea, who served iced tea from a pitcher, asked Steve where he grew up and he said, "Lemoyne," a town not five minutes away. Despite the absence of an accent, she'd still been hoping to hear something exotic, Cairo or Dubai.

At one point, Cassie asked Jim what was on his arm, and he rolled back his short sleeve to reveal a circle of thirteen stars. "Those are for the original colonies. Are they teaching you about America at school?"

Cassie shook her head.

Jim curled his lips. "They ought to be. She's the greatest nation there ever was, God bless her."

Andrea wiped some pizza goop from Ellie's chin. "Cassie's only just heading in to third grade this year. They haven't done much history yet."

Jim set down his slice and sat back. "Nothing's more important. We're forgetting who we are in this country, I can tell you that."

"Who are we?" Cassie asked, and everyone laughed.

After they finished the pizza, Andrea got the girls ice pops, and she was delighted when Steve took an orange one. The men gathered their things and drove off, and Andrea left the girls in the backyard to play on the jungle gym. She went into the kitchen and inspected the work, which looked nice as far as she could tell. The ceiling had been made whole. Along the edges of the patch job was a thick white compound. Suddenly Ellie, sun-baked and thirsty, appeared at her side. Andrea retrieved a juice box and asked, "It looks good, doesn't it?"

Her daughter sipped on the straw.

"Those men, they were nice guys, huh?"

Ellie nodded and stopped drinking. She pointed to the ceiling, the corner by the fridge where Steve had been working. "Rag-head," she said.

Andrea caught her breath. "What?"

Ellie, beaming, repeated the word.

Andrea wasn't ten seconds into the phone call with Mike when he said, "Calm down now," which she always found belittling. "Are you sure that's what she said?"

"No Mike. I'm calling you at work just to annoy you, just cause I've got nothing better to do." She hung up the phone.

That night, after leftover pizza, Mike bathed the girls, read them bedtime stories, and tucked them in. By the time he found Andrea on the couch, a short glass of red wine sat on the coffee table before her. She aimed the remote control at the TV, changed the channel. "I'm sorry," he said. "About when you called."

She kept her eyes on the screen.

"So let's say this guy did say that and Ellie overheard it. What do you want me to do?"

Andrea took a sip of her wine. "I don't want that man back in our house."

"Hang on now," Mike said. "Krupka told me he was his best guy, pulled him off a new construction job in Mechanicsburg to help me out. Tomorrow he's only got to be here for a bit. Be in and out in a couple hours probably. Then he'll be gone."

"I never want to see him again. And I don't want him near our daughters."

Mike ran a hand through his hair. "Sometimes guys say things. They don't mean anything by it."

"Is that what guys do, Mike? That's part of the man code?"

Mike plopped down in the Lazy-Boy and stared at the TV. A female reporter said that NASA was monitoring a Chinese communications satellite that had lost power. It was expected to burn up in the atmosphere, but some worried that small debris could rain down across the southeastern United States. Mike said, "Look, I'll call in to work in the morning. There's some things I can shuffle around. Would it make it better if I were here? If you didn't have to talk to the guy again?"

Andrea drained the last of the wine. "I don't want him near the girls. I'll take them to the park when he shows up."

But in the morning, it was raining. So when the pickup truck pulled along the front curb, Andrea shepherded the girls into the garage and headed for the mall. As she backed down the driveway, she saw Jim and Steve crossing the lawn, crouched against the rain. Steve was carrying the toolbox.

As she wandered the Camp Hill mall with her daughters in tow, Andrea's eyes kept falling on those not like her. Browsing at the entryway to a bookstore, an Indian woman with a red dot above her nose;

an Asian man working at a kiosk selling hot pretzels; at the indoor playground, two African-American mothers with children about the same age as Ellie and Cassie. The kids fell in together easily, talking and playing without regard for skin color. Andrea wondered if the mothers, who were both beautiful in the same way, could be sisters, but she didn't want to ask such a personal question.

An older man Andrea identified as Mexican came hobbling into the playground pushing a stroller with a sleeping child, likely his grandson. He parked the stroller and pulled out a cell phone. Andrea knew that every one of these people she saw at the mall, the people not like her, had surely dealt with men like Jim, narrow-minded men who judged in ignorance. Andrea saw the sisters whispering, and when she glanced at the grandfather, he averted his eyes. She became overcome by the strange sensation that the sisters and the grandfather somehow knew what she had done, or rather hadn't done. They were all talking about her right now. Andrea decided they'd be right to be disappointed. She would no longer be bullied into silence in the face of hatred.

So even though the two hours wasn't up, Andrea summoned the girls and told them to put on their Crocs.

As she drove home, she mentally composed the email—or even better, the certified letter—that she would send to Tony Krupka. The phrases floated through her mind: "unacceptable in this day and age," "utterly repulsive behavior," "tainting the innocent soul of my daughter." She would demand action, insist that Jim be disciplined or fired or forced into diversity training.

When she turned the corner onto Beverly Drive, the pickup truck was still in front of her house, and Jim and her husband were standing by it, smiling the way men always did. The rain had passed through.

Andrea didn't look their way as she pulled up the driveway into the open garage. She released the girls into the living room, telling them they could watch one show while she prepared lunch.

Steve was in the kitchen, alone, sweeping up the floor. The countertops were immaculate, the ceiling pristine. The teen didn't lift his head when she walked in on him. He bent and extended one hand with a dustpan.

"Thank you for cleaning up," Andrea said. "It looks great."

"Glad you like it, ma'am."

"You do good work."

"I'm learning."

Between them, there was a silence. Mike came in the front door, and the two of them heard him chatting with the girls. Steve finished sweeping, returned the broom to its closet, and moved toward the exit.

"Wait," Andrea said, lowering her voice. "I have to tell you something."

Steve stopped in the threshold and turned.

Andrea inhaled once, deeply, then let out the breath. "I'm sorry."

"Sorry for what?"

"For not sticking up for you yesterday. But I'm going to now. I'm going to do the right thing, like all of us should. I'm going to write a certified letter. People like you don't deserve people like him."

After a moment, Steve scratched the back of his neck. "I'm not sure what you mean. People like who?"

"Jim," she whispered. "He's horrible to you. And I know the kind of language he uses. That's hateful and cruel and is absolutely unacceptable in our day and age."

She felt a lightness in her chest as she delivered this line.

Steve shrugged and said, "What now?"

Andrea pressed her palms together and it was decided. She spoke the word, saying it as if she was spitting out something foul.

Steve stared at her and she said, "That's what my daughter said. My sweet little girl called you that because that's what she heard Jim call you. He's teaching her hate, right in my home. I teach my children not to judge others."

Steve's face scrunched up, as if he were trying to work out a complex mathematical equation. Finally he said, "Ma'am, that dude's an asshole for sure and for certain. He runs me pretty hard, but I get paid under the table and I've learned a ton this summer. Yesterday he gave me serious shit cause his cutline was smooth and mine was all ragged. He had to cut mine again himself, even it out, and he was explaining it all to your kid, my screw up and everything. She was in here painting then. Jim was really rubbing it in, pointing at his line and mine and repeating *smooth* and *ragged* over and over."

Andrea could think of nothing to say, so she said, "Oh."

From out front, a truck horn blared. Steve stood there for a few seconds, then turned and walked away.

After he was gone, Mike joined Andrea in the kitchen. With his face tilted up, he said, "They do quality work." Andrea, who was wiping down the already cleaned countertops, didn't answer. Mike stepped up behind her and said her name. She stopped and turned around and her husband put a hand gently on either shoulder. "For what it's worth," he said. "I think you were right about that guy. He gave me the creeps. Out front just now, he kept ranting about our sacred duty to America as the land of the free. He even has a bumper sticker, one of those *America, love it or leave it!* deals." Mike grunted and shook his head. "People like that. I'll never understand them."

Andrea slid into her husband's chest and let his arms close around her. She knew she'd never tell him the truth.

As Mike embraced her, Andrea's eyes lifted to the ceiling, which was restored and flawless. Except for the slight shift in whites, it was impossible to tell where the patchwork ended and where the original was. After Mike painted, it would be good as new, forgotten.

The Complete and Illustrated Guide for Meeting Your Most Sacred Obligations as an Altar Boy

AFTER WHAT HAPPENED DURING LUNCH period, Thomas Mulligan wasn't surprised when he was summoned via intercom to Sister Anita Joseph's office. His sixth grade teacher, Sister Cecelia, paused from the penmanship exercises she was slanting across the chalkboard and waited for him to leave while all his classmates watched. He made eye contact with no one, staring instead at his black shoes, which though he'd polished just that day with his father's can of Kiwi, were already somehow dull with smudges.

Thomas took the long way, down past the gymnasium and the music room and his old kindergarten classroom, where he recalled his tender crush on Ms. Podgornik and drawing pictures of rainbows and butterflies. Every Friday afternoon before dismissal, the children who hadn't had their names put on the board for being disruptive at some point during the week were allowed to select an item from the treasure box. All day Friday, Thomas would try to decide if he would pick a rubbery finger puppet or a baseball card or an eraser shaped like a space robot. The instant he got home, he would show it to his mother and she would squeeze him tightly and tell him what a wonderful boy he was.

When Thomas arrived at the principal's office, he found her sitting sternly behind the huge oak desk, hands folded. He sat in a straight back chair before Sister Anita Joseph, who began, "Merciful Christ Jesus guide me," before offering a brief sermon on honesty and integrity. Thomas was recalling the widespread rumor that the nun wished she were a priest when she asked him what he knew about Peter Gordon. Thomas stared at a framed photograph of the pope, John Paul II, on the wall. On the day last spring after his shooting, every student at Most Precious Blood had spent a full afternoon in prayer in the church. They knelt in absolute silence for two hours.

"Peter Gordon," she repeated. "The cafeteria bathroom."

Thomas shrugged and said nothing.

Sister Anita sighed and said, "You've become quite the cross to bear this year. If not for your mother's heart, no doubt I'd have you expelled."

She lifted the receiver from the phone on her desk, dialed a few numbers on the rotary, then said, "Yes, Patricia. If he's available, I'll be sending the boy over. Very good."

Thomas watched her pull out a sheet of paper and write several sentences, pausing now and then, for the right word the boy thought. Then she folded it neatly and tucked it into an envelope, which she licked and pressed tightly shut. She wrote something on the back, then handed Thomas the envelope. "Bring this to Monsignor McGinley."

Thomas hesitated, then took the envelope. In elegant cursive that Sister Cecelia would surely have admired, the principal had written,

"In Christ's name" across the flap, a kind of wax seal to prevent tampering. Sister Anita Joseph stared at him, unmoved, and said, "In the rectory."

Without his coat, Thomas folded his arms against the cold as he followed the fractured sidewalk around the church. He climbed the rectory stairs he'd passed for a decade but never gone up. Once through the double wooden doors, he located Monsignor McGinley's secretary, who barely shifted her eyes from her typewriter before saying, "He's expecting you." She glanced toward an open door to her left, then went back to rapid fire clattering, punctuated every few seconds by a *ding!* that made Thomas twitch.

Monsignor McGinley, a lanky man with thin graying hair, stood at the window in slanting sunlight. He picked dead leaves from a potted plant on the sill. Thomas offered him the envelope, which he took before saying, "My ficus might not make it to spring." He walked to his desk and dropped the envelope into a pile. Thomas was surprised he didn't open it immediately. The priest sat and asked, "How's your brother Brendan, Mr. Mulligan?"

Still standing, Thomas said, "Fine, sir."

"Nose guard at Shippensburg?"

Thomas' eldest brother played right tackle at Kutztown, but Thomas simply nodded, not sure how to correct a senior priest without seeming disrespectful.

"He was scrawny when he was here. Boys mature late, you know. That's something for you to keep in mind."

Thomas, neither small nor big for his age, wasn't sure how this applied.

"And what about Edward and Joseph? Both at St. Catherine's, correct?"

"Yes, sir." Edward was directing the high school play, *Brigadoon*, and Joseph—though just a junior—was co-captain of the wrestling team. Thomas waited for Monsignor to bring up the past glories of the Mulligan clan, all of which seemed like distant memories in the here and now, but the priest held a brief silence. Thomas looked at the red cushion of the high-backed chair in front of him. The seat looked like a pillow, but he hadn't been invited to sit. The priest again considered the envelope from Sister Anita but set it back down a second time, still without opening it. "Quite a financial sacrifice for your mother and father," he said, "putting you four boys through a Catholic education."

"I know," Thomas said, wincing a bit at the mention of his parents. He rested a hand on the back of the red cushioned chair and prepared himself now for the lecture about appreciating his blessings, honoring God's call, bearing witness to His works, living up to one's potential as a soldier in Christ's holy army. Over the last year, versions of this had been dispensed by each of his brothers, his father, and even Mr. Reinhaur, Most Precious Blood's janitor/gym teacher, who pulled Thomas aside one day after an especially lackluster attempt at kickball and asked him when he was going to stop wasting his God-given life. It was a question Thomas had asked himself, wide awake in the bottom bunk, long after the others in the house were asleep.

But instead of lecturing Thomas, Monsignor lifted a yellow sheet from his desk. "I noticed that your name is not on the roster of altar boys. Don't I recall you going to the retreat last year? You took the class, did you not?"

"I did," Thomas said. "I failed the test."

"You failed the first time," Monsignor said. "Christ believes in second chances." He opened and shut several desk drawers, then finally pulled out a booklet and stood, handing it over the desk to Thomas. He remembered the cover. A cartoon boy on his knees smiled up at a cross, above which were the words, *The Complete and Illustrated Guide for Meeting Your Most Sacred Obligations as an Altar Boy.*

Monsignor said, "Study this over the weekend. You can ask your brothers any questions. They were all excellent servers. I'm putting you down for next week's six-thirty masses. I'll see you in the vestibule Monday morning at six sharp."

After saying this, the priest nodded, then sat and picked up a pen, which he began to scrawl rapidly across a legal pad. Thomas realized the meeting was over, and he'd never even sat down. "I'm not sure how I'll get here at six in the morning."

Monsignor didn't stop writing. "Christ didn't ask how He would accomplish His responsibilities. He simply did them."

Holding the booklet, Thomas turned and walked past the secretary, back out into the cold. Only then did it occur to him that Monsignor McGinley had never mentioned what happened with Peter Gordon.

AT LUNCH EACH AFTERNOON, THOMAS sat at a table with Niles Shaeffer and Harold Janoso, who talked almost exclusively about their Ataris and Dr. Who. He wasn't really friends with them, but he could eat in relative peace. Earlier that day, while working his way through a peanut butter and jelly sandwich, Thomas felt a twinge of the gas pains which occasionally meant an evening spent in a fetal tuck.

The cafeteria bathroom was down a thin hallway, past the coat check room they used when the cafeteria was employed as an auditorium for school plays or meetings of the Knights of Columbus. Thomas was pleased to find the bathroom empty, and he took the stall on the end. Just as he was finishing, he heard the squeaky hinges of the outer door. He waited for one of the stall doors to open or the flush of a urinal, but there was only silence. Then there was a sniffle, followed by another, and Thomas was soon certain he heard muffled weeping. When he flushed the toilet and left the stall, he found Peter Gordon leaning into a sink, looking surprised to see him. Peter was a fifth-grader, pale-skinned and paunchy. The two boys had passed dozens of times in the hallway and library, but never spoken. Peter wiped at his eyes and turned on the faucet. Thomas washed his hands and did not look when Peter sobbed, even as he splashed water on his face. Thomas activated the new hand dryer that sounded like a lawn mower. Inside the mechanism, the red coil glowed with heat. When it shut off, Thomas heard Peter behind him, crying still. He turned and said, "Stop that."

Peter didn't acknowledge this. He gazed into the mirror and watched himself cry. Thomas raised his voice. "Come on," he said. "Cut it out."

This only seemed to make matters worse for Peter, as he began now to blubber. There were tears and his chest heaved as he tried to catch a breath. He looked at Thomas with his wet, red eyes and seemed fragile and desperate.

Thomas stepped over to Peter and shoved both hands into his shoulders. "I said stop!"

Peter fell backwards onto the floor, then did a kind of crab crawl away from Thomas, who advanced on him. The trembling boy backed up under the sink and curled into himself, covering his face with a chubby arm. For a moment, Thomas glanced at the door, and he even took a step in that direction. But then he heard Peter sniffle again and he turned back. Sometimes in the dead of night, Thomas found himself awake and suddenly alert, unable to sleep. On one such night this past summer, he'd snuck downstairs for a glass of water and found his mother at the kitchen table in the dark. She held her head in her hands, elbows planted, and she was quietly weeping. From the shadows, Thomas watched her, frightened. Instead of going to her, he crept noiselessly back up the steps.

Thomas, who could boot the kickball clear over the playground fence if he wanted to, drove his foot into Peter's ribs. For balance, he gripped the sink.

FRIDAY NIGHT, THOMAS' MOTHER ROSE from the dinner table to answer the ringing phone in the kitchen. She came back a moment later and said her husband's name, then took her seat again. Thomas looked at her, read her concerned expression, and knew. He heard his father talk low, then set the phone back on the receiver. When he returned, he went back to eating, and Thomas' brothers re-engaged an argument about the merits of soccer as a sport. After a few minutes, Mr. Mulligan set down his steak knife and fork. "That was Monsignor McGinley," his father said, turning to face Thomas. "Seems you'll be needing a ride early on Monday morning."

"I was going to ask you on Sunday," Thomas said.

His father was quiet. Then he picked up his fork, stabbed a piece of the London broil. "This boy. Did he start the fight?"

Mrs. Mulligan cleared her throat, but said nothing. She brought her napkin to her mouth, touched the edges, then dropped it back onto her lap.

Thomas recalled Peter's eyes on his, the way he looked so pathetic. "He did."

Mr. Mulligan chewed and swallowed. "All right then. Mulligans don't start fights. We finish them. Right?"

All three boys, familiar with this expression, nodded in unison. Mrs. Mulligan held her hands on her lap and looked there, as if for an answer.

Over the weekend, Thomas helped Edward rehearse lines for his play, acted as a dummy for Joseph's wrestling moves on a gymnastic mat in the basement, watched a Godzilla creature double feature, and used an old World Book encyclopedia to scribble out a few lines for a social studies project on Africa. His mother marked it for grammatical errors and returned it to him for corrections.

Now and again, Thomas would flip through the altar boy booklet. There was a list of questions to determine if you were mature enough to serve. *Can you sit without fidgeting? Are you prepared to audibly say all the prayers and responses? Do you strive to be an exemplary Catholic?* There was a step-by-step explanation of the mass and the role of the altar boy at each stage. In the back was a glossary with terms that seemed like magic words: cincture, cassock, cruet, paten. On Sunday, from the pew he watched the altar boys swirl around the altar at the ten o'clock mass. Father Coyle was the celebrant, and just as he needed something, one of the altar boys stepped forward. Even taking into account the instructions in the booklet, it seemed to Thomas that they were all following a mysterious and unknown choreography. Thomas expected to go in on Monday morning, fail some test, and then deal with the consequences.

HIS FATHER, A UNION LAWYER with clients like Mack Truck and Bethlehem Steel, pulled up in front of the church at 5:55. He told Thomas to do his best, and Thomas climbed out into the frigid air. He could see his breath as he climbed the stone steps, and the metal knob on the great door felt like a hunk of ice. When he pulled on it, it didn't budge, and Thomas turned to see his father already a block away, the turn signal blinking. Locked out, Thomas grew colder and angry, so much so that when at 6:10 the door finally opened, he snapped, "Freezing out here," and brushed quickly past Monsignor McGinley.

Inside the church, it was only a bit warmer. The air was very still, very quiet. As he followed Monsignor McGinley down one of the side aisles, he found himself growing calmer. The priest, dressed plainly in black pants and a black shirt, led him to a room with a wall lined with closets. Together they selected a red cassock with a white surplus that fit overtop. Thomas struggled with the white rope he knew was supposed to function as a kind of belt. There were tassels at the end. The priest glanced at his watch and said, "Are you prepared to serve God?"

Thomas played with the belt and said, "I really didn't get a chance to study that book so much."

"I see," Monsignor McGinley said. "Finish up then. It's almost time."

He followed the priest to another room, where the old man slipped on his own holy vestments. Thomas watched him kiss the stole, which he then slid around his neck like a scarf. They stepped through a door onto the altar and Thomas saw that there were now people in the pews, maybe a dozen, all of them bent in prayer. Monsignor McGinley showed him how to light the four candles that surrounded the altar, and he brought him to a table on the side. He pointed to the shining items, glass and gleaming gold, and in a low voice named each one and explained its function.

Lastly, he picked up a golden disk with a wooden handle. "Paten," he said. "At communion, keep this under the host while I place it in the recipient's mouth. No sliver, no crumb, no speck, must touch the ground. Keep it under the recipient's chin until they've closed their mouth entirely. Do you understand?"

Thomas nodded.

"At the moment of consecration, those wafers become the body of Christ. The entire mass is a celebration of this miraculous act. As an altar boy, you are guardian of the body of Christ. This is no small obligation, and it calls for the most serious commitment. For the body of Christ brings nourishment to the soul. It is hope and it is renewal."

Each week at Sunday mass, Thomas plodded up the receiving line and took communion, but he hadn't thought about it for some time. The priest was staring at him, waiting for some response. Thomas said, "I understand," even though there was a great deal he knew he did not.

During mass that first morning, Monsignor spoke under his breath, guiding Thomas around the altar. *Stand there. Bring me the red book. Remain kneeling.* When he wasn't busy following the priest's instructions, Thomas found himself staring out at the scattered members of the congregation, all sitting far apart from each other. He wondered what would compel them to come here, to leave behind the warmth of their beds so early on a weekday winter morning.

Several times, he was struck by the purity of a singular moment. The warmth of the priest's hand when they shook at the Peace of Christ, the hardness of the marble floor when he knelt on it, the flickering white flame of one of the candles. As he was preparing to bless the hosts, Monsignor had Thomas bring him a tiny glass pitcher and a deep glass plate. The priest held his fingers over the plate and said, "Pour a little water." As Thomas did this, the priest closed his eyes solemnly. In a voice so quiet Thomas barely heard him, the priest said, "Wash away my iniquities. Cleanse me from my sins." He wondered what wrongs Monsignor McGinley was thinking about when he said those words.

He watched the priest lift one large host, snap it in two over the chalice, and continue through the consecration. He saw him take a host into his mouth, then he turned and said, "Bring the paten." Together, the two of them went down to the center aisle. Standing at the priest's side, Thomas watched the aged and bent parishioners amble forward in the half light. Three used canes and one leaned into a walker. Mixed in with the seniors was one man in his forties, wearing a threadbare business suit. Thomas looked into their faces when Monsignor McGinley said, "Body of Christ," and each one seemed transported when they spoke the amen. In the backmost pew, a woman did not rise from her knees.

But for the ones who did come forward, Thomas was careful to hold the paten beneath their mouth, and he watched closely after communion, when Monsignor McGinley returned to the altar, took the paten, and brushed whatever invisible bits remained of the body of Christ down into the chalice. He added some water, swished it around, and drank. He recalled reading in his booklet that a special sink was used to clean any of the items that came into contact with the Eucharist, one that emptied not into the sewer but into the pure and sanctified ground beneath the church. Clearly Monsignor McGinley was cleaning up, concluding. Thomas felt the sudden sense that he'd somehow screwed up again and forgotten something crucial. He stepped forward, dipped his head to keep his voice low and asked, "When do I receive communion?"

Monsignor McGinley calmly finished what he was doing, set a gold plate atop the chalice and turned. As he stepped toward his throne-like chair he said flatly, "When you are ready."

Thomas apparently wasn't ready on Tuesday, Wednesday, or Thursday morning either, as Monsignor never paused to offer him the Eucharist. Thomas recalled a story his brother told, about a homeless man who walked into a church in Easton. After the priest gave him communion, the man spit it on the ground and stepped on it like a cigarette. As he turned to leave, the priest dropped to all fours and took the crushed host into his mouth, then charged after the vagrant, tackled him, and licked the sole of his tattered sneaker. Thomas wondered if the story was true.

As the week went on, Thomas did find himself being less clumsy, less uncertain about his duties. It was a simple ceremony taken step by step, and at night he consulted certain passages from his altar boy booklet. He found himself looking forward to two moments most: when he helped Monsignor wash his fingers, and when the gathered came forward for communion. As an altar boy, he was virtually invisible, and he found he could stare point blank into their faces and they'd never notice. He could almost sense it, the weight of something terrible driving them forward, how tightly they interlaced their fingers and how their eyes brightened when Monsignor held up the host and declared, "Body of Christ." And the depth of conviction in their voices, the breath that escaped when they responded, "Amen."

He wondered how many, in the midnight darkness, were awake and afraid like him. He wondered if any sat at their kitchen tables crying in the night.

Perhaps most upsetting was the figure who never rose from her knees in the back. When they recessed at the end of mass, he'd glance over at the withered woman, wrinkled and small, and try to look into her face. But it was always bowed.

At the end of his week of service, after mass, Monsignor stepped over to Thomas in the sacristy. He said, "Were you paying attention today?"

"Yes, Monsignor," Thomas answered.

"Tell me something about the gospel."

Thomas searched his memory, but nothing came.

"Which apostle wrote it? Who was the central figure? What was it's meaning to you?"

Thomas, crestfallen, could only stare at a BB gun hole in the stained-glass window. Finally he said, "I can't answer. I'm sorry."

"Sorry is an interesting term. Forgiveness is at the heart of Christ's teachings. Do you know that? And each of us needs forgiveness because each of us sins. To be human is to fail, no one escapes that. We fail over and over again. That isn't the question. The question is what you do after you realize your failure."

Thomas thought about what the priest said. He wasn't sure how to respond, and finally he came up with, "Thank you."

The priest nodded, but did not smile.

"Did I do a good job this week?" Thomas asked.

"You're improving," Monsignor McGinley told him. "But surely next week you'll do even better."

Thomas did a double-take. The priest took a step toward the main part of the church and said, "See you Monday morning."

On Saturday morning, after watching two hours of cartoons and shoveling snow from the steps while Joseph ran the blower over the sidewalk, Thomas pulled a thick phone book from a kitchen drawer. He flipped through the pages and found that there were six "Gordons" in the city. He wondered which one was Peter's, and briefly considered calling them all. Since the bathroom incident, he had only caught fleeting glimpses of him in the hallway or cafeteria, and always the pale boy quickly turned away.

On Sunday at the ten o'clock mass, when those in his pew rose from their knees to receive communion, Thomas sat back and made space for the others to pass. His father and brothers shuffled by, and only his mother gave him a questioning look of concern. After his family joined the line in the center aisle, Thomas lowered the kneeler and returned to prayer. He prayed to do better in school, to be more like his brothers. He prayed to make his parents proud. He prayed to be a better altar boy. He prayed to understand the strained silences between his parents that only he seemed to notice and why he cried at night in his bed and why he'd been so cruel to Peter Gordon.

At Monday morning mass, Thomas listened closely to all three readings, which came from Leviticus, Corinthians, and the gospel according to Luke. Afterwards, he was ready to be quizzed, but no questions came. On Tuesday and Wednesday too, he fought against his early morning drowsiness and concentrated on the words as Monsignor McGinley read them. After mass each day, the two of them spoke briefly, once about a misstep Thomas had taken, but otherwise about trivial things. The televised launch of a space shuttle for another orbital test flight, the upcoming Superbowl. Thomas was surprised that Monsignor McGinley was a Steeler's fan.

All week long, he watched as the faithful took communion, wondering with each one about his or her secret sins. A teenage girl appeared one morning, and her hair was dyed a bright shade of red. Thomas could imagine the many things she'd done wrong.

If the monsignor's words were true, then even the priest, Thomas realized, even the priest himself was wicked in some way. Up on the altar, Thomas found himself mouthing the words, just moving his lips along with the monsignor, when he begged, *wash away my iniquities, cleanse me from my sins*. And all week long, the tiny woman in the back pew sat in silence, looking to Thomas not just penitent but crumpled, defeated.

In the fall, there had been a change to the mass, something so rare and unexpected it seemed impossible. But, because of some ruling Thomas did not fully understand, it was now permissible to receive communion in your hand and then slip the host into the mouth yourself. When Sister Anita Joseph explained this to the auditorium full of students, it was clear she was offended by the change. But she told them all that you were to hold your left hand cupped under your right, both upturned, and that once you had the host in your palm—which should obviously have been scrupulously cleaned just before mass— you should step to the side, continue to face the altar, carefully pick up the host, and insert it into you mouth with respect and reverence.

Later that same day, Sister Joseph visited each classroom so the students could rehearse this new technique. They practiced with wafers that had not yet been consecrated, with Sister Joseph playing the role of priest.

At mass two days later, the feast of the Immaculate Conception, almost all of the kids received communion in this way, mostly for the novelty Thomas thought. Once the initial excitement passed, about half the younger generation used their hands, but almost all the older folks remained faithful to the old ways.

This is why Thomas was doubly surprised on the Thursday morning of his second week of serving the 6:30 morning mass. When the dozen congregants came forward for communion, Thomas saw the withered woman—risen at last from her back pew—shuffling deliberately up the aisle. And not just that, but she had her hands cupped and out-stretched.

Monsignor McGinley seemed undisturbed as he lifted the host and offered, like a question, "Body of Christ?"

With her head still dipped, the withered woman said, "Amen," and extended her cupped hands up to her forehead. Monsignor deposited the host in her wrinkled palm. As she stepped to the side, directly in front of Thomas, Monsignor scanned the pews to be sure no one else was coming forward. But Thomas watched her reach her right hand into the palm where the host was, pinch at the air, and bring an empty hand to her mouth. All the while she stared at the tiled floor. The hand still holding the host quickly closed and slid down to her pocket, and she kept it there as she turned and went back to her pew. Monsignor strode up to the altar, leaving Thomas paralyzed where he was. There was nothing about this in the *Altar Boy's Complete Guide*, which by now he'd all but memorized.

Monsignor cleared his throat and drew the boy's attention, and Thomas stiffly returned to his duties. But once the priest had finished at the altar and they'd returned to their cold marble seats, he could contain himself no more. He leaned over and whispered, "Monsignor, that woman—"

"I know," the priest said, keeping his eyes out on the congregation. "She's still here. Let's just finish the mass."

And that is what they did. Only a minute or two later, they were walking down the aisle, past the somber churchgoers, and heading toward the sacristy where Thomas and the monsignor had their talks after mass. But the priest veered away at the last pew and unexpectedly sat down with the old woman who'd stolen the communion. Thomas, unsure of what to do, retreated to the sacristy and from there he watched everyone else leave the church, almost all of them nervously glancing over at the strange scene in the back pew.

When the priest rose a few minutes later, he turned and motioned for Thomas to come over. "Thomas," he said, "this is Mrs. Cosgrove. I'm going to ask you to sit quietly with her for a moment while I gather a few things. Can you do that for me, please?"

Thomas nodded and sat. Mrs. Cosgrove gave no sign that she knew he was there. He wondered what her punishment would be, and he wanted to ask her why she'd tried to steal the host.

When Monsignor McGinley reappeared, he wore a winter coat and had Thomas' gripped in one hand. He passed it to him and said, "You'll come with us."

The withered woman rose and said nothing to either of them. She ambled through the vestibule and out into the bitter cold. On the church steps, which had been salted to melt the ice, Thomas stepped forward and offered his arm, but she gripped the black iron railing instead. In silence, Thomas and Monsignor McGinley followed her slow progress through the parking lot that doubled as a playground. It had been plowed and so Thomas could see the hopscotch board as well as the game of Prodigal Son that had been painted into the asphalt. Even when they reached the back of the parking lot, where there were no cars, the old woman kept walking, and only when she left the lot and turned on the sidewalk did Thomas realize they were walking to her house.

It was two blocks down, a row home one from the end. The painted wood of the front porch flaked, desperate for a new paint job, and a swing hung lopsided, dangling from a single chain. Stacked up along the wall by the door were dozens of newspaper bundles, wrapped in plus signs of twine. The withered woman opened the creaky door and walked through. The priest and the boy followed.

Inside, the air was musty and dark. The antique furniture, ornate carved wood, gold framed photos, reminded Thomas of objects from a museum. As they mounted a staircase, Thomas heard above them an odd sound, a low mechanical hum.

They moved down a thin hallway, toward the rear of the house, and entered a cramped bedroom. Even as he stepped in, Thomas smelled something sour and unpleasant. In the center of the dimly lit room was a man propped up in a bed with hospital railings. His face was gaunt and his eyes were fixed directly overhead, so intent and concentrated that Thomas followed his stare to a water-stained ceiling. The stains bubbled out like storm clouds.

"Pardoname," said a woman Thomas hadn't seen. She rose from a rocking chair by the window and spoke in hushed tones for a moment to the withered woman. Monsignor McGinley moved to the head of the bed and Thomas looked around. On the nightstand, a collection of pill bottles looked like a skyline. In one corner, a purring humidifier huffed steam, and Thomas recalled his mother smearing Vicks VapoRub on his chest when he was sick in second grade.

The woman who spoke Spanish excused herself and slipped away, and the withered woman took a position across from the monsignor. The priest motioned to the space next to him and Thomas made his way there, having to bump passed a strange looking chair that was nothing more than a large white bucket with metal rails. It took Thomas a moment to realize its function.

The old woman settled a hand on the man's bony shoulder. "Franklin," she croaked, the first word Thomas heard her say. "Franklin, the priest is come."

The man blinked, as he had been blinking, but did not take his eyes off the ceiling. Thomas thought he might be smiling, but realized it could be his imagination.

"Hello, Franklin," Monsignor McGinley said in a clear voice. "It's Ed McGinley. We met years back, when I officiated at your daughter Jeanie's wedding."

"Jenny," the old woman corrected. She picked up a brush from the nightstand and combed out the man's wispy grey hair.

Thomas looked at the man's mouth, slightly open, and wondered if he had teeth. His whole face seemed on the verge of caving in on itself, so tight was the skin and so sunken the cheeks. The woman reached for a glass of water, held it with one hand, and with her other she inserted an eye dropper, the kind with a big blue bulb on the end. She dipped the eye dropper into the water, tapped it on the side of the glass, then brought it to the man's cracked lips. Perhaps instinctively, he pursed his lips around it and the woman pressed gently. The man licked his lips, worked them with his gums, and then he said the words, "More . . . please."

The woman gave him two more droppers full, and when she finished, he turned his head on the pillow and faced Monsignor McGinley. The priest said, "How are you, Franklin?"

Franklin blinked and said, "Well, you're here."

The priest slid a hand through the railing and set it gently on the blanket, over the outline of an arm. "Would you like to pray?"

Franklin nodded, and without blessing himself, he began to recite the Hail Mary in a raspy voice. When Monsignor joined in, Thomas did as well. Together they got through that and an Our Father, but half way through the Apostle's Creed, Franklin fell silent. He shook his head at the lost words. The others finished it for him.

Monsignor slid a hand inside his coat and withdrew what looked to Thomas like a tiny tobacco tin. He said, "I'm going to anoint you now." He unscrewed the top and passed it to Thomas, then dipped a thumb inside the container and brought it to Franklin's forehead. He made the sign of the cross and whispered, then said, "Amen." Thomas repeated it.

Monsignor gave the chrism to Thomas, who put the cap back on, then the priest leaned in close to Franklin's face. "Have you done wrong things in your life, Franklin?"

In the corner of the room, the humidifier wheezed. Almost imperceptibly, the old man nodded.

"And do you regret those acts? You don't need to name them Franklin. That isn't necessary now. Just put them before Jesus. Ask for His forgiveness."

"I'm sorry," Franklin said. "I'm sorry. I'm sorry. I'm sorry." He continued to repeat it, and each time he seemed more insistent. It was difficult to watch, but Thomas did not turn away.

Finally, the priest patted him on the arm and said, "That's fine, Franklin. That's very good." He lifted two fingers and positioned them over Franklin's face. He drew the sign of the cross in the air and said, "I absolve you of all your sins in the name of the Father and the Son and the Holy Ghost."

The priest again reached into his coat and pulled out a second tin.

From this one, he retrieved a single host. At the sight of it, the woman crossed herself and knelt. With great care, monsignor broke off a tiny splinter and said, "This is the body of Christ." Franklin, staring at the water-stains still, opened his mouth just enough for the tip of his tongue to emerge.

Monsignor placed the sliver on the man's tongue and said to the woman, "Perhaps some more of that water."

She obliged and together the three of them watched Franklin chewing the tiny fragment with great effort. Finally he swallowed. He sighed, then after a few moments of quiet, he focused once more on the ceiling. Again, Thomas thought he saw him smile thinly. "Do you see them?" Franklin asked.

Almost instantly, the priest said, "I do not see them. But I know that they are here." After a moment, he added, "Pray to hear God's will, Franklin. And when you hear it, obey His will. If He calls you to rest, it's all right if you rest. I'll come see you again in a few days, if that's all right?" He looked to the withered woman for an answer, but she was still on her knees, looking down. It occurred to Thomas that she might be crying, or that she might be thinking about what the next few days would surely bring.

They saw themselves out, Thomas following the priest. They heard the Spanish woman running water in the kitchen but did not talk with her. Without speaking to each other, the two of them went back down the broken sidewalk and crossed the church parking lot. At the back door of the rectory, Monsignor McGinley turned to the boy. "Do you have any questions?"

Thomas considered this, then shook his head.

"Very good. Saturday penance service is available from 3 p.m till 4:30."

126

Thomas nodded. He remembered the cramped darkened chamber, the red cushion of the kneeler, the woven screen and the deep quiet.

"All right then. Thank you for your help. Go and join your classmates."

Thomas went down to the cafeteria, where the kids gathered on cold days before classes began. Some were racing around but most sat in groups at the tables. Thomas found Peter Gordon sitting on the stage steps by himself reading a book. Peter lifted his eyes from the book, saw Thomas, then began to scan the auditorium. But Thomas, who had come to apologize to Peter, held up a hand and said, "Don't worry. I want to ask you a question."

Peter folded the book on his lap and looked blankly at him. And Thomas leaned in and quietly asked, "Tell me please. What was making you cry?"

Henry Wants to Know Your Name

I

JUST AFTER TWO A.M. AT the all-night CVS, Henry pulls a blue bottle of sleeping pills from the shelf and studies the warning about recommended dosage. In his other hand, he holds a box cutter with a brown handle that he found in aisle six. Henry's thinking it may be easier on his landlady if he's simply in bed, apparently resting. Unable to decide, Henry carries both to the front counter, where a middle-aged man with braces asks him if he's found all that he needs. But Henry's eyes fix on a tiny booklet in a white rack. On the cover, a chubby infant smiles. Henry and his wife bought a booklet similar to this one two summers ago while on vacation in the Outer Banks. But here and now, in this CVS at two a.m., Henry doesn't think about the sons and daughters denied him. His mind turns to you, not a child he'll never have but a man he'll never meet. Henry wants to know your name.

Sitting in his car, the only one in the dark parking lot, Henry pulls the booklet from the bag. He cracks the door so the light comes on and he begins flipping pages.

You can't be a Michael, he decides. Or a Carl or a Matthew or a

Scott. None of these names from his grade school classes or the roster of his many brothers. No, it must be something unfamiliar, something never before encountered. Aramis has the right sound, perhaps Rutledge. Henry scratches at his beard, untrimmed now for over a week, and ponders Lucian, but the connotations are all wrong. Shamus rings more true, and when Henry says it aloud in his cold car, "Shamus," the sound of his own voice startles him. He has not spoken to anyone since this morning at 7 a.m. when he called in sick for the third day in a row.

Back at his apartment, Henry puts on a pot of coffee and wonders what to do with you now that he has your name. Guided by habit more than design, he unfolds his laptop on the kitchen table. Once online, he pulls down the favorites menu and selects the web address for Dr. Frank's Recovery Club. The home page features a bright red tree house with "No Girlz Allowed" scrawled across the wooden door. At the prompt box where he normally inputs "N-Ree," his fingers hesitate. He inhales deeply, like a magician about to try an incantation for the first time, and types in S-h-a-m-u-s. Tapping ENTER brings him into the main chat room, where the show is already in progress.

Dr. Frank: Have you tried warm milk Buf? Maybe yoga?

Buffalo72: No matter what, I think about Julie all night long.

Jaybird: Call the bitch. Make her cry. That always helps me sleep better.

Dr. Frank: Non-productive behavior J. The secret—for all of us—is not letting the bitterness enter our heart. It's like an enemy army once it's encamped.

Two weeks ago, Henry stayed awake with Buffalo72 even after Dr. Frank signed off, reading his tale of betrayal and offering what comfort he could. And Jaybird's hostility is really a flawed coping mechanism for dealing with unhealed emotional wounds. That's Dr. Frank's assessment, and Henry agrees. Henry scrolls through the evening's chat and sees no sign of Oxman, a fact that concerns him.

Greetings Shamus, Dr. Frank writes. *Glad that you could join us. :) Would you like to share your story?*

Henry sips at his coffee, then types in, No. *I'm here to apologize.*

Dr. Frank: For what?

Shamus: All the pain that I have caused.

Buffalo72: Share with us.

I'm him, Henry types, and he feels a strange surge rising. *I'm the one who brought you here. I'm sorry I guess but look, the way I see it, I just gave your wives what you couldn't.*

Henry lifts his hands from the keyboard and leans back in his chair. Jaybird writes, *hacksaw your balls cocksucker.*

Before booting Henry from the room, Dr. Frank writes, *Whoever you are, consider the destructive repercussions of your actions. Mend your ways.*

Exiled from the recovery tree house, Henry is faced again with the wooden door on his screen, though now it has a "KEEP OUT" sign on it. But Henry does not feel excluded. He feels fine and good. Something hums warmly in his chest, a sense of power and satisfaction that he immediately identifies as yours.

Ad boxes flash along the side of the page. An "X-Skirt Service" with chapters in 34 cities runs its number: 1-800-AllforU. The ad beneath it features a digitized cartoon wolf licking his chops. His caption reads, "Looking for Lambs? Click Here for Hottest Personals." While Henry has never pursued such diversions, he decides that you probably do, and he rolls his mouse and clicks.

He hungers Shamus, for more of you.

The site is vast, thousands of entries, and as he reads Henry marvels at the sheer scope of the lost and lonely:

Pretty Woman
DWF, 46, Julia Roberts look-a-like,
ready 2B your fantasy.

Simple Life
Friendly Mother of special needs angel.
Just want someone to share life with to the fullest.
Smokers A-ok.

Scout's Honor
SWF 34, independent, energetic,
enjoys hiking, tofu, and gentle anal.

After a while, Henry can't help but imagine his own ad. *DWM with slight beer gut seeks patient woman who enjoys flea markets, old bookstores, and walks in the forest.* It is bland and typical and he knows it. But then he realizes he's become distracted by reality. He's forgotten he's you right now. He opens the submission box and, after several drafts, sends in the following:

Total Package
SWM, 37, Discrete. Rich.
Ready to give you everything he can't.

$$* \qquad * \qquad *$$

STRANGELY ENERGIZED, HENRY STARTS WONDERING about the rest of your life.

After looking at four college websites, he decides you went to Duke. He studies the descriptions of the majors and settles on a business degree for you. You pledged Kappa Alpha. You were vice-president of Future Business Leaders. You were formally accused of date rape, twice.

At a travel website, Henry completes a contest entry form for a trip to France. He fills in your full name as Shamus B. Thorn. The B is for Benedict and he thinks the whole thing is really quite clever. He decides during this exercise that you never married, you enjoy golf, tennis, and horse racing. A checklist of appliances makes Henry pause. He leans back in his chair, pictures your house, your living room. The upstairs bedroom.

Henry types in new parameters for the search engine. He wants to decide where you live.

A dozen local realtors have webpages. All promise new beginnings at reasonable rates. But when he downloads the homepage of Coker Realty, Henry sits up. Brett and Rita Coker stand side by side, his arm around her shoulder, a "Just Sold" sign staked in the grass, a moving truck backed up to the door and a happy little family cheerfully carrying taped boxes. "Your Dream is Our Dream," their slogan reads. Brett is beaming, chest puffed, chin raised. Rita smiles, but something in the strain of her cheeks catches Henry's eye. He thinks she might be sad or a little lonely. But he also sees what he knows you would see Shamus: opportunity.

Henry selects "Homes Over $300,000," and is presented with a list of six offerings. He knows you'd never live in a beach house. Too public. The second entry looks promising: a restored farmhouse in the county across the river. Fenced yard. Secluded. Just rustic enough to qualify as romantic. A click enlarges the photo and reveals an upstairs window with a rounded top. The glass reflects passing clouds, but what Henry sees in the puffy forms is a man standing in a white bathrobe, surveying his property. Henry decides the man is you.

Henry decides this is afterwards.

He stares at the image for three minutes and then shuts off the computer.

Lying on his bed in the dark, Henry can't help wondering what the two of you talked about, in the quiet after you finished. Henry wonders what she told you about him. Do you know that when they first tried to make love back in the dorms, Henry came before he got his jeans off? Do you know that during their rained-out honeymoon in the Bahamas they spent two naked days in their cabana? That he's saved the tickets from every movie they've been to for seven years? That on long car rides they do crosswords together? Do you know Shamus, that when his wife began sleeping on the couch Henry asked her if he was snoring? That, of course, was long before he knew about you.

When his alarm clock sounds, Henry calls in sick for the fourth day in a row and notices the black smudge burning in the bottom of the coffee pot. His shower is long and scalding. Distracted, he shampoos twice. Standing before his sink, Henry rubs the fogged mirror with his towel, and in the misty circle something seems wrong with his face. He focuses on the vision of you in the farmhouse window. You have neither moustache nor beard. He removes the attachment from his trimmer and it buzzes pleasantly against his skin. The shaving cream is cool and the razor is quick. Henry has not seen his bare chin since before the wedding, and it startles him. But he likes the look and runs his fingertips over the smoothness, and he imagines his wife doing the same to your chin. The trimmings stay in the sink.

Henry dresses in his finest suit, the blue one he wore to court six months back because he knew she'd be there. He ties the tie three times until he's satisfied with the knot. Sitting at his breakfast counter, he flips through the phone book. He will call Coker Realty and make an appointment to view your old farmhouse. He will tell them his name is Shamus B. Thorn and he's new to the area. He will tell Rita that he's prepared to take immediate action.

II

At 10:55, Henry locates the dirt road and steers through the thin pine tree forest. He pulls around the horseshoe driveway in the black Lexus he rented with his Visa from a place by the airport and parks behind a BMW. The moment he shuts off the engine, Rita Coker opens the front door of the house and waves as if she's welcoming him home. Henry climbs from the Lexus and thinks how nice it would be to return to such a smile each day. But as the realtor crosses the tightly trimmed lawn on long legs, Henry feels Shamus' reaction: she's the kind who'll like having her hair pulled. The realtor extends a slender hand. "Rita Coker," she says. "Call me Ree."

"Shamus Thorn," Henry says as they shake. Rita's ring has three diamonds, two more than the one in the box under Henry's bed, still in the UPS box addressed in his wife's handwriting. Henry looks over Rita's shoulder. "I thought Mr. Coker would be joining us."

"Brett got called away on an inspection. Wood rot hiding in a sill beam."

Henry laughs nonchalantly, the way he imagines you would in this situation.

"We'll start inside, alright Mr. Thorn?" She flashes bright teeth.

"We can start anywhere you'd like," Henry says. "But call me Shamus."

His eyes rise to the window with the rounded top where you stood in the white robe and for a moment his smile thins. But this, Rita does not notice.

As they tour the downstairs, Henry listens intently while Rita points out the pine hardwood floors (original, 1875), the delicate twin antique ceiling fans (brought back by a son from WWI), the stone fireplace in the living room (mined by hand from a local quarry in 1894). After Rita tells him that the built-in bookcases in the study were fashioned by a carpenter named Carpenter in 1965, Henry says, "Now Ree, either you've got a memory on loan from M.E.N.S.A or you're making all this up."

Rita laughs, genuinely amused, and the sound of her laughter fills the air of the empty house. The way she laughs, without restraint or embarrassment, makes Henry think that when she makes love with Brett—if in fact she is still making love with Brett—she is not quiet. After this has occurred to Henry, he decides it is an observation that you would make. He is surprised by how easy it is to be you.

While touring the living room (north wall replaced due to fire damage in 1928), Rita makes plenty of eye contact as Henry concocts a past: he's from the north, an independent financial advisor.

"So what kind of advice do you give?" Rita asks.

"Buy low," Henry says. "Sell high."

Again, she laughs.

A series of swift beeps sound from Rita's back pocket. She slides out a cell phone and looks at the screen. "I need to take this quick, okay?"

Henry nods, and Rita unfolds the phone to her cheek. "What's the damage?"

Henry pictures the muscular Brett, fresh from under a home on pillars, where he prodded a wooden beam with his fingers, tugged away small chunks of a foundation that will crumble without swift intervention.

Rita nods. "Uh-huh. Uh-huh. Get Kendall to come give an estimate. No not Gary. Kendall." She folds the cell shut.

"Trouble in paradise?" Henry asks.

"Nothing Brett can't handle. He's a big boy."

"I'm sure he is."

Rita breaks eye contact and points at some crown molding. "That's all original," she says.

"It's beautiful," Henry says, which brings a slight smile back to Rita's face. He feels certain now that she desires him and it makes him feel prized, chosen. He wonders Shamus, if you have felt this way. Once he saw a TV special about Nigerian nomads who steal each other's wives at an annual festival. They paint their faces orange and take part in a frenzied dance to demonstrate their virility. At the time, Henry thought they looked insane. He recalls now that he watched this from bed, with his wife asleep next to him, on her side, turned away.

In the kitchen, Rita waves a hand at the stale air and unlocks a window overlooking the backyard. She tries to push it open but can't. Henry steps directly behind her, stretches his arms on either side of her, and with the heels of his hands shoves on the window. After a groan, it shimmies up. Still inside his arms, she turns. "It's the humidity," she explains. "This far south, you get that a lot." She looks into his eyes, but does not slide from his arms. "It gives the place country charm, another selling point."

Henry says, "You like this, don't you Ree?"

Rita dips her chin and blinks. "I enjoy matching personality and property to create a unique and positive synergy."

Henry steps away, walks over to the double sink. "That's from the realtor handbook, and I know it. I mean what you do. You like showing other people's homes."

Rita, still against the window, inhales and exhales. "This is nobody's home now. It's just a house."

"But before."

"Those people are gone now. That's how I see it."

She opens the stainless steel fridge and he peers in, nods his approval of the impressive square footage. A corner of paper on top of the refrigerator catches his attention and he pulls it from the thin dust. The post-it note's handwritten list reads: sun-dried tomato bagels, Fat Bastard, my milk, double-A batteries, 87-95-23.

The list makes Henry feel strangely like himself. Rita sees him reading the note. He says, "But you know about them, all these people who lived here once?"

"Everyone kept the house in good shape. The folks who just left are latter day yuppies from Cleveland. The Halseys. They converted the place into a B&B but couldn't keep it afloat after their tech stocks tanked. Before that the Carpenters, Liz and Frank. Started with a newborn baby when they bought in the sixties, moved out west with six kids in 1988. According to the abstract, they bought it from the Metoyer family, who owned the land since this was all farm country. Three generations. We could look over the paperwork together if any of this matters."

Henry takes a deep breath, as if he's inhaling all that Rita is saying. He returns the list to the top of the fridge, bothered now that he disturbed it. He looks around the room, stares hard at the walls. "Just one house," he says, his voice growing softer. "Just wood and stone. It's a wonder it can hold so much."

Rita steps closer. "So much what?"

"Think about it. Husbands and wives came through that door carrying bags of groceries. On that counter they cut up vegetables from the garden. In that sink they washed and dried dishes. From these cabinets they pulled coffee cups, wine glasses, baby bottles. Right here, this is the drawer they came to for candles when the power went out. Do you understand? On a table in this room, checkbooks were rebalanced. Bills were juggled. Inside these very walls, people swore, lied, took oaths, broke promises. A phone plugged into that socket rang one morning with terrible news, or it didn't ring the one night when it had to. On that refrigerator, a lover left a note—maybe a dozen small words—that changed everything."

Henry finds himself standing at the open window. He looks out over the grass into the thin pine trees beyond the fence. He is feeling suddenly a lot like himself.

Rita stays behind him, and for a long time, they are silent. Finally Rita speaks. "One time I sold a condo for this couple, the Breckenridges. Their daughter died in her sleep, just didn't wake up one morning. They couldn't keep living in the house, of course. And every time I showed the place, when I'd get to the second bedroom with the perspective buyers—"

Henry turns. "Did you tell them?"

Rita looks at the tile floor. "No. Brett said it was better that way." "To lie?"

"To keep it a secret," Rita says. "I don't know why I'm telling you this." Her eyes stay on Henry.

He feels you stir inside him and thinks how you would answer. "You're telling me because you want me to know, Ree."

She shrugs. Henry looks at her and she looks back. Henry feels you again Shamus. He says, "Let's head upstairs."

The Halseys of Cleveland fixed up four bedrooms nicely. Bright colors, restored crown molding. A communal bathroom features a stained glass skylight salvaged from a church. But Rita keeps the best for last, the master bedroom. When Henry steps through the doorway, he sees the window with the rounded top and is immediately drawn to it. While Rita opens a closet door, he walks to the spot where you stood in your white robe and places his feet where yours once were. Henry tries to imagine what thoughts turned in your mind as his wife laid in bed behind you. Was she sleeping peacefully? Was she getting dressed? Was she coaxing you back?

"The master bathroom has a Jacuzzi," Rita says. "Self-cleaning."

He turns to her. With her slender arms and her slim neck. He needs to know how you felt. "Ree, does Brett compliment you?"

"Brett?"

"Does he appreciate you?"

"I'm not sure what—"

"There's no need to be shy. Or anxious. I'm just asking. I'm making casual inquiries."

Henry advances on Rita and she backs into a corner by the bathroom. Pressing her shoulders to the wall, Henry kisses her. For a moment her lips seem to part, but then she twists her face to the side. "No," she says. "Not here."

Their eyes meet. Henry says, "I can get a hotel."

"No," she says. "I don't do this."

Henry speaks in a tone he's convinced is yours: "You do now."

Rita flattens her palms against Henry's chest and pushes. Though the pressure isn't much, he steps back. She slides into the bathroom with the self-cleaning Jacuzzi and shuts the door. Henry hears the click. The faucet runs.

Henry leans into the door. He feels confident that if you were here Shamus, you could lure her out. "Ree," he says. "You can decide what happens now. You can stay in there or you can come out. But I promise you one thing: your husband never has to know."

The water stops and Henry hears three cell phone beeps. Briefly he imagines his shoulder splintering the wooden door. He wonders how capable of violence you are and has a disturbing image of Rita in the Jacuzzi. And then, just before he turns and leaves, he pictures unsuspecting Brett out there talking with Kendall in some driveway discussing wood rot. Stupid bastard, Henry thinks, he has no idea.

III

In the dim light of Gentlemen's Jungle, Henry thinks he sees freckles on his waitress' breasts. She tells him the special today is chicken fried steak with gravy, two veggies and a lap dance. $49.95. Henry almost orders a beer and a burger, but realizes that you wouldn't have such common fare. "Bring me a steak," he demands. "And a rum and Coke. We'll talk about dessert later."

She disappears. On stage, a man Windexes the floor length mirrors that line the wall. Other than Henry, there are five men and one woman having lunch here today. Henry keeps picturing Rita in that bathroom, cradling her cell phone. He wonders what she told the 911 operator. He wonders what she'll tell Brett and imagines his suspicions—that she led the stranger on, that laugh of hers, the flash in her eyes. Maybe tonight, maybe tomorrow, accusations will be made. Henry is surprised when he realizes he's not feeling guilty about any of this. Then he remembers he is you. So he feels no remorse, no regret about what happened, except for what did not. This absence feels wrong. He should feel regret. You should feel regret.

"How do you want that?" his waitress asks, her freckled breasts looming suddenly in front of his face. "Your steak. How do you want it cooked?" She puts down his glass and the ice tinkles. "You didn't say."

"Rare," Henry tells her, though he prefers medium. He holds her with your smooth eye contact while he tastes the drink and then asks, "Any chance there's still a pay phone in here?" Henry is thinking *AllforU*.

THREE HOURS LATER THERE IS a knock on the door of room 324 of the Ramada, one interstate exit east of Henry's apartment complex. Henry puts down his drink and hurries to the door, opens it, and she stands there, a short blonde in jeans with a small black purse. "Hi," she says. "You Shamus?"

Henry smiles. "Come on in."

As she's closing the door, she slides the "Do Not Disturb" sign to the outer knob, a smooth, professional move that impresses Henry. He also notices her long red nails and wonders if they are real.

"What you watching?" she asks, lifting her chin at the TV. She sits on the edge of the bed and stares at a financial analyst explaining the risks involved in investing too heavily in one stock.

"Checking up on my portfolio," Henry lies. "The guy I talked to didn't tell me your name."

"Call me Tabitha. Unless, you know, if you've got something else in mind, super."

Henry considers speaking the other name. But that would be too much. Maybe later, he decides. "Tabitha. Would you like some wine?"

"Not really. Got any beer?"

"Sorry."

"I'll have the wine then."

Henry pours and Tabitha starts flipping channels. Henry hands her a glass and she says, "So Marty explained everything, right?"

"Of course," Henry says. He walks to the night stand drawer and opens it, pulls the bank envelope from beneath the Bible. When he hands it to Tabitha, she puts down her wine and the remote control to count.

"Super," she says and tucks the envelope into her black purse, which she places on the nightstand between two unlit white candles. "My purse stays here. There's no reason for you to touch it at all. Okay, Shamus?"

He nods.

She smiles. "I need for you to say that back to me so we're clear. This is what I need for us to have our fun."

"There's no reason for me to touch your purse. It stays on the night stand."

"Super." She sips more wine, clicks the TV to blackness, then sits cross-legged in the middle of the bed. "So how do you want to start?" She pats the mattress.

But Henry arranges the pillows at the head of the bed and settles in as if he's about to read. He steadies his wine glass on his stomach. "I want to talk for a bit."

Tabitha shrugs. "It's fine if we talk, Shamus. But that cuts into our fun time, okay? I'm seriously on the clock the minute I walked through that door."

"That seems fair." Henry lifts his glass, feels the warmth spread into his body. His confidence is slipping, and he tries to think of what you might say. "You must learn a lot about people in this line of work."

Tabitha sips her wine. "You've got very nice teeth."

Henry doesn't know how to respond.

"Your teeth. They're very nice. One time I took these Dental Assistant classes. The whole thing didn't work out, but now I notice teeth. You've got nice incisors."

"Well thanks. Your teeth are really nice, too."

They each drink their wine and Henry gets the bottle, refills hers then his, returns to his spot. "I really don't want to turn this into an interview, but I have a question that I need to ask."

"I'm totally clean," she says. "Marty gets us tested once a week."

"No. Listen. A lot of your clients. Are they married men?"

"I suppose. Some guys mention wives. You got one?"

"Does it matter?"

"Not to me."

Henry looks away from her, down into his wine. "What is it that makes married men call you? What makes someone in love turn to somebody else?"

"I don't know," Tabitha says. After a few seconds of silence she shrugs and adds, "Some folks really just like to fuck."

Henry nods. "There are a couple things in the bathroom, Tabitha. I'd like you to put them on. If that's okay."

Tabitha cracks a sly smile. "From one to ten, how weird is this gonna get?"

"I don't know the scale," Henry says. "But not a one and not a ten."

"Super." Tabitha lifts her black purse from the nightstand and struts into the bathroom. Henry brings a match to each of the candles and turns off the lights. He finishes his wine, undresses and gets under the covers.

When Tabitha steps into the flickering half light, Henry tries to pretend. She stands at the foot of the bed, naked except for one of his white dress shirts.

Back in the dorms, years ago, Henry's wife said she loved to have his scent wrapped around her. "It fits?" Henry asks, and Tabitha raises her left hand, where a diamond ring sparkles on her ring finger.

"I want you to imagine that you're married. To a good man. A man that you care for. But now you find yourself here. Do you leave the ring on or take it off?"

Tabitha shakes her head. "Role-playing's cool, but Marty didn't—"

"Leave it on then."

He pulls back the sheets and she slides in next to him. Henry is already aroused.

In the bed in room 324 of the Ramada, Henry and Tabitha tumble and roll, and for a while, Henry disappears into the physical delight of it all. When Tabitha whispers, "Are you ready?" he nods and she reaches to the black purse on the nightstand and retrieves a condom. She rips it free of its pouch and unrolls it down his erection. Henry maneuvers himself on top of her, and once he's inside, he begins the familiar rocking, their faces side by side. He says the other name once and whispers, "I know what you're risking, to be here with me. I know that he could find out."

"Yeah, super," Tabitha says. "Fuck me like a rock star."

"Now tell me that it's worth all the risk."

"You're worth all the risk, Shamus. You're worth all the risk." Her nails dig into his ass, urging him on.

"Henry's a good man," Henry says. "But he's not enough, I understand. Why should you feel bad about having your needs met?"

"C'mon," she says. "Give it to me good." Tabitha looks at the second glass of wine that she didn't have a chance to finish.

Henry notes the dullness of her tone, its half-hearted enthusiasm. He knows she doesn't want to be here with him like this, and this notion shifts the fantasy. "Tell me you want me to stop," he says, no longer whispering. "Tell me you love your husband and you can't do this."

This new idea, that his wife was not complicit, that in the final moments before betrayal she was true in her heart, ignites in Henry. He hasn't noticed that Tabitha is no longer moaning and her hands have stopped. He rocks his hips faster.

"Hey," Tabitha says. She pushes into his shoulders. "Not so rough."

"Good, that's great. Now try to make me stop."

Tabitha shouts, "I mean it," and rakes her fingernails down Henry's chest. He arches back and she claws again. A red fake nail snaps off and Tabitha is watching it tumble in the air when Henry slaps her once, turning her face in the pillow. They both are still in the silence. Then Henry lowers himself and continues. Tabitha sniffles.

"Tell me to stop," Henry says. "Tell me you can't do this to your husband."

With his eyes closed in near ecstasy, Henry doesn't see Tabitha reach to the small black purse on the nightstand, and he doesn't see what she pulls out. He only feels the sharp shock on his temple. His body rolls next to Tabitha's, and she kneels up, raises her hand and brings it down. Henry's body drops off the side of the mattress, collapses between the bed and the wall.

Tabitha snatches her clothing from the bathroom and stuffs her legs into her jeans without putting on her panties. "Motherfucking prick," she says. "You got maybe ten minutes before Marty and Randolph show up and do their impersonations of pissed off violent offenders."

After the door closes, Henry finds himself unable to concentrate. His arms are like jello. His penis is flaccid inside the condom. There is a dark spot in the center of his spinning vision. Above him, a dozen candle flames float in the air.

Later, when the door opens, his eyes roll and focus on white sneakers and black boots. The door locks. The TV snaps to life, and the volume rolls quite high. An analyst shouts something about the Dow Jones Industrial Average. The black booted figure stands over him. He is about to kick Henry's ribs until three of them crack. He is about to break his fingers in the nightstand drawer where the Bible sleeps. But before any of this, the smaller man mutes the TV for a moment and leans over the bed. "Shamus, consider this a lesson in consequences." And Henry, hearing your name coming from the lips of another, smiles and nods and waits for the righteous beating he knows he's got coming.

Holding Your Peace

ON THE DAY AFTER ROSALIE FERGUSON files for maternity leave, Elijah is summoned from his cubicle to a meeting where Rosalie's district gets divided up among the other book reps in the region. Eli's share comes to about a dozen schools, including a handful of the PASSHE universities and a community college in Harrisburg. Most are along major highway corridors—78, 81, 83—and, while his fellow workers grumble about the new assignments, Eli doesn't mind. It doesn't really mean more work, just a longer interval between visits to his established clients, almost none of whom remember him despite the long years, nearly ten, that he has spent stopping by their office hours, providing them with free desk copies, listening to their stories about idiot students and ignorant administrators. The idea of something new almost appeals to him. He puts fifty bucks in the office pool for the baby shower, signs a card, and sends Rosalie an email that reads, "You take care of that sweet baby. I'll take care of your customers."

And so, three weeks later, after a night in a LaQuinta with better than average free coffee, buoyed by a certain spirit of possibility, Eli wanders for the first time through the halls of Harrisburg Area Community College. As he's done at the other new schools, he makes impromptu stops at several department heads and slips a photocopied "introduction" sheet into almost one hundred faculty mailboxes. On the sheet, a photo shows a cramped but smiling Eli sitting in a wooden desk, the kind he used to have in grade school. Beneath his contact information, his interests are listed: reading, audible books, travel. All this is intended to add a personal touch. After the photocopies, armed with a folded campus map, he makes his rounds, roaming the catacombs of faculty offices, prowling for open doors. His eyes drift past posted office hours, notes left by procrastinating students, political cartoons. He chats with a dozen professors of varying rank, among them a historian with a bad head cold who is all-but-dissertation and a painfully thin poet, who asks if Eli's publisher might be interested in an innovative approach to free verse.

On his silver laptop, Eli shows his company's website to everyone he sits down with, noting some new editions of classic bestsellers along with more recent books. He touts the affordability of electronic versions, the online guides that students really really love, and the tech support that is available 24/7/365. While he doesn't secure any new orders, he does get a few requests for desk copies, not a bad start for a first visit, especially one at the beginning of the semester.

In the afternoon he visits Messiah College, where he stops by to check in on some of his regulars, then he does a fly by of Elizabethtown, where their textbooks are chosen by committee. Though he could make it back to his home outside Hazleton by nightfall, he decides to crash in a Red Roof Inn along route 83. Over the years, Eli has come to prefer the anonymity of the highway. The midnight desk clerks, the waitresses at Ruby Tuesday's or Applebee's, the staff at the rest stop offering free coffee, they are none of them in the job they dreamed of. But these are Eli's people, and he likes to lift them up. He always makes a point of reading their name tags, making genuine eye contact when offering his heartfelt thanks. He makes a point of trying to forge a quick connection, even if it's just some bland personal question—"Always this busy?" When he can, he likes to offer a sincere compliment. Eli likes to think such things makes a difference, albeit a small one.

The other advantage to being on the road is that he is not home. His apartment building is the same as all the other apartment buildings in his compound, a stale beige. And though Eli doesn't know his neighbors beyond a wave and a smile, he is sure that their apartments are essentially the same as his, identical and stale. Alone in his home, he feels confronted by his own mediocrity. Even the one distinct piece of furniture, a lawyer's bookcase left to him by his father and filled now with novels and poetry collections from his days in grad school, serves only to remind him of what he no longer has. At the center of his life, Eli feels an absence.

After dinner (Olive Garden, a fine dish with sausage and pasta), Eli returns to his hotel room in the Red Roof Inn, a bit more relaxed with the two and a half beer buzz he is enjoying. His waitress, Simone, had tipped his last bottle of Corona, spilling half of it across the table. As they each worked at drying it up, she apologized and insisted on getting him another. But Eli said, "That's okay, all the alcohol is in the bottom anyway." Simone had smiled at his attempt at humor, but hadn't laughed.

Eli isn't looking forward to a night with the remote control, but the idea offers him a certain familiar comfort. Lying on the bed in his boxers, he clicks to a movie he's seen parts of before about a scientist accidentally sent back in time to the days of King Arthur. Long ago, Eli accepted that there was no shame in seeing a movie alone, though he still tended to sit in the back corner when he went to a theater. On his hotel bed, Eli props the laptop across his thighs and, with a vague sense of dread and anticipation, checks his email.

There are a half dozen from the company, including a reminder from HR to get a seasonal flu shot, along with a few requests from various instructors across the state. But one with the subject line, "Can't Believe I Miss You," draws his attention.

As soon as he opens it, he sees he's misread. The words are "I Can't Believe I Missed You," and it's from Jeremy Kincaid, a would-be novelist who was a year ahead of Eli during his grad school days at Bowling Green. They had taken a writing workshop together, one with a professor who seemed to suffer through every page. The email explains that Jeremy, who teaches Freshman Comp at Harrisburg Area Community College, had been shocked to find Eli's introduction and card in his mailbox. He goes on to note that he is still working on his second novel ("in between grading essays about alcoholic fathers and bad boyfriends") and asks if Eli is still writing. One line reads, "You were good." This makes Eli pause for a time. In the next sentence, Jeremy mentions a story Eli had all but forgotten, actually his only publication, a piece about a young boy watching a bridge being built over a river near his small town.

At the end of the email, Jeremy insists that next time Eli comes through, he gives him a heads up so they could visit properly. "You could even crash with me, meet the wife and kids."

Here Eli's mind rolls to Rosalie Ferguson, who gave birth to a little girl the previous week. Christine. Eli had meant to send a note congratulating her, a gift certificate for something, but he had forgotten.

Eli feels bittersweet reading the email, warmed by the affection of a lost friend, upset by the disturbance of long slumbering dreams. He recalls with pride how he'd felt when his fiction was accepted by that online journal. In the story, the bridge is part of an interstate highway system, one that promises prosperity for the isolated town. Even the influx of money from the construction company alone brings treasure. The boy's uncle gets a job with them. But the boy sees too the corrupting influence of progress and decides that in order to preserve his town, he will steal dynamite and blow up the bridge. Eli recalls getting the phone call that the story had been accepted. It felt like it was the beginning of something grand.

Strangely now, he finds he can't remember the story's title. After a few minutes of straining his memory, he does recall the online journal's name—*Wishbone*. But when he punches in the URL, he finds the site has been taken down. There is an apologetic message from the editors, who thank all the writers and readers.

On the Red Roof Inn television, a commercial for tires promises a twenty foot difference in stopping distance. "You can't plan for disasters," the husky man says. "So we do."

Eli turns back to the email a second time and only then does he discover the p.s., buried down below the sign off. "I can't believe Tyler is getting married."

Eli slaps the laptop shut, so hard it stings his legs.

Tyler was the writing program's golden child, a tall blonde boy out of Wyoming with a thick accent, insane talent, and a photographic memory. Even drunk, he could recite whole passages of Shakespeare or the first paragraphs of his favorite novels. Half the stories in his thesis were published by upper-tier literary journals, and he received a fellowship when he entered the PhD program at Rutgers.

Eli and Tyler started the program at the same time and formed a quick, easy friendship. Over crooked pool tables, they engaged in the great debates of grad school—Shelley or Keats, Hemingway or Faulkner, Baldwin or Wright. On Raymond Carver, they agreed. They shared teaching assignments and figured out their schedules together, and when Eli's marriage turned sour midway through their third semester, it was Tyler who did his best to comfort him. He insisted Eli get help at the counseling center on campus, let him sleep on his couch for two months. There was a night one November, the worst of it, when Tyler kicked down his own bathroom door and found Eli naked on his knees, scrambling to collect dozens of red pills that had scattered on the tiled floor.

Eli's wife returned to Baltimore at Christmas, and Eli didn't come back for his fourth and final semester.

Eli hasn't spoken to his ex-wife in seven years. It has been nine since he talked with Tyler. But sometimes late at night, in hotel rooms like the one he's sitting in now, with his face bathed in the laptop's glow, he would wander the web. There was a single picture of his ex-wife he found through Google Images, at a picnic for the insurance company where she worked in Cary, North Carolina. As for Tyler, there were glowing reviews of his two books everywhere, and accolades of his life as a teacher at Old Dominion. During his last book tour, Tyler had an event in Allentown and Eli had been sorely tempted to attend. The novel was about a good man who sleeps with his best friend's wife, ruining the lives of all three. As a work of fiction, it was compelling and well crafted. Eli read up to the scene, about two-thirds the way through, when the narrator stops his despondent friend from jumping off a bridge, but he could read no more.

Now, Eli stares at the laptop and the words of Jeremy Kincaid's email. Jeremy had graduated before everything turned in Eli's marriage, though he must have known Eli never finished. And it was no surprise that he mentioned Tyler—the friendship Eli had with him was well known to all, a centerpiece of that small group. Tyler's pending marriage was remarkable mostly for the fact that, during grad school, he seemed entirely uninterested in dating, despite the many opportunities that came his way. Some speculated that like a bullfighter, he was abstaining to keep pure. Eli came to know better.

Eli begins typing out a cordial response to Jeremy but then abandons the effort. When the computer asks if he wants to save a draft of the file, he chooses no. The scientist on the TV, bespectacled and wearing a white lab coat, charges across an open grassy field, chased by a dragon that breathes fire upon him from above.

The next morning, rejuvenated by a Denny's Grand Slam breakfast, Eli sends a reply to Jeremy. It is professional and concise, noting two new anthologies that were designed to help freshmen see the value of writing. He promises to stop by next time he comes through and congratulates Jeremy on his continued dedication to his fiction. Using a p.s. to make it seem like a casual afterthought, not the main reason he's writing, Eli adds, "Good for Tyler! I wonder who the lucky girl is."

The truth is that all night, though he realized it was highly unlikely if not impossible, Eli had imagined Tyler and his ex-wife standing at an altar. They were smiling, holding hands, waiting for the priest's permission to kiss. Though of course, over the years Eli had imagined them doing much more explicit things, this public acceptance of their union, this holy sanction, enraged him like nothing else. Somewhere in the long night, the old ulcer, a dime size piece of burning coal, ignited under his right rib cage.

For two days Eli checks his email for a reply from Jeremy, often even between visits with professors. But it isn't until Eli is back in his cubicle processing orders that Jeremy finally writes back. It isn't much of a response, just a token couple sentences and, without comment, a link to a website, MonicaPlusTyler.com.

Eli glances around the cubicle, as if someone were about to witness him visiting a porn site, and clicks on the link. And there is Tyler and an attractive blond woman, with long eyelashes and an almond-shaped face. Eli does not recognize her, but clearly, she is the guiding force behind this website. It is an impressive production, giddy and sweet. Beneath the tab "Our Journey!" is what looks like a children's book. Cartoon renderings of the bride and groom are accompanied by simple sentences like, "See Tyler. See Monica. See Tyler see Monica."

The proposal, apparently, involved a balloon ride. Beneath "Picture Gallery!" is a slide show of gauzy photos with the two of them on a beach, hiking a mountain trail, dressed up at a party as Homer and Marge Simpson. Eli peruses through their two "Want Lists." One from Target, one from Finer Things. Among the many items already purchased are an ice cream maker, a digital camera, a picnic basket, matching roller blades. Eli guesses that Monica is eight to ten years younger than Tyler, and realizes it's quite possible that they met when she was Tyler's student. It is easy to imagine her in the front row, listening in rapt attention while Tyler lectured about the organic symmetry of the sonnet, the intricacies of a Joycian epiphany. In all the pictures, she beams bright-eyed, young and fresh. Undisappointed by life. It looks like a fairy book romance.

Eli learns that the wedding is to take place in three weeks in Richmond at a reclaimed train station that had been abandoned for years. There are photos of the majestic building with sunlight slanting through tall windows. A block of rooms with discounted rates has been set aside at the Richmond Hilton, where several other events, including the rehearsal dinner, are to take place.

Also on the website, he finds a guest book where visitors have signed in with sentimental regrets like, "You'll have to party without us, but we send big love from Hawaii!" or enthusiastic praise—"Never known two people so in love. You deserve each other!"

But Eli, reading this last statement, isn't at all convinced. Looking through the site, he's felt a growing kinship with Monica, who deserves better than Tyler. She seems bubbly and naïve—all those toothy smiles in the photos, all those exclamation marks. Eli recalls his first workshop story at Bowling Green, how the professor had called the characters "sugary sweet" and said that overall, it had the emotional depth of a Hallmark card. Was it so wrong to believe in love? Staring into Monica's clear eyes on the computer screen, Eli feels a stirring in his chest, something that feels like obligation.

When he clicks on the "Sign our Book!" button, he isn't sure what he'll do next, so it shocks him when his fingers begin to tap the keyboard and the sentence expands across the page: "Monica, about ten years back Tyler screwed my wife. I wouldn't trust him. Thought you should know."

Rolling the mouse, he maneuvers the blinking arrow over the box that reads, "Submit!" He holds a single finger over the enter key, and tries to imagine what would come next. Someone, not Monica, would read his message, and this person would email or phone or text the bride to be, who would be horrified, indignant. She'd excise it from the site before anyone else could be poisoned by such libel. And then over dinner she'd tell Tyler about the weirdos on the internet, how some people have such twisted minds. It's likely she'd never entertain the anonymous message as the truth. But the insidious seed would be planted. A tiny crack would appear in her perfect world.

Should Monica actually suspect the truth, Tyler, silver-tongued, could persuade her of almost anything. After all, this is the man who had convinced Eli's wife to sleep with him. No, if Eli wanted to save Monica before the wedding, he'd have to do something more than send an anonymous cyber note. He deletes his message and closes the website, then goes to Mapquest and learns that Richmond is only six hours from Hazleton by car. After this, he reaches in his filing cabinet for the form his company uses to request personal days.

There is a moment when he pauses, right at the line for "Reason for Request," as he questions his motivation. Eli wants to save Monica, but he knows too that this will hurt Tyler. Eli isn't the kind of person who takes pleasure in other people's misery. But, Eli realizes with a start, he isn't all that happy with the kind of person he is. Maybe, he thinks, it's time to be somebody new.

Three weeks later, wearing a baseball cap and sunglasses, Eli stands at the front desk of the Richmond Hilton. He had considered booking one of the rooms set aside under the wedding party discount, but was afraid the little joke wasn't worth the risk of being discovered. The concierge, a balding man in his sixties, takes his credit card information and passes over a key card. "Just down the hall to your left. Elevators are on the right."

Eli pulls out a blank piece of paper, folded into a square. "Could you see that Monica Hogan gets this?" he asks.

The clerk dips his head and eyes up the computer screen before him. He nods and takes the paper. "Of course sir."

Till that moment, Eli isn't sure that the bride is actually staying in this hotel. Eli knows that, to avoid hijinks, brides are often secreted away off site. Now the last piece of his plan has been secured. All that remains is execution.

Eli goes up to his room, takes a long, hot shower, then tries to nap. He had awakened at three in the morning on the heels of a vivid dream, one that gave him a profound erection. After that he had been unable to sleep, and the long drive south had been tiring.

At five-thirty, he drives to St. Mary of the Holy Veil, where the wedding rehearsal is being held at six. Eli knows that inside there would be only a handful of people, so if he goes into the church he will certainly be noticed. So he remains in the parking lot, in the corner, under the shade of an overgrown oak. From here, he watches like a cop on a stakeout. When he feels like a stalker, he reminds himself that he's doing all this for Monica's good.

The cars come in, and as the people head for the church, Eli tries to guess who is who. That older couple walking hand in hand, is it Tyler's mom and dad? He has the urge to cross the asphalt, block their path, and say, "Your son is an adulterer." All those giggling ladies, surely bridesmaids, and the thick men are of course ushers. None of them knows the truth about Tyler.

Eli has that written down, a single folded sheet sealed in an envelope back in his hotel room. He has worked on the letter every day since he found their website, and as much as one can be proud of such a document, Eli is. Some phrases, "she was the brightest object in my sky," "brothers of the soul," "betrayal on a scale I had not imagined," he finds especially accurate. In the end, he is certain not to tell Monica to leave Tyler, but merely to be aware of the true nature of the man she is marrying.

Tyler pulls into the parking lot alone, five minutes late, and he barely stops the car before leaping out and charging towards the church. His hair has thinned and he has put on a few pounds. Yet still, jogging comes naturally for him, and his body is strong and graceful. For an instant, Eli imagines running him over. But then he feels it behind his breast plate, how the sight of his old friend lifts him back to when they were close. Those drunken nights discussing Toni Morrison, the long hours spent together in the library stacks, the football games they walked to together, bent toward one another in the cold. It has been years since Eli felt the weight of missing Tyler, and feeling it now makes him angry.

He wonders again if it would really be so melodramatic to forego the letter and actually attend the wedding tomorrow at ten, sit in the back pew like a sniper on a grassy knoll and wait for the priest to ask if anyone had reason that these two should not be bound together. Eli can picture that quiet scene in the church, the half breath of silence when all who had gathered smiled thinly and pretend to look around. Into this stillness, Eli could rise. This, Eli thinks, is how it would happen in a movie or a novel.

But scandal is not his goal, he reminds himself. He needs to save Monica, to keep her pure and unharmed. If she and Tyler become husband and wife, it is inevitable that he will wrong her. Eli is sure of this. He doesn't really want to make a scene or ruin Tyler. He could've done that in a dozen ways over the years. But, loyal even in the face of betrayal, he has held his peace, kept the secret his intoxicated wife told him one night, a 3 a.m. phone call that woke him from a pleasant sleep. Tyler and Eli hadn't spoken after that, and Eli, though he had many opportunities, never divulged it to anyone, not to his two sisters, his dying mother, his therapist. Even as he grew distant from his circle of grad school friends, he knew it was because of what he withheld from them. Maybe this, the fact that what happened had never been put to words—is why the white envelope contains such raw power. It is a physical acknowledgment of the piercing truth, the wrong that he had endured.

During the rehearsal dinner, Eli waits in the hotel lobby. He reads a USA Today behind which he can hide if he needs to. To his left is the room reserved for the party, and earlier Eli had snuck in, confirming that there were no other exits. To his right are the elevators. Eli's plan is simply to trail Monica back to her room, get the number, then return late in the night to slide the white envelope under her door. In his imagination, she wakes early in the morning, anxious and excited. She throws back the curtains, flooding the room with light, and then stumbles toward the bathroom. She doesn't see the envelope. Instead she steps on it, feels its cool texture beneath her bare toes. And as she bends for it, reaching with delicate fingers, she has no idea how her world is about to be changed. Again, Eli is aware of how much this feels like a scene from a novel.

A bridesmaid with a baby slung on her hip emerges from the rehearsal dinner, followed by a wearied man carrying a diaper bag.

Behind them the rest of the crowd trickles out in twos and threes, small groups huddled together, smiling and nodding, clearly under the warming glow of pending nuptials and alcohol. Tiny children dart back and forth, and the grey-haired elders of the families trudge along at their own pace. There is a brief flash of memory in Eli's mind, a moment from the rehearsal dinner before his own wedding when his wife's mother came over to him, clutched his shoulders, and whispered, "Take care of her. She's a lovely girl." He felt it like a warm blanket thrown over his shoulders, the weight of that wondrous obligation.

When Eli sees Monica, he's so excited that he rises and takes two steps across the huge lobby before realizing that she's walking next to Tyler. The two of them stride toward the elevators, and Eli freezes. He can't get into those close quarters with Tyler, who will surely recognize him. And before he can think too long on this, he's moving again, in pursuit. So what if Tyler sees him? What can he say? Eli is tired of hiding and being silent.

But at the front desk, Tyler pauses, lifting a hand toward the concierge. Monica moves ahead to catch up with a small group nearing the elevators, and Eli has to quicken his pace. As he passes behind Tyler, he hears him say, "Just be sure—" but doesn't catch the rest.

At the elevator bay, Eli says, "Hold that door," and the woman with Monica, the bridesmaid with the baby, stops it with one hand. Eli thanks her and steps inside.

He moves to the back of the elevator, next to the diaper bag dad. Eli glances down at the row of round buttons. Leaning into a side wall, the bridesmaid asks, "Which floor?"

Only two are lit up, rimmed in yellow: Seven and Ten. Eli hesitates, and the doors slide shut. "Sir?" Monica's friend asks as they begin to ascend. Her finger hangs in the air, poised to press a button.

"Seven," he says, mostly because the silence had become impossible to bear.

All this time, Monica has been looking down. Her chin nearly touches her chest and there is no smile on her face. The bridesmaid touches Monica's arm and says, "You've got to realize that right now, everybody's under a lot of pressure."

At the seventh floor, Monica steps out and the bridesmaid says, "I'll be down after I change and we'll figure this out. Okay?"

"You bet," Monica says as she exits quickly. Eli follows, giving her a little bit of a head start, just a few steps so as not to crowd her. He keeps his face aimed at the carpet and allows himself only the slightest glance at her feet as she paces ahead of him. After two turns down the labyrinth hallways, she begins to slow, and Eli decides it would be awkward not to look up and make note of the odd coincidence. He is prepared to smile and say, "Small world," but Monica is focused on her key card. Eli's eyes catch the room number and he walks on for thirty feet, pausing at a random door before reaching into his own pocket. Monica steps inside her room, and the hallway is empty.

Eli returns to his room and retrieves the letter. He re-reads it and thinks about changing "overwhelming" to "devastating," but decides it isn't worth another trip to the hotel's cramped office center. So he folds the letter back in its white envelope and tucks it into his inside jacket pocket.

In the hotel bar, he has two tall drinks but does not feel the looseness of inebriation setting in. He eavesdrops on the conversations around him, hoping to overhear some snippet of chatter about Tyler.

But nothing comes his way, and his attention floats from the décor to the customers to the game on TV, as it often does when he finds himself sitting on barstools like this. He hunches forward, weight on his elbows, and wishes things were different. He feels the heat of the envelope in his pocket and considers just going back to bed. Rather than relaxing him, the beer has only made him weary. He is tired and it feels late. Tomorrow after the deed is done, he'll treat himself to a day in Richmond before driving home. Surely a city of this size has a decent art museum, or maybe a zoo. It's been decades since Eli's been to a zoo.

Two guys next to him, both in business suits with ties slid down, trade lewd comments about the bartender, who is young, tall, and pale. Eli had seen her nametag, "Marija" and noted it. "Hey honey," one says. "Me and my buddy are trying to figure out where you from with that pretty accent."

She smiles professionally and says, "Croatia."

"That so?" the other one says. "That where you learned to make such shitty screwdrivers?"

Her smile vanishes and she turns away. The men laugh.

Eli would never confront another man, but normally in such a situation, he'd make some comment to Marija, something to help her shake off the insult. Eli searches for this impulse and doesn't find it. Given what he's about to do though, who he is on this night, he isn't surprised.

In the elevator, he stares at the round buttons. Tomorrow, after his mission is complete, he wonders how he'll feel when he returns to his life, driving the highways between arrogant professors who make polite conversation with him only so they can get free desk copies, most of which they sell to book buyers anyway. Maybe he'll be more confident, more self-assured. Maybe it's time life stopped pushing Eli around.

He reminds himself this isn't about revenge—he's not out to take Tyler down. He only wants Monica to be safe. If someone would have been in a position to prevent him from feeling all that pain, wouldn't he have wanted it?

He taps 7 and the elevator ascends with a jolt.

Pacing down the hallway, he slips out the plain white envelope. He eyes up the room numbers, and when he reaches Monica's, he pauses. After a moment, he bends to a knee. Under the door, a slim bar of light escapes. Inside he can hear voices, and he imagines that bridesmaid. He wonders what they were talking about before, and when he listens closely, he's sure he can hear crying. On the night before her wedding, Monica may be weeping. And rather than disturbing Eli, this excites him. He is thrilled that she's upset. It occurs to him that now, if she's doubting the marriage, his note will land like a bomb. He'll slide the envelope under the door like in all those old British novels, and he'll walk away a changed man.

Eli tilts one edge under the door and takes a breath, as if he's about to plunge underwater.

When the door swings open, he's facing a pair of large sneakers. He looks up and sees Tyler standing in the doorframe. Eli stands and comes eye to eye with his old friend. Tyler's mouth opens but he does not speak. More than shocked, he looks confused, as if he can't make sense of who he is seeing. Monica comes up behind him and Eli looks at her reddened eyes, the slightest puffiness around them. Nobody speaks for a few breaths and finally Monica asks, "Can I help you?"

"I'm an old friend of Tyler's," Eli says. "And I'm very sorry, but I won't be able to stay for the wedding tomorrow. Urgent business back home."

Tyler has gone pale and is frozen. Monica sniffles and says, "That's too bad. I'm sorry I don't know your name."

Eli reaches into his pocket and pulls out the envelope. "I tracked you all down so I could give you your wedding present." He's happy with this line, something that sounds scripted and perfect. And now he envisions the scene that will come next, as if it were written on a page. He will hand the envelope over to Monica—Tyler cannot stop him, he is helpless—and Monica will open it and her life will be shattered. The light in her eyes will dim, the smile on her face will tighten, and her quiet moments will never again be peaceful. Eli has this power, and he knows that in a story, this is the moment when he would take his righteous revenge.

But he sees the real faces of these real people before him and understands that none of them are characters. And he passes the envelope to Tyler, who accepts it nervously and stammers out a ragged "Thanks."

"That belongs to you," Eli says. "Sorry I can't stay." Here, he places a hand on Tyler's shoulder. "I miss you."

Tyler looks at the envelope, then back at Eli, and says, "Me too."

Eli smiles at Monica and says, "Tomorrow's going to go great."

With that Eli turns and heads for the elevators. Even though it's late, he plans to check out, leave a large tip and compliment the front desk clerk on the hotel's quality. It's a long drive up I-95, but along the way, maybe he'll stop for a bite to eat at some random diner. Perhaps he'll chat with the weary waitress, tell her how much he appreciates the coffee. Eli knows the story took a turn he wasn't expecting, but he feels just fine, heading back to the life he's crafted.

What Walter Lost

EVERYBODY IN CAMP HILL who knew Walter knew he was a nice guy. At his job across the river in Harrisburg, where he analyzed highway traffic patterns for the state, all his coworkers smiled warmly back at him when he passed on the way to his windowless cubicle. During meetings he was seldom called upon, but on those occasions he cheerfully offered his opinions. The other parishioners at Trinity Assembly of Christ returned Walter's sincere handshakes and good wishes on the steps of the church after Sunday service. His wife of seven years, Melissa, would sit by him on the couch at night, and she would watch shows about vacation getaways and dream weddings and home improvements while he skimmed technical reports or read the latest book on new developments in science. Melissa was Walter's second wife. In his younger days, Walter had developed a fascination with quantum mechanics, string theory—the mysterious underpinnings of the universe. He had majored in physics at Bloomsburg, but without the money to go after a PhD, the pursuit was relegated to a hobby.

One Friday night, when he was just beginning a new book on dark matter, the phone rang, startling both Walter and Melissa. Up on the TV screen, a man in denim overalls took a sledgehammer to a blue kitchen countertop, and a small box appeared with a phone number and the name "Bartowski, Philip." Walter closed his book. "That's Phil," he said. "From Bridges and Overpasses."

Melissa asked why he'd be calling, a question Walter wondered himself. He stepped quickly into the kitchen, caught the phone on the crucial fourth ring. When he came back to the living room a minute later, Melissa wanted to know if everything was all right. Walter nodded and said, "He wants me to go shoot pool tonight. With some of the other guys from the bureau I guess."

"Can you shoot pool?" Melissa asked. She reached for her glass of white wine.

Walter shrugged. "I did back in college. The frat next door had a table." He sat down on the couch and picked up his book. "Actually I wasn't half bad."

"Well what did you tell him?"

He stared at the back cover. "I said I was busy."

On the screen, the contractor began shaking his head at a problem in the wall. "You aren't busy," Melissa said. "You should go."

Walter opened the book but did not begin reading. After a few seconds he asked, "Why?"

Melissa aimed the remote at the TV. The images on the screen flashed by—a woman wearing a diamond necklace, two vultures pecking at an unidentifiable carcass, a bald infant in a hospital bed. "It'd be good if you got out more, Walt. Go on. Go have fun."

Walter looked at the child for a moment. Its gender was difficult to determine. "Do you want me to go?" he asked.

Melissa turned away from the screen. "Why in the world would I want you to go? It doesn't matter to me. It just sounds like it could be nice. You know, I've got book club and Bunco, coffee with Cindy. It's important for a man to go out with his friends."

Walter thought, *They aren't my friends*, and nearly said it, but he realized how pathetic it sounded. He wondered then just who he would list as his friends, if compelled to.

Ten minutes later, he came down the steps and stood in the living room doorway, his arms outstretched. He was wearing beige Dockers and a blue polo shirt. "How do I look?"

Melissa put down her wine and shifted on the couch. "You look fine. This isn't a date you know. If you put cologne on, I'm going to start getting suspicious."

Walter walked over to her, bent, and kissed her on the cheek. "Enjoy your shows," he said.

"I'll be here when you get back."

Walking to the car, Walter replayed his wife's last comment. Where else would she be?

Overtime! was a sports bar planted in the mall parking lot. As Walter circled, looking for a spot, he thought back to when, as a kid, he would take the bus out here for a quarter. He'd meet Eric Zincenko and Chris Dickert, along with John Rusin, who was close enough to ride his Schwinn. They would play in the mall arcade for hours, wander from store to store in air tinged with Musak, slurp Orange Juliuses and read comics sitting cross-legged on the floor in Waldenbooks. They'd pitch pennies into the fountain at the mall's heart, watch it shoot water up toward the glass-paneled dome ceiling. Walter remembered that from outside it looked to him like an observatory.

Since it was a Friday night, Overtime! was especially crowded. Walter excused himself as he turned sideways and gently shouldered his way through those waiting for a table in the dining rooms. He kept repeating, "I'm meeting someone inside," as an explanation for his rudeness, though no one seemed to care. At the bar, which he leaned into with one elbow, he surveyed the area where people congregated around pool tables. He did not see Philip, or anyone else he recognized, and he felt awkward standing alone and empty-handed in the middle of people enjoying each other's company, smiling and laughing. When the bartender, a kind-faced woman in her forties, raised her voice to ask him what she could get for him, Walter asked what she had on draft. He listened to her rattle off a series of exotic sounding microbrews, nodded as if he'd tried each one many times, then said, "That pale ale sounds good."

When she brought the glass, it was much taller—and more expensive—than he'd thought it would be. He noted that he would have to limit himself to one drink, if the drinks were this big. He sipped at the beer and, though it had more bite than he expected, it went down easy. Immediately he felt a bit less anxious. He paid for the drink and carried it into the crowd, holding it with both hands.

As soon as Walter made eye contact with Philip, tucked away in a corner booth by the pool tables, his coworker tapped the shoulder of the man sitting with him and pointed at Walter. They both watched him slip past four big guys holding pool cues like spears, standing over a cluster of balls around a side pocket. Walter was careful not to spill his beer, which was still quite full. When he reached the table, Philip stood and said, "Walter, this is Ken, new in Signage. Ken, this is Walter." Walter put down his beer and shook hands in turn with each man. He slid into the booth.

"Glad you changed your mind," Philip said. "You find the place okay?"

"Right where you said it'd be," Walter replied. The other men smiled and Walter was pleased.

"Like I was saying," Ken said to Philip, "I told her if that was the best she could do, I'd do it myself."

Philip slapped the table and laughed loudly. Ken beamed. Walter glanced at Ken's ring finger, saw it was bare, and forced a polite grin. He took a sip from his beer. "So I thought you guys were playing pool."

"We were," Philip said. "Till the damn fire brigade showed up." He cocked a thumb toward the tables, and Walter looked again at the four burly men he'd come past. They wore matching blue t-shirts with red insignia and lettering. As they moved, Walter read "Firefighters" on one and "Eternal Brotherhood" on another. Above them, a crown of oversized TVs showed Mixed Martial arts, basketball, and a cooking competition. On one screen, Walter saw a blue screen with white words asking the question, "Which island was originally a British Penal colony?" The possible answers were Ireland, Puerto Rico, Madagascar, and Australia.

A man Walter recognized but could not name appeared at the table. "Ireland," the man said. Walter knew he was wrong, but remained silent. Philip said to him, "You remember Dale from Planning?"

Walter and Dale nodded at each other, then Walter slid deeper into the booth to make room for him. Dale said to Ken, "I left your cell number on the bathroom wall. You like it doggy style, right?"

"No, no," Ken said. "You've got me confused with your mom."

The other three men began discussing the recent trend of remaking classic TV shows. There was a new *Knight Rider*, a *Wonder Woman*, and a *Charlie's Angels*. Dale said, "They got some other Star Trek movie now with a new Captain Kirk. Fucking crazy. William Shatner is Captain Kirk, nobody else."

"Damn straight," Philip said.

Dale agreed and all four of them drank, as if it were a kind of toast. Walter didn't have strong feelings about the matter, but he drank anyway. Squeezed in the back of the booth between Ken and Dale, he felt a bit cramped, trapped even. As Philip began to describe a recent negotiation with a car dealer, Walter started to wonder if, had he stayed home, he and Melissa might've gone to bed together. If this were one of those Friday nights when, wordlessly, they would have reached for each other across the cool sheets between them.

When Philip finished, Dale told a long story about floating beneath a bald eagle during a recent kayak trip on the Conodoguinet Creek. Walter was envious, trying to imagine the sight of a majestic bird in the wild. That's when Dale held his hands up as if holding an invisible rifle and said, "Well within range."

Ken, newly divorced, offered a series of anecdotes from his adventures in internet dating. "Some of these forty-something chicks are just so fucked up," he said. "They've been in these shitty marriages and think they can show their independence by getting freaky. Thank god for Cosmo. One brought her own goddamn vibrator. I'm telling you. Thing was bright blue." This made Dale almost spit out his beer.

Philip said, "Watch out with those things. She might figure out she doesn't need you."

As for Philip, he shared his dread at an upcoming trip to Disney being planned by his wife. "The girls love it," he said. "But what's really magical about the place is how fast your money disappears.

Other day she asked me what I thought about Breakfast with the Princesses. Sixty-five bucks a plate."

"Guess you'll be leaving your balls in the hotel room," Ken said.

"Yeah right. I wish I could leave my wallet. Joys of fatherhood."

Five years ago, Walter and Melissa had tried to conceive. Once they realized there was a problem, they followed the familiar route from doctor to specialist. They'd even made a series of trips to New York City. The experts offered many theories, but no one was able to pinpoint the problem. One grey-haired woman, after reviewing their files, examining them both, and consulting new test results, simply shrugged and said, "It's one of those things. Science can't explain everything." After an unsuccessful in vitro procedure, they briefly discussed a surrogate. Walter saw the history of their laptop fill up with sites about agencies desperate to pair potential parents with babies from China, from Bangladesh, from West Virginia. He never asked Melissa about these sites.

Philip thwacked Walter on the back and said, "How about you?"

"How about me what?"

"Dream concert. Van Halen or Bon Jovi?"

"Oh, I don't know," Walter said. "That's a tough one."

"Damn straight," Dale said. "Like asking Boston or Journey."

In a room just past the bar, someone named Teddy Midnight opened the karaoke machine up. Immediately two women began crooning out "Margaritaville." A round of drinks appeared on the table, and Dale and Philip thanked Ken. Walter winced for a second at the idea of having a second drink, but once he started, found that it felt just fine.

As the men traded tales, Walter tried to think of a story he could tell, one that would make him feel part of this group. Using a video on "YouTube," he had managed to replace the mother board on his refrigerator last weekend. And the previous Friday, his wife ha seen their neighbor's landscaper taking a piss in the huge azaleas that separated their properties. Then of course there was his father's stroke. He was recuperating in a rehab over in Hershey. Earlier in the week, when Walter had visited, his father kept asking him to get him some riding boots. It took Walter twenty minutes to unravel that he wdas trying to get some vanilla ice cream. None of these stories seemed right for this crowd, so Walter held his beer with both hands, listened to them talk, smiled or laughed when the others did. Meanwhile, he secretly played along with the trivia game on the screen across from him. He knew that Sun Tzu wrote *The Art of War* and that the capital of Nebraska was Lincoln. He did not know that baby dolphins are born striped. He kept waiting for a question about science, about the big bang or the expansion of the cosmos or unknown forces that churn at the center of a black hole.

"You know Walt," Philip said. "I've been meaning to ask you something."

Walter turned to him. He noticed that Ken and Dale were silent, looking into their beer. Philip said, "The usage reports on I-83 north, down by the turnpike. They've got a real bearing on my unit, and I was wondering what they were looking like."

Walter said, "Those reports are due in two weeks. We're still gathering data."

Phil folded his hands. "I know what you're gathering. That's what you guys do so we know where to build stuff, right? What I'm asking for here is a little heads up. Something off the record."

Walter looked at him.

Dale leaned in and said, "You know. Between friends."

Walter was still looking at Philip when his gaze shifted. A large figure stepped to the edge of their table. It was one of the thick firemen, holding his cue like a walking staff. He lifted his chin and said, "Feel like shooting a bit?"

Philip, Dale, and Ken exchanged looks. The fireman, bald with a thick beard, said, "Eight ball. The other guys got tired of getting their asses kicked."

Ken said, "Yeah, that doesn't sound like fun."

Walter rose. "I'll give it a shot." He pushed into Dale, who had to slide out. As he carried his drink away from the booth, Walter didn't look back at Philip.

One of the things Walter used to enjoy about billiards is that, while there are a great number of variables, that number is fixed. At its heart, the game is a simple matter of physics. The ball goes in the hole or it does not.

The rack had already been set, and as Walter rolled a stick on the table, testing it for any defects, the fireman said, "I'll give you the break. You want to say five bucks a game?"

Walter raised an eyebrow.

The man said, "Just to give the game a little edge. C'mon. It's five bucks."

On the break, Walter sank a striped and a solid. The loud crack and the scattering of balls was satisfying. After surveying the table, he chose solids and dropped three more before leaving the six ball on the lip of a side pocket. The fireman nodded and went to work, piecing together a run of five balls that only stopped when he scratched. Walter retrieved the cue and said, "I didn't think that would fall."

The fireman said, "It wasn't supposed to."

They made quick eye contact, smiled, and nodded at each other.

Walter eyed up the nine ball, imagined where he'd want the cue to end up after that shot. The trajectory of the cue—the path he wanted it to take from ball to ball and bumper to bumper over the next several shots—formed a constellation only he could see. He placed the cue ball down, gently, then bent and leveled his stick.

A few minutes later, after Walter sank the eight, the fireman shook his hand and said, "Double or nothing?"

Walter paused, wondered if he were in one of those movies where a gullible schmuck falls prey to a savvy pool shark, but he said, "Why not? My name is Walter."

The man said, "Bill."

As the winner, Walter broke the next rack, though nothing fell. Bill dropped three stripes before playing a safety of sorts. With the balls clustered more, the game became a bit of a defensive effort, with each man trying not to give the other an advantage. They took each other's measure and, when Walter managed to bank the one ball lengthwise on the table, Bill tapped the heel of his stick into the floor to show admiration. Walter had a chance to win and was lining up the eight ball when Ken and Dale stepped over to the table. "Things look pretty intense over here."

"Everything's good," Walter said.

Bill just stared.

While Ken and Dale watched, Walter ran the eight into the corner of the pocket and it bounced free, but not far enough that Bill couldn't easily tap it in.

"Tough break," Dale said.

Bill broke the rack for the third game, a tie breaker they agreed to play for twenty bucks, and somehow Walter's beer went from being empty to full. Philip, off to the side, saw him notice and said, "Liquid courage. You're playing for the honor of the Interstate Highway Bureau." Walter turned away from him but lifted the beer.

During the game, a couple of the other firemen stood just past the end of the table. They offered Bill encouragement.

Soon Walter's beer was nearly empty and there were only three balls left on the table—the eight, one solid, and one striped. Walter stood behind the eight ball, which was in close proximity to the eleven, his last. As he walked around to the cue, he announced, "Combination." Two of the fireman shifted their feet and leaned their heads closer together. Walter knew it was a difficult shot, one he might not try if he were entirely sober.

He chalked his stick and blew across the powdered tip. Then he lowered himself and struck the cue with an easy stroke. The ball ran into the side of the eight, which ricocheted into the eleven, driving it with force into the corner pocket. Both the cue and the eight rolled gently down to the rail, where they rested lined up for an easy winning shot. Ken and Dale whooped as if they were responsible.

But as Walter moved to position to finish the game, Bill stepped toward the same space. "Scratch," he said.

"Scratch?" Dale asked.

One of the other fireman said, "Eight ball's not neutral."

"It is where I learned the game," Ken said.

Bill shrugged. "Guess you shouldn't have learned to play in Dip-shitville."

Walter was standing over the cue ball, where Bill needed to be if he were going to shoot. Quietly, Walter said, "You saw me lining up the shot. I called it. Why didn't you stop me?"

"You seem like a big boy," Bill told him. A couple of the firemen snickered, and Walter glanced over at Philip, Ken, and Dale. He thought about dropping a twenty on the table in disgust. He imagined shoving the eight ball into the pocket. He pictured himself saying, *In a dispute, all bets are off.* Instead of any of these things though, he handed his stick to Bill and turned from the table, then walked into the crowd.

Outside there was a light rain, and the air was cool. Walter took measured, even strides into the parking lot, away from the building but not really toward anything. He had to stop when he realized that he wasn't exactly sure where his car was. It quite likely was, he decided, on the other side of Overtime! Above him, a passenger jet from the airport in Harrisburg rose into the storm, just high enough that it made no noise. Walter watched it disappear and wondered where it was going.

After taking a few steps back toward the building, he passed an oversized red pickup truck with a siren on the roof. Along the side, he read the arching words, "Volunteer Firefighter, Mechanicsburg." Walter stood in the rain for a few moments, then his eyes fell on the parking island the truck was nosed up to. A street light sprang from a landscaped bed of river rocks. Scrawny weeds poked through those stones. When Walter picked up one of the rocks, it felt good in his hand, like a baseball. He realized there was no way to be sure this was Bill's truck, but that didn't seem to matter as he stood over the hood, considering the weight in his hand. Slim raindrops ran down the windshield.

When Walter hurled the rock, it bounced off the glass, clattered onto the wet asphalt. The windshield didn't shatter, but a crack splintered down the driver's side, like a bolt of lightening.

Walter's heart was pounding.

Voices from the bar drew his attention, and he turned away from the building and the patrons hustling his way in the rain. He walked along the cars, retreating, but soon saw he was running out of parking lot. Rather than turn back, he continued on, crossing the street and stepping up onto the sidewalk of the mall. A steady stream of people were coming out of the exit, and a man with a tan jacket held the door and said goodnight as each passed. Walter took hold of another door and the man said, "Sir, the mall's closing in ten minutes."

"It's okay," Walter said, and he slipped in without looking behind him.

Inside, the lights were dim and many of the shops had closed their rattling gates. Between the bars, Walter saw shopkeepers and minimum wagers putting away displays, closing out cash registers. He couldn't recall the last time he was actually in this mall. Had he come to a jeweler here to look for an engagement ring for Melissa? As he walked on, he was struck by how much had changed, how few stores he recognized. There was a gold and silver jewelry kiosk where he and his buddies used to get Orange Juliuses, and where he expected to find the record store, there was a place that sold cell phones. He knew of course that the arcade would be gone, but when he saw the Dollar Tree in the old location, his disappointment was bitter. Just outside of it, an old man, thin and wearing a blue jump suit, plugged in a floor waxing machine. He looked at Walter with curious eyes.

Walter walked away and found himself suddenly eager to see the fountain, the centerpiece at the mall's main intersection. The memory of being there with Dickert and Rusin and Zincenko, it came on so strong he felt transported and light. He began to walk more quickly, until he was nearly in a jog, trotting past all the closed stores. He pictured not just the fountains that every fifteen minutes sprayed in a choreographed pattern set to music, but the brass turtles that sat in the center of the water. Everyone used to try to pitch pennies onto their curved shells, make them land just so, pretending that success would bring the granting of a wish. The floor of the fountain shimmered with coins, each one a dream unfulfilled, and Walter recalled a summer day when he and his friends all brought a hundred pennies and they sat together on the edge, grinning and beaming, taking turns at the impossible. Victory seemed inevitable, just a matter of time.

When he reached the center of the mall, he thought he must be in the wrong place. There were no brass turtles, no fountain even. There was only a circular information booth with metal blinds pulled down in the windows. On the side was a brightly colored map with a "You are here!" red arrow confirming that Walter was, indeed, at the main intersection. Still, he hardly could believe this, until he looked up and saw the glass ceiling, comprised of all those octagonal panels. It was the same. He was exactly where he thought he was. He squinted to see the stars, but the clouds from the storm obscured the night sky.

"Can I help you, sir?" came from behind him.

Walter turned to see the man in the tan jacket, the one from the entrance. He was holding a walkie talkie. "The mall is closed."

"I know," Walter said.

"Is there something I can help you with?" The man looked at the map. "Do you know where you are?"

"I do," Walter said. "I'm just—I lost something, okay?"

The man snapped the walkie talkie onto his belt and pulled out a ring of tingling keys. He stepped toward the door of the booth. "They got a big box of unclaimed stuff in here," he told Walter. "What are we looking for?"

Walter didn't answer. Instead he came up behind the security guard, who hoisted a blue plastic bin up onto the counter. Walter removed a flannel jacket, fished through a handful of scarfs, hats, a single mitten. There was a handbag, a pair of sunglasses, two tiny umbrellas, and a water bottle.

"Well?" the security guard asked. "Any luck?"

Walter wanted to know where the fountain went. He remembered the brass turtles so clearly, and how they spit water from their mouths. But he didn't want to seem foolish. "No," he said as he returned all the items to the bin. "None of this is mine."

"Okay," the guard said. "Tell me what you lost and give me your number. We'll keep an eye out for it."

But Walter was already turning, already picturing the exit and the cool rain. "Forget it," he said. "It's not the kind of thing somebody would find."

The Dad in Question

MATTHIAS IS ON HIS KNEES, trying to unclog the nacho cheese machine, sleeves rolled up, fresh burn singeing the back of one wrist, when Keyanna leans over the snack stand counter. "You said to let you know if that skinny dude showed up."

He sets down the pliers and turns to Sharon, standing behind the register. "No nachos," he says. "Make a sign so people don't get their hopes up."

Walking with the confident stride of upper management, Matthias passes the four royal throne rooms, glancing in to be sure all is well with the birthday parties in progress. He sees the plastic crowns atop the heads of the birthday boys and girls, piles of wrapped packages, fathers snapping pictures. In the last room, children swarm around Gary the Dragon as if he were Christ returned. Matthias makes a note to tell whoever's in the Gary suit to dial down the arm swinging, which seems hostile, threatening. One tot flees behind his mother's legs.

Matthias weaves through the canyon of enormous inflated slides and obstacle courses. He dodges sweaty, wide-eyed children darting from ride to ride, ignoring his teen workers endlessly droning *no running.* As he and Keyanna near the entrance, they cross a three-foot plywood drawbridge that arches over a carpet moat decorated with grinning alligators. They pass through a tiny gate, and he scans the entryway for the dad in question. Morgan, who still has facial stubble despite a written warning, snaps a neon admitt. bracelet on a pony-tailed girl and says, "He just left."

"Great," Matthias says. "Guess he got the message."

But then his eyes fall on a thin-armed boy with an uneven crew cut. Carl smiles, flashing a wandering set of teeth that Matthias guesses will need a few grand in orthodontia one day. Carl says, "Can I have pizza again?"

"You let the guy pay?" Matthias asks Morgan.

The teen scratches at his stubble. "You told us to tell you if he showed up."

"Nothing about not letting him pay," Keyanna adds. Matthias keeps reminding himself that this generation of teens seems determined to do exactly what they are told, literally, and very little else.

Last Saturday, for what Matthias suspects was not the first time, the dad in question dropped off his son and left him at Kids Kastle for the whole day—unattended. Around six-thirty, one of the staff brought the boy to Matthias in his office and explained that he was asking for food but didn't have any money. Now, Matthias reaches for the boy's scrawny wrist. "C'mon Carl."

In the parking lot, Matthias is blinded by the sunlight, but soon enough, his eyes fix on a solitary figure out on the asphalt. He's crossing the vast expanse between the Kastle and the Camp Hill Mall. Directly ahead of him are a Sears, a JC Penney's, and Overtime!, a sports bar where the waitresses wear referee uniforms one size too small.

"Pardon me," Matthias yells. The dad, distant, doesn't turn. Matthias tugs Carl along, and once they're free of the cars parked in the shadow of the building, he breaks into a bit of a jog. At his side, Carl is not unwilling to come along, but he drags his heels just a bit.

Matthias recalls getting frustrated at his own son, Noah, who was perpetually late for kindergarten. Noah, in fourth grade now if Matthias has it right, lives out west with his mother and her boyfriend Nelson. For a while, Noah sent his father two sentence emails once a week.

As Matthias gains on the dad in the parking lot, he shouts, "Sir!" Then, when he doesn't acknowledge him, Matthias lets loose with a good, "Yo, Buddy!" Now the dad pauses and glances back, and Matthias sees he's smoking a cigarette. He hangs his head to the side and waits, looking a whole lot like a kid outside the principal's office. If Matthias had to guess, he'd put him in his mid twenties. Matthias thinks of the mistakes he made at this age, but only for an instant.

Approaching the dad, Matthias catches his breath, releases Carl's wrist, and says, "Look, I told your wife last week, you can't leave your son alone. We're not set up as a babysitting service."

The dad draws on his cigarette and stares at Matthias, huffing. "She ain't my wife. And I seen shitloads of kids in there alone."

Matthias nods. "Sure," he says. "Kids that are thirteen. That's posted out front." The 8 *Rules of the Royal Kingdom* were one of Matthias' additions when he took over last year. Other highlights include restrictions against rough play, cursing, and cleats. Lastly, all subjects are commanded to have fun.

The lanky dad aims his cigarette at Carl. "He's thirteen."

"Come on," Matthias says. "He's nine, maybe."

"Carl, tell this jackhole how old you are."

"I'm thirteen!" he says, beaming.

"Seriously?" Matthias asks. He posts his hands on his hips, feels the sun on the back of his neck. "Do you even think about the lessons you're teaching your son?"

The man leans into Matthias, enough that he can smell the sweet tang of nicotine. Matthias rears back but doesn't step away.

Carl's dad says, "The boy's got some growth issues. Kind of a runt. Small bones, some shit like that. Now look, I paid my six bucks and I got somewhere to be. Carl, you walk on back with this guy to the bouncy playground. Don't make no trouble. No bugging anybody like last week. You hearing me?"

Carl nods, cowed but smiling. His father turns to walk away, and Matthias says, "This is the last time."

"You're the boss, Big Man," the dad says, and without turning he flips Matthias the bird.

After a moment, Carl says, "Do you know what that means?"

"I sure do," Matthias tells him. He watches the dad striding toward Overtime!, where Matthias figures he's a bartender or cook. But Matthias could also imagine him going there to party. This other dad may well spend the day draining pitchers, laughing with high school buddies, playing pool or darts, watching a marathon of college football. All while his son plays alone. The thought, one Matthias has had many times before, crystallizes: *Some people don't deserve to have kids.*

Matthias and Carl start hiking back across the parking lot. After twenty feet, Carl reaches for Matthias' hand. This part of the lot is empty, and there is no need for extra caution, but Matthias takes the boy's hand. Together, they head for the bright red and yellow spires of the Kastle.

Nearly a year ago, on an autumn morning much like this, Rodney the owner walked Matthias around the huge warehouse, big enough to house aircraft. The concrete floor was nearly covered with enormous deflated balloons, rainbow blobs that looked to Matthias like emptied skins. Rodney activated the massive fans and Matthias watched, mesmerized, as a fantasy world rose up around them, pumped full of air. "The customers aren't really the kids," Rodney told Matthias. "It's the parents who pay. At Kids Kastle, the moms can bitch about the other moms while sipping fancy coffee and the dads can watch baseball on the widescreens." Rodney pointed here to the new Keurig machines and the HDTV flat screens, which received over 200 channels. "These days, nobody trusts babysitters, and what with broken glass and dog shit, who wants to go to a park? We're a substitute for parks, the next best thing. That's our business model."

Rodney had already given Matthias this speech when he was a sales rep for Z-104, the Thunder, Camp Hill's country radio station. This had been a good job for over a decade, one which had helped Matthias finally pay off his student loans, be a good provider for a time. When the station manager told Matthias he was being let go, he phoned a few of his clients to say goodbye, a clear and desperate fishing expedition. Rodney at Kids Kastle bit. At the end of the interview/tour, Rodney shook hands with Matthias and said, "Hey, I never even asked. Have you got kids yourself?"

During his tenure as manager, Matthias has witnessed the ugly side of parenting. Fathers scowling at their children for a spilled drink, a lost shoe, a broken retainer. Mothers yanking kids by the wrist, smacking the bare backs of legs or even cheeks. It's always disturbed Matthias, the way red rises on a child's skin. Like an instant sunburn.

184

There's a quick sting in the palm, followed by a brief heat. And the things he's heard: "Jesus, just play like the other kids." "Stop pretending you're hurt." "You're such an ungrateful snot." All the while, the children wither under the assault. The awesome authority of a parent is godlike to a child, something parents often forget. Matthias knows this, understands this. In extreme cases, he's tried to gently intervene. He's developed a handful of lines: "It's easy to get frustrated." "Maybe I can help?" "I've heard the king frowns on that kind of thing." At the very least, this redirects the parent's anger.

Two hours after the encounter in the parking lot, Sharon knocks on Matthias' door and pushes inside. She's got a hand on the back of Carl's neck, and the boy is staring down at the flattened carpet. She says, "Guess who bit someone inside the Mystic Mountain?"

Matthias turns away from the inventory on the computer screen, tries to make eye contact with the boy. "That true?"

"She cut in line," Carl says. "I was next."

"Cutting in line isn't allowed. But that's hardly a good reason to bite someone."

Carl lifts his face. "What's a good reason?"

This strikes Matthias as a reasonable question. But he says, "That's not important now. Did you apologize?"

Carl nods his head. Sharon shakes hers.

Matthias asks, "Any blood?"

Sharon says, "None I saw."

"How are the parents?"

"Mom's freaked out. Dad's oblivious."

Carl asks, "What's oblivious?"

Matthias says, "Okay. Bring them an Incident Report and see if they want to fill it out. Be sure they sign. Check the wound again. If skin was broken, get me involved."

Sharon roams off, and somehow Carl is left behind, forgotten. He looks around Matthias' cramped, windowless office. "You have a computer," he says. "Cool."

"It's for work," Matthias explains. "There are no video games on it."

"We got one at school like that. Only dumb games with math and a robot bunny."

Matthias tries to picture Carl at school. He imagines him with a smudge of dirt on one cheek. At recess, he's the kind of kid who tears around the playground, inflicting mayhem, but not attached to any group. "Math is very important. Listen, you can't stay here if you don't follow the rules. The king won't allow it. One of the rules is no biting. Are we clear?"

"I thought you were the king," Carl says.

Matthias looks away. The spreadsheet on his computer screen shimmers.

Carl says, "I know how money works. If you want, I can work for you."

"Doing what?" Matthias asks.

"I can clean dishes, tie up garbage bags, wipe down the tables. Lots of stuff. You can pay me in food."

Matthias eyes the boy. "What did you have for breakfast today?"

"Brownie cereal with chocolate milk."

Matthias wonders again about calling protective services. Earlier, when they'd first returned, he'd even looked up the phone number. But the publicity of a police car pulling up to the Kastle, right in the middle of a busy day, that didn't seem worth it. Some parent would surely snap a cell phone picture, and rumors would be all over the web. Who knows what stories could spring up. Rodney would hear and want to know why it wasn't handled in-house. Plus, Matthias recognized that he was angry at how Carl's dad had ignored his authority, mad that he hadn't handled the situation differently. These days, Matthias tries never to make a decision in anger. For a few years, when he felt his temper coming on, he'd snap a rubber band that he wore on his wrist. This was an idea his wife had suggested, something she heard from a radio talk show. "Stay here," Matthias tells Carl. "Don't touch anything."

Out in the warehouse, the late afternoon is in full swing. Screaming children climbing over the sides of rides, exhausted parents sipping coffee to stay awake, an obese man sprawled on the couch watching ultimate fighting, the new kid (was his name Sam?) reluctantly mopping up vomit in the Enchanted Forest. When Matthias comes back to his office, he finds Carl sitting in his chair. The boy is maneuvering the mouse, clicking closed a website. He swings the chair around and says, "Your browser is slow."

Matthias sets down a bottle of water and a slice of pizza. "You were told not to touch the computer."

"I didn't break it. Check for yourself."

Matthias inhales, exhales. Carl does not break eye contact. Matthias glances at the food and says, "Pepperoni, right?"

Carl nods. "I like Coke."

"Your body doesn't need Coke. It needs water."

Matthias unscrews the top and Carl lifts the bottle with both hands, takes a long drink. He reaches for the pizza and says, "Who's that kid?"

Matthias looks over his desk at the photograph, which is faded and worn. It is tacked up next to the calendar, nearly covered by schedule requests from the workers, invoices, sticky notes scrawled with minutia. Matthias sees the toddler face peaking out at him. He considers lying to Carl but then says, "Noah."

Carl takes three bites, chews with his mouth open, and says, "Noah looks happy."

Matthias remembers feeding the geese at Silver Spring, how Noah ate a handful of the smelly pellets they got from a quarter machine. "Noah was happy," Matthias says. "That day."

Carl asks if he can wear the dragon costume. Matthias looks in the corner, where the body slumps like an empty tent and the huge head sits on its side, decapitated. "No," Matthias says. "It's too big."

"It'd be cool to be a dragon."

For a moment, Matthias imagines himself huge and winged, with claws and the ability to breathe fire. He pictures Overtime! in flames. The radio tower at Z-104 burns. For the second time today, he reaches for his wrist.

A hunk of pizza falls to the carpet and, before Matthias can tell him not to, Carl snaps it up and pops it into his mouth. Matthias watches him chew and asks him what year he was born. Carl's knee-jerk answer confirms two of Matthias' suspicions. One, that Carl is indeed not thirteen. Two, he was born the same year as Noah.

"Where do you live?"

Carl rattles off an address that Matthias doesn't recognize. He says, "That's not in Camp Hill."

Carl shakes his head. "Harrisburg. We take bus five."

With evidence that Carl is underage, here under false pretenses, it would totally be in his right to call the boy's house or bring in protective services. Matthias says, "I'll bet you know your phone number."

"Uh-huh," Carl says. He sing-songs the memorized numbers and Matthias writes them down, only to realize that he's coming up one short. Carl only said six numbers. Matthias is pondering his options when Carl says, "Where is Noah now?"

Matthias looks at Carl, then turns again to the photo. He starts to reach for it, but then lets his arm fall to his side. "Colorado," he says. "Far away."

Around dinner, there's always a lull, even on a Saturday. Matthias emerges from his office and helps with one of the parties, carrying the flaming birthday cake himself. In the arcade, he settles a dispute about the true owner of a horde of fun tickets. He sees Carl at the far end of the dark room, crouched inside a video game cockpit. The huge screen before him flashes with tentacled aliens, and laser fire explodes them into bloody guts. Matthias considers redirecting the boy, suggesting skee ball or air hockey, but then lets him have his fun.

At the snack stand, he's taking another crack at the repair job to the nacho cheese machine when he wonders where Carl got the money from for that game. After he hears an order for popcorn, he rises to pass a box to Sharon, who gives it to the woman on the other side of the counter. Once she's gone, Matthias says, "Things are kind of calm. I'm taking dinner."

Sharon turns from her register. "You never take dinner."

"I'm hungry," he tells her. "I won't be half an hour."

Sharon shrugs.

"Carl's in the arcade last I saw. Be sure he gets something to eat."

She looks at Matthias, eyebrows raised.

"The biter," he says.

"Gotcha."

"No Coke—and no charge."

"Sure thing," she says. She picks at something on the back of one hand, maybe a scab.

Out in the parking lot, Matthias is surprised that the air has cooled so much, and the walk is actually pleasant. Overhead, the late evening sun lights up the underbellies of the clouds, and Matthias wishes that Carl were here to see the sight. He would point out the half moon to him, perhaps explain the basics of the lunar cycles. He would be slow and patient.

Inside Overtime!, Matthias pushes through the lobby, crowded with people clutching beepers and looking at their watches. He tells the trio of blonde girls at the front desk—could they be triplets?—that he's meeting somebody and then slips inside. Everywhere, TV screens beam sporting events. There's baseball, football, Nascar, girls softball. It's enough to induce a seizure. Surrounding the pool tables, men stand with sticks around high back stools, slosh beer from pitcher to frosty mug. But Matthias doesn't see Carl's dad among the customers. He has come with a calm spirit, not to threaten or scold, but merely to remind him of the obligation he has as a father, the amazing opportunity he has to shape a young life. He wants to explain to him how much he takes for granted.

Matthias selects a seat at the bar that gives him a good vantage point. He checks the face of each passing waiter and peers through the cut out to the kitchen. Cooks drop plates onto a counter and shout out numbers. None of them is Carl's dad. In response to the bartender, a woman in her forties with a kind smile, Matthias orders a mixed drink, and when it is finished, he orders another. He is beginning to think that perhaps Carl's dad has left, abandoned his son, and that the boy is now fatherless. What will he do, he wonders, if no one comes to pick Carl up?

And just then, as he is deciding between a third drink and leaving, his eyes catch on a familiar gaunt face. Carl's dad cuts through the crowd of drinkers holding an empty grey tub. At a booth not five feet away, he clears the clattering plates and glasses, and Matthias is surprised by his speed and efficiency. He watches his hands reach and grab, reach and grab again. As they flash back and forth, his quick fingers pinch a single dollar from the handful left behind for a waitress. Then the dad straightens and heads for another table, and Matthias follows him, watching closely.

When the man rushes past the bar, carrying the grey tray now loaded with dirty dishes, Matthias turns away, afraid he'll be recognized. He squints through the prep window to the kitchen, where he sees the man in the back, hunched over a sink with steam rising from it.

The bartender asks Matthias if he's up for a hat trick, and he says, "That skinny guy bussing tables. What's his name?"

She glances over her shoulder, then back at Matthias. "Malcolm," she says. "How come?"

Matthias stuffs a hand into his pocket, peels a twenty from his money clip, and drops it on the bar. "No reason," he says.

Back at the Kastle, Matthias wanders from one inflated ride to the next, scanning for Carl. He checks the arcade, where he interrupts two teens making out in the photo booth. He checks the snack stand, where Sharon confirms he ate two hot pretzels and an ice cream sandwich. Finally, Matthias finds Carl curled up in one of the oversized easy chairs, staring blankly at the enormous TV. On the widescreen, a gladiator hacks at a Roman centurion while a woman in a ripped robe tries to cover her exposed breasts. Two men watch from easy chairs of their own on either side of the boy. Matthias blocks the screen with his body and says, "Where's the remote?"

One of the men, a guy with a shaggy beard, points to a coffee table strewn with magazines about hunting and automobiles. Matthias snaps up the remote and changes the channel to a cartoon, something with talking sharks. He turns to the men and says, "This is a family business. Sporting events or children's programming only, okay?"

Both gaze absently at him. Even Carl just blinks.

Matthias says, "You really think that show was appropriate for a little boy?"

The bearded man rises up, taking some offense. He steps into Carl and tilts his head toward the other dad, slender and bald with a single silver earring. "I thought the kid was his."

Matthias looks at the bald man, who shrugs and says, "That show was on when I got here. He had the remote." His accusing finger points at Carl.

Matthias says, "Was that a good show for you? Are you allowed to watch shows like that in your house?"

"Goddamn cable guy shut it off," Carl says, clearly repeating something he'd heard.

The other two men stifle their laughs. The bald one with the earring sets a hand on Carl's head and shushes his hair. "You're something special, ain't you?"

Matthias ignores them and says, "Carl, you shouldn't talk like that."

"Like what?"

Matthias remembers the phrase he used when he apologized to Noah. "With rough words."

"How can words be rough?"

The bearded man and the guy with the earring wait for Matthias' answer. After a moment, he says, "Look, just watch this show, okay?"

All of them turn to the screen, where a cartoon baby seal is being chased by a killer whale. The bearded guy stays on his feet. Matthias says, "Be sure he doesn't change the channel, alright?"

The man rolls his eyes. "Not my kid, man."

"What?"

"I said he's not my kid. I mean, really, screw off. He's not yours either." And here, the man aims a single finger, jabbing it towards Matthias' chest.

Matthias' hands flash upward, and he clenches that finger in a fist. His other hand takes the man's wrist, hard. He bends the finger back into the joint—just a bit—and shoves forward. With only a little heat, he asks, "Know how easy it would be?"

The big man lets out a little whelpy sound and tries to retreat, but he stumbles on the coffee table and falls backward. Matthias watches him drop, then turns to see Carl staring at him. The boy is standing, skinny arms at his side, a silent witness. The bald man with the silver earring has draped an arm across the boy's shoulder, as if to offer protection.

As the big man clambers to his feet, Matthias walks away. Behind him, he hears the man cough and shout out something that includes the words *asshole* and *lawsuit*.

After taking some time to cool down in his office, Matthias takes over for Sharon at the snack stand, which mostly means clean up duty at this hour. He oversees the last two parties as they wrap up, then makes the announcement over the loud speaker. "The Kastle will be closing in ten minutes. Please enjoy your final magical rides." At the front gate, a small gang of older kids gathers, waiting to be picked up. Items left behind in the throne rooms—spare goodie bags, small presents, two cell phones—are collected. Matthias asks Keyanna if she's seen Carl. She shakes her head and asks if she can leave early. He scans the thinning crowd of kids, glances over at the TVs. "Sure," he tells her. "Just help Morgan and Nicky bring down the slides."

At his office desk, Matthias goes through the day's receipts, comparing the revenue to last year's and then to this year's projection. He inputs these numbers for corporate. After that, he fills out a deposit slip. The bank is on the way home to his apartment, which he pictures as still and empty. Tonight, he knows, he will lie on the couch and watch TV until he falls asleep. His attention is pulled away from this by raised voices in the hallway outside his office. When he opens the door, he sees Carl's dad by the arcade, shouting at Nicky. Carl's dad sees Matthias and the two men approach each other. "Where's my kid?"

Matthias looks at Nicky, who doesn't have any answer.

"Quit screwing around," the skinny dad says. "I'm about two minutes from missing the last bus."

"I don't know where Carl is," Matthias says. "He's not here. I thought you came and got him earlier."

"He got picked up?"

"Like I said. I don't know. This is exactly why—"

"Fuck me," the dad says. "If you dipshits lost him."

"What about his mom?" Matthias asks. "Somebody else?"

194

Carl's dad shakes his head. "Out of town."

Matthias runs through the possibilities. "Nicky," he says. "You and Morgan checked the rides before you deflated them?"

Nicky says, "There was nobody in them."

"But did you go through them?" he asks. A walk through is written protocol, part of their required training. Matthias stresses this at weekly safety meetings. Nicky doesn't answer, and in a moment, all three of them are sprinting into the warehouse's main hall. They move quickly but carefully over the rubber, like men rushing over thin ice. Matthias scans the rubber skin for a small bump that could be a suffocated boy. Each of them calls out Carl's name, and it echoes off the high walls.

After a few minutes, when they've each zig-zagged the hall three times over, they've still found nothing. Relieved, they check the snack stand, the arcade, both bathrooms. At the front gate, the three of them gather. In the wall of cubbies, a single set of tattered sneakers. The dad says, "Ain't like him to just wander off."

Nicky says, "You think somebody took him?"

"Who would take him?" Carl's dad asks.

Matthias pictures a single silver earring, that bald man's arm around Carl's bony shoulder. He says, "It's time to call the cops." Together, they run up the hallway to his office and the phone. But just as he's snapping up the receiver, Matthias sees the blackened bottoms of Carl's socks. Over in the corner of the room, the boy is curled up on the floor. His legs extend from inside the mascot head of Gary the Dragon. For an instant, Matthias is frozen, staring at the tiny minotaur-like creature, half child, half beast.

His dad shouts, "Carl!" and the boy snaps to life. He tries to sit up but only whacks into the inside of the huge head. As Carl crawls free, his dad drops to his knees and embraces the boy. Carl sets his bony chin on his father's bony shoulder. But then the dad grips him by both arms and yanks him back. "What the hell were you doing back here?"

Carl looks away. And his dad's one hand pulls back, opened for a flat slap. Carl flinches but does not try to retreat. His dad's right hand hangs in the air. His left still grips his son's thin bicep. Matthias winces, expecting the swift strike. He says, "He's safe now. Everything's okay. Come on."

Carl sniffles and his dad says, "Don't start up with that crap now." He shakes his head and releases the boy, then stomps from the office, reaching into his pocket.

Nicky asks Matthias if it's okay if he heads out, and then leaves the three of them alone. Carl stares at Matthias, wipes his wrist under his nose and says, "I wanted to be the dragon."

"It's alright," Matthias tells him. "Your dad's just upset. He was worried you were lost. We both were worried."

Carl seems to process this, then he walks past Matthias, who follows him out of the office. They find Carl's dad on the sidewalk out front. He tosses a cigarette into the parking lot, then glances at his watch.

Matthias says, "I need a few minutes to lock up. Then I can give you a ride."

Carl's dad flashes him a look like this is some kind of trick. Matthias tells him, "Really, it's no trouble. I'm happy to help."

Ten minutes later, Matthias slides behind the steering wheel while Carl and his dad climb together into the cramped back seat. Matthias says, "Sorry I don't have a booster seat or anything." He waits to hear the click of seatbelts, but the sound doesn't come. Like a taxi driver, he asks Carl's dad the best way to get to his address.

Up on Route 581, just as they're coming onto the bridge that spans the Susquehanna, brake lights begin to wink and flash. Matthias slows down and takes his place in the stalled traffic. "Must be an accident," he says.

The three of them sit in silence. When Matthias asks if they'd like the radio, there is no answer. A few minutes pass and a police car zips by on the shoulder, strobing lights but running without a siren.

Later, a couple cars up ahead sound their horns. Matthias hears a snap hiss in the backseat, and even before he turns he smells the smoke. Looking over his shoulder, he sees the cigarette's red tip. Carl's dad, on the passenger side, has one arm across the seatback. Carl is nestled in the crook, his head on his father's flat chest. The boy's eyes are open, but heavy.

Matthias almost asks the dad not to smoke but decides he doesn't care. The smell reminds him of nights at the periwinkle house on Poplar Lane, when he'd go out back for a drink and a smoke, try to think of how to get a handle on the situation.

Without being asked, Carl's dad cracks the window. A while later, Matthias hears it go up.

Finally the traffic starts moving. And in no time, they are across the river, whisking eastward. Mathias keeps an eye out for an ambulance, a tow truck, an overturned vehicle or skid marks. But there's nothing. No sign of catastrophe. He says, "Crazy how it's like that sometimes. All that trouble, and you'll never know why."

When there isn't even a grunt from the back, he glances in the rearview mirror and sees them. Carl's dad has his head tilted down, resting on his son's head, which is resting on his father's chest. As they cruise beneath the highway lights, their faces are brightened for an instant, then cast into shadow. But Matthias is certain they are both asleep, and for now, they look peaceful, serene.

When he reaches the exit that leads to their home, Matthias accelerates by in the passing lane. Above him, the billboards shine with whole families outside brand new homes, an infant beaming with care at a new pediatric unit, a mother and daughter—screaming with arms extended overhead—as they rise over the apex of a roller coaster at Hershey Park. Matthias has no clear plan, no expectation of atonement or penance. He knows only that the scene in his backseat brings him temporary warmth, and though he's sure it must end, for now he'll do all he can to preserve it.

Trials of Isaiah

A S SOON AS ISAIAH AWOKE, he knew he was in his father's home. Being in his boyhood room—blinking at the blank walls where once he hung comic book posters, where his father laid beside him and they took turns reading from the *Epic of Gilgamesh, 1001 Arabian Nights,* Tennyson's *Idylls of the King*—did not produce any sense of disorientation. The reality of his immediate circumstances was something he felt keenly aware of, and it came to him instantly. He was a middle-aged man, urgently summoned to a house he had not stepped into for six years.

The tightening along his temple made him recall his father's stash of vodka which he'd plundered last night, right under the kitchen sink where a bottle always seemed to be. If not for the headache and the need to piss, Isaiah might very well have spent the morning right there with his heavy head deep into the pillow. As it was, he dragged himself to the bathroom, where bright light drove pain into his eyes. He blinked it away and saw the lipstick message on the mirror. "Come over when you get up. Sorry about last night."

The chunky letters could've been any of his three sisters', each of whom lived here in Harrisburg within a few miles of this home where they all grew up. The lipstick messages were a common means of communication between his sisters back when they were all teens living here, in the days before white boards, sticky notes, emails, or texts. This was a time before the neighborhood slid onto hard times. All three of them, Donna, Julie, and Isaiah's twin Margaret, had been with Isaiah last night, here in the nearly empty house.

Opening the medicine cabinet, he saw the clear, clean shelves. He opened a drawer only to find virgin floral facecloths, folded perfectly in case a potential buyer got nosey. According to Donna, his eldest sister, the new realtor wasn't doing much better than the old one at selling the house. Even the big idea of "staging" the property hadn't produced much interest. Like so many homes in the area, the house was viewed as a grand old dame with "good bones", full of potential for someone who wanted to take on a major restoration project.

Isaiah headed for the oversized master bedroom, passing through rooms with foreign furniture he'd never seen before, matching sets of dressers and framed art and perfect accent pieces. But in his father's room, preserved in time like a museum exhibit, things felt entirely familiar. Here was the old square TV where they'd watched Tuesday night boxing, and here the ancient dresser with the feet chewed by Beowulf the dog before he drowned in Conodoguinet Creek. Though impossible, Isaiah smelled the faint hint of cigars. Yet even in this sacred space, there was an anomaly—evidence of the abject wrongness of all things. A second bed, this one motorized with a mattress bent nearly in two. Next to it, a white-bucketed toilet.

Forgetting about his headache, Isaiah approached the nightstand, where a red spiral notebook rested. It was the same kind he'd used for algebra homework in seventh grade, which his father would review with him after dinner, while his mother cleaned the dishes by hand. Isaiah recalled his frustration when his father would only put a question mark by the wrong answers and not simply solve them. On the cover of this notebook was scrawled, "Day Nurse Notes." He picked it up and flipped to a random entry: *Wednesday, March 3. Up at 5:15. Voided bowels. Productive bm. Morning meds. Sp. Bath. Back to bed till 9. Oatmeal brkfst, coffee. 10-12 watched news. Lunch Lentil soup. Choc. milk. Attempted physical therapy exercises (8 plz x 12). Afternoon nap. Patient refused to play cards, do crosswords. Watched Judge Judy.* Isaiah skimmed through the pages, nearly a hundred such entries. And of course, there might be other books.

When he lifted his head, his eyes fell on a series of hairline cracks in the wall. Like veins they arched down the plaster. On the ceiling above, the thick cloud of a water stain. Isaiah couldn't tell if it was old or a result of last night's downpour, the one his sister Julie, the youngest, had fled into crying.

After locating some Tylenol in his father's bathroom, he decided a shower might clear his head. He let the hot water scald his neck and back, but clarity did not arrive. When he twisted the silver knob, he noticed the showerhead leaked. It was also filthy with black grime. He dried, used his father's comb to settle his hair, then climbed into the same clothes he wore yesterday. The lump in his jeans pocket brought his hand there, and when he pulled out his cell phone, he saw he had a text message from his twin sister Margaret. "Up yet?"

Down in the kitchen, with a strangely immaculate fridge and a perfect table (never crayoned or scratched by pencils), one with four matching seats and bright cushions, Isaiah tried to locate a coffeemaker.

When he found the Maxwell House Instant, he recalled his father's incomprehensible preference. What kind of English professor prefers tasteless coffee? Despite his feelings, Isaiah put a mug of water in the microwave, making a mental note to buy a real cup later. For years after college, when he lived here until he met his wife Marie and found a decent job down in York at a firm that published yearbooks, Isaiah jokingly argued with his father about "real coffee." Isaiah dreaded the bland taste, but expected too it would bring back warm memories. His cheeks bunched up as he smiled. Yet as soon as he hit the power button, the microwave went dark, as did the overhead kitchen light. The notorious circuit breaker, unfixed for decades.

Marching into the basement, Isaiah had to brush back cobwebs along with the memories of the train station he and his father had constructed down here, the model airplanes, and the devices that together they took apart to better understand. Radios, an Atari joystick, a dehumidifier, old clocks. With a screwdriver and patience, listening to jazz on the radio, in a fog of cigar smoke, together they revealed the inner workings of things. Often they chatted about literature, and Isaiah recalled long talks about the difference between the Greek gods and the Roman, the trials of Hercules, the epic journey of Ulysses.

Isaiah was so distracted by his memories that he didn't see the water before he stepped into it. He stopped and looked down. It was more than a puddle, at least an inch deep, and he wondered how long it had been standing. The sheetrock on an interior wall, unfinished, was stained with a floating mountain range of moisture. It would have to be replaced. As for the outer wall, the concrete foundation was crumbling. Isaiah brushed his hand along it, and it flaked off in chunks. He glanced at the plumbing overhead, then looked toward the hot water heater, but there was no sign of a leak. Finally he sloshed his way to the basement door in the corner. When he pulled it back, sending a tiny flood across the room, he saw the source of the problem.

At the bottom of the concrete steps outside was a small landing, and at its center was a storm drain. It was clogged by sticks and leaves, clumps of pin oak bits and the whirligigs that spun from the branches each spring. Isaiah reached down into the murky water and used his fingers to rake free the debris. Immediately, as in an unclogged toilet, the water began to swirl downward.

In the corner of the landing was an ancient Maxwell House tin, the bottom rusted out, trampled. Isaiah picked it up for inspection and saw the holes drilled through the sides, summoning the memory: he and his father together in the workshop, crafting this makeshift grate. This had been thirty years ago, and Isaiah doubted this was the original. More likely his father had made a series of them as each one became worn. But still, the lettering was awfully old, and the label proclaimed, "Approved by leading doctors!"

Back in the basement, he sat on a cooler and watched the waters recede. They exposed the bottom of the doorframe, rotted, and Isaiah again looked at the walls the whole house was built on. The rust, the rot, the crumbling foundation. How long till the whole thing collapsed? Rising, he wondered if the neighborhood hardware store could possibly still be open.

Seven years ago, a few years into his marriage, Isaiah attended a company retreat in the Poconos. On the second night, he drank too much and slept with a new sales rep, a woman from Ohio with long blonde hair. In the morning when he woke, he was horrified to see her in his hotel bed. But when she rolled over into him and began to slide her hands over his body, he had succumbed. Sober and aware, he had failed.

He told Marie a month later, began sleeping in the guest room, and they signed up for marriage counseling. After a year, Marie forgave him, but somehow this only compounded his guilt and he found he couldn't forgive himself. Perhaps to drive her away, he was again unfaithful, this time with a teacher at the preschool where their daughter Haley was enrolled. Marie filed for divorce. Isaiah didn't contest, not even when she decided six months later to return home to Kentucky. In a small town like Camp Hill, rumors and gossip were hard to escape, and not long after Marie left, Isaiah quit his job in York and resettled in Norfolk, where the yearbook company had a branch that was expanding.

His father drove down once to see his new place and visit with him. For two days, they didn't speak of his ex-wife, the daughter who now lived hundreds of miles away. They went to bookstores, a movie about horseracing, a maritime museum. But in every silence between them, Isaiah could hear the question. Finally consumed by regret and guilt, on the night before his father was to return, Isaiah drank and drank until he found the courage to be truthful. At the kitchen table, with an empty bottle between them, Isaiah stared at the floor and said, "So I cheated on Marie. That's what happened."

His father was silent for a time. When he stood his chair scraped the floor. He said, "I'm going to bed." At the doorway he paused and turned, steadying himself with one hand on the frame. He looked back at his son. Isaiah was looking at his shoes when his father added, "I raised you to be better. I raised you to be a hero."

Al's Hardware and Supply was, remarkably, still open at the corner six blocks away from the family home. The pizza parlor next to it was now a Subway, and the old arcade had transformed into a laundry mat. But Al's, where he and his father had trekked many a Saturday for supplies for their weekend list of projects, still survived. Stepping inside was like stepping back in time. The door chimed behind Isaiah, and he settled a hand on the gumball machine at his side, recalling the thick crank, the sugary satisfaction. No one was at the counter, and the store seemed empty. The wooden floor creaked beneath him. Tall shelves surrounded cramped aisles, and as he walked down them he had the illusion that the shelves were curving in at the top, threatening to topple. At the pay-by-the-pound bin, Isaiah shoved the metal scoop into a pile of penny nails. He wandered a bit aimlessly by the plumbing section and picked out a showerhead. A tortoise shell cat with half its face mangled trotted over to him and studied him with its one good eye.

His cell phone buzzed, startling the cat. Isaiah reached in his pocket and pulled it out. The text was from Donna, and it read, "Get here. The doctor says he's close."

At the check out, a grey-haired man now sat on a stool reading *Fish and Stream*. When Isaiah approached, he stood, remaining the same height as he'd been while seated. He limped the two steps to the register and asked if Isaiah had found everything he needed. Isaiah shook his head. "I need a grate to cover a drain. Something big." He lifted his hands up as if holding a basketball.

The old man nodded and limped back into his store, and Isaiah followed. He walked him down an aisle of grass seed, then paused before some gutter covers. He pulled what looked like a wire light bulb down from a hook and said, "If you put this in the spout, it'll catch all the leaves and gunk."

"It's not for the gutter," Isaiah explained, not impatient. "The drain outside the cellar door gets clogged all the time. The basement floods." He lifted his hands again, showing the size he needed.

The shopkeeper nodded. "Industrial grade. I don't carry anything like that. But I can special order it. Hang on." He hobbled back to the front and slid through a grey curtain, into an office maybe. When he returned carrying a thick book, the cat followed him. He dropped the book on the counter and flipped the thin white pages before coming to a stop. He spun it around and aimed a crooked finger at a picture of exactly what Isaiah felt he needed.

Isaiah leaned over and said, "How long till it would be here?"

The man shrugged. "Three to five days. But it's $139 dollars."

Isaiah straightened. "That can't be right."

"Look for yourself. I'd be giving you my price. Mostly only contractors order stuff like that."

"Contractors," Isaiah said. He thought of the Maxwell House coffee tin, how even if he made another one, that in time it would decay. He thought of the rotting wood in the basement, the mold and the crumbling cement foundation. Putting the showerhead on the counter, he said, "Just this."

After the old man rang him up, Isaiah handed over his credit card and the owner glanced at it, then up to Isaiah's face. He paused, then continued. Once he'd put the receipt and the showerhead in a plastic bag, he gave it to Isaiah and said, "I knew you looked familiar. You look a lot like him, you know."

Unsurprised, Isaiah nodded. His resemblance to his father had plagued and delighted him all his life. Plus his name, also the same, was on the credit card. He said, "So I've been told."

The old man worked something in his mouth. "You even sound like him. Your voice."

Isaiah held his silence.

The shopkeeper dipped his head. "I heard about what happened. I'm very sorry. He was a good man."

It unnerved him to hear his father spoken of in the past tense. Isaiah was trying to decide if he should tell the shopkeeper that his father was still alive when his phone erupted. It wasn't the buzz of a text but the sharp ring of an incoming call. Startled, the two men looked at each other until the shopkeeper asked, "Ain't you gonna answer that?"

Isaiah shook his head. "I know who it is." He reached into his pocket and turned the phone off, then he left the shop.

Two days ago Isaiah had arrived on the three o'clock bus from Richmond and walked the half mile to the hospital complex, which overlooks the river. On the walk, as he had on the long bus ride, as he had for six years in his most private moments, he rehearsed what he might say. He knew he would tell his father he was sorry for the distance that had settled between them. They had spoken on the phone, sat at the same holiday meal table at his sister's home a few times, but never really talked since that night in Norfolk. Isaiah wanted to thank him for his childhood, for the many sacrifices he'd made and the blessings he'd bestowed. Isaiah was pretty sure he'd forgive his father for the harshness of his judgment regarding his infidelity, though he doubted the old man was seeking absolution for that particular sin. What Isaiah couldn't decide was whether or not he'd release the venom, the poison he'd been carrying in his gut since he was in college, home on winter break his junior year. At the time his mother was in the hospital recovering from her surgery. Nine months later the cancer would take her. But that day, Isaiah was in the kitchen when the phone rang, and when he answered it, the female voice said quietly, "I need to see you. Can you get away?"

Assuming it was a wrong number, Isaiah asked who it was.

"Isaiah?" the female voice asked.

And, truthful, he said, "Yeah. This is Isaiah." After a moment, he added, "Isaiah junior."

The next thing he heard was the dial tone. He wondered if that woman ever told his father that she'd given away their affair, or if she'd kept the secret the same way he had. And walking to the hospital from the bus station two days ago, Isaiah rehearsed all the lines he might use to reveal what he knew. "You cheated on mom." "I talked to your girlfriend once." "Guess I'm not the only one who isn't a hero."

But when he arrived, his father was curled up in the bed, crooked legs propped by pillows, wrists turned inward. Without his glasses his face looked empty, and the skin across his cheeks was taunt. Blue veins forked like rivers. His eyes, wide open and cloudy, fixed on the ceiling straight over his head, and he didn't respond to anyone. He only blinked and stared and breathed through his mouth. The doctor and his sisters spoke as if Isaiah's father was not in the room. This second stroke was much worse than the first, and no one had discovered him for quite some time, too long for TPA to have any effect. "We'll just keep him comfortable now," the doctor said. After he left, Donna inserted a dropper in a glass of water and brought it to her father's open mouth. Instinctively, he wrapped his flaking lips around it as an infant would a baby bottle, and Donna pressed the plunger and their father sucked the water, swallowed. His sister Julie reported that their father had called out in his sleep for his grandmother, that earlier in the week, still somewhat lucid, he had reported seeing people who were not there: his parents, his older brother who died in the war, his wife. Isaiah's sister said these spirit visions, whatever they were, had comforted their father. In the window, taking in what light it could, was a bouquet of a dozen pink roses. Isaiah wondered who would send such a thing at a time like this.

Including a quick stop at the house, where he dropped off the showerhead, the walk from Al's Hardware took about forty-five minutes, and Isaiah reached the hospital in a light rain. He dried off in the bathroom on the first floor, passed the receptionist's desk and the coffee cart and the gaudy-bright gift shop. In the elevator on the way to the third floor, Isaiah considered his cell phone, which he hadn't turned back on. He knew that right now, it may contain a message that would alter his life. But he didn't want to hear such a thing in that way.

The doors split open with a pleasant ding and Isaiah stepped through, but instead of heading down the corridor, he paused at a large window by the elevator bay. There was a tree with plastic leaves in a plastic apple basket. Rain trailed down the glass, though not so much that he couldn't see outside clearly. On the roof just outside the window, huge air conditioning units hummed. He could see their fans spinning. Rain water puddled around a large vent, pumping steam. Beyond the edge of the roof, the river ran beneath the six bridges. A train chugged across one, and on another traffic was stopped heading into Lemoyne. Isaiah thought about the room he was about to enter, what he was likely to see and hear. He knew too that what he'd wanted all these years, a confrontation, reconciliation, forgiveness, an explanation, were all now impossible.

There was nothing to do now but bear witness.

As this settled over him, Isaiah's eyes fixed on something on the roof. The rain was coming down harder, and as it pooled and gathered, it ran towards a central low point, where it passed through a familiar-looking metal grate. Isaiah squinted but was sure of what he saw. Without thinking, he reached up and undid the twin latches of the window and shoved it up with his palms. Cooler air eased in. Isaiah climbed up through the opening and stepped out into the thickening rain.

His feet sank a bit into the spongy black surface, and overhead an emergency helicopter on the roof began to spin its blades. He started to walk toward the grate, about fifty feet away. But after he wiped his eyes to clear some rain, he looked to the side and saw pink roses in a window. He paused. Something drew him towards that window. The pull was like a current, and he did not resist it.

When he reached the window, he cupped his hands to his forehead and set them on the cool, wet glass. Inside, he saw the backs of Donna and Margaret standing at his father's bedside. Julie sat on the far side of the room, bent elbows to knees. Isaiah wondered if they were crying softly or praying or if they were silent.

Margaret stepped away, and suddenly Isaiah could see his father, turned on his side, facing the window. His gauzy eyes were open, and they fixed on Isaiah through the glass. He blinked, and his eyebrows lowered as he peered intensely. Isaiah wondered, through the delirium, through the medication, without his glasses, if the old man could make him out at all. He wondered if his father thought he was another apparition sent to ease his passage. Isaiah smiled, tight-lipped, and set a hand flat on the slick glass. He nodded.

Perhaps it was coincidence, but his father, almost imperceptibly, nodded too. And Isaiah decided his father saw him and knew who he was. The two men recognized each other.

His twin sister returned to her position, holding something, and blocked Isaiah's view. In the rain, he turned from that room and made his way to the center of the roof. The water flowed evenly through the grate, swirling into the holes of a drain. Isaiah reached down and clutched the metal, but when he lifted, it did not budge. He pulled harder still with the same result, and it came to him that the thing might be bolted down. Next he squatted with bent knees, and with both hands he took hold of the grate. And now he tugged and heaved, lifting his face into the rain, straining so that pain pierced his back, but he did not stop. From his father's evening tales, he remembered the would-be kings testing themselves at the sword in the stone, and he tugged all the harder, even though it did no good.

Kol Nidre (All Vows)

"IT WAS ONLY ONCE," BARRY confessed to Nicole as they sat in mismatched chairs across the desk from Rabbi Coleman. "Just that one time."

Nicole broke the strained eye contact she'd been holding with her husband and turned to the window, where the earliest fall leaves had begun to turn. The actual number attached to the infidelity was new, but Nicole had known of Barry's adultery from the start, nearly three months ago. These last six weeks of counseling sessions with Rabbi Coleman had been painful though not entirely unpleasant as she watched Barry squirm his way toward this revelation. At home and during these meetings, she'd tried to find ways to prevent him from telling her, as keeping it a secret meant she wasn't compelled to take action. Being Nicole, she had devised a solution of sorts as a contingency, but it involved taking an enormous risk, one that even she couldn't quite calculate.

"Nicole," Rabbi Coleman said, "you heard what Barry shared just now, yes?"

"I did," she said.

Barry leaned into the space between their chairs and spoke to the side of her face. "I'm telling you this now so I can explain to you how sorry I am and ask your forgiveness, so we can stay together and raise our boys. I want to get back to us."

Nicole said nothing to this line, which was probably scripted. She pictured Max, Aaron, and Jacob, by now picked up by her sister-in-law and probably playing video games with their cousins on the far side of Camp Hill.

"You may ask anything you'd like," Rabbi Coleman said, adjusting his black glasses with both hands. "That's part of the healing process. Barry is prepared for full disclosure."

"I am," Barry added, nodding deeply.

With a flat expression, Nicole told them, "I have no questions."

Rabbi Coleman and Barry exchanged awkward glances. Clearly, this was not going according to plan. Part of her husband's expiation was obviously a detailed accounting of his sin. Prompted by Rabbi Coleman, Barry asked, "Don't you even want to know—"

Nicole rose. "I know you screwed her. One time. Just that once. You said that, and I heard you. I also heard you say you were sorry and ask for my forgiveness." As she turned to the door, she slid her purse strap onto her shoulder.

"Hang on," Barry said. "We still have fifteen minutes."

Gripping the doorknob, Nicole paused. "I'll be in the car."

Hastily, Rabbi Coleman got up and opened a desk drawer. He pulled out a white envelope and passed it to Barry, who took a few quick steps and held it out to his wife. "We wanted to review this together. Think of it as a path forward."

Nicole tucked the envelope in her purse. "Just come out when you're finished. But it'll be sundown in a couple hours. I'm sure Rabbi Coleman has preparations to make." She looked at him, standing behind his desk. "Thanks for all your help." Then Nicole left the men alone.

Behind the steering wheel of their minivan, which smelled of melted granola bars and French fries, Nicole used a key and jaggedly sliced open the envelope. The two page "Marriage Contract" involved fourteen proclamations, including "Barry agrees to let Nicole call him on his cell phone at any time and inquire as to his whereabouts to help repair the trust he shattered" and "Nicole may discuss this matter with anyone she chooses, including Max, Aaron, and Jacob, but Barry would like to be present." It was actually an impressive little document, she had to admit. At the bottom Barry had signed it already and there was a space for her token signature.

Nicole wondered fleetingly whose idea it was. Was this crazy notion something that floated around the hallways at the law firm where Barry worked mostly on intellectual property disputes, or did Rabbi Coleman propose it as some half-baked scheme to preserve their marriage? No matter. Nicole had thought of a better way.

After Barry finally joined her, Nicole navigated in silence through rush hour traffic. This time of day in Camp Hill was always frustrating, with the bypass choked by Harrisburg commuters. The two of them drove mostly in silence, punctuated by occasional pleas from Barry, who wiped his tears with a white handkerchief and now and then used obscenities to try and capture the depth of his regret. Nicole turned off the air conditioning and lowered the windows, letting in the cool autumn air.

At his sister's house, Barry ran inside for their sons alone. As Nicole drove home, the boys reported on their adventures at school and each other's bad behavior and misdeeds at Aunt Deb's. At one point, Barry reached across the console and set his hand on Nicole's leg. Gently, she removed it, and with the same motion turned on the news. There had been a massive explosion at a gas plant in China. Exotic toxins had been released into the air. Hundreds were already dead and more were likely to be killed. Officials were already on the scene investigating the cause, but the focus for now was helping the survivors.

A RUSHED HALF HOUR LATER, after Barry and the boys had loaded up on a quick dinner ahead of the twenty-six hour fast while Nicole ate nothing, Barry walked into the bedroom to prepare for the evening service at temple. Nicole had been careful to avoid being alone with her husband, and they hadn't discussed the latest development in their fifteen-year marriage. Even as they sat at table, Nicole didn't look him in the eye. Now he found her zippering up a small suitcase on the bed. "What's this?" he asked.

"I don't want to sleep here tonight."

"But where will you go? How long will this last?"

Above them, their sons banged around their bedrooms, supposedly getting dressed in nice clothes. "Don't panic," she told him. "I'll be back in the morning before the boys even wake up."

Barry gathered himself, and Nicole imagined him recalling some sage advice from Rabbi Coleman. Finally he said, "Of course. You need space and time to process. I respect that. I want to give you everything you need."

"Alright then," Nicole said, lifting the suitcase.

"Only what do I tell the boys? At temple tonight, what do I say to my mother and sister when they ask where you are?"

Nicole didn't turn or slow down. As she rolled the suitcase across the hard wood she said over her shoulder, "Anything you like. You could even try the truth."

A DEAL IS A DEAL. This is one of the things Nicole's insurance agent father had instilled in her from the earliest age. All through her childhood, he spoke to Nicole openly about the rightness of things, doing good, being good. "When you make a promise with someone, you make it with yourself first. To break it is a betrayal of them, yes, but more importantly, you have broken with yourself. Later, in your most private heart, this you will always know." In the hospital room where he'd died two years ago, she'd heard her father share these words with her eldest boy Max, and she recalled the lesson from her own youth.

Maybe the man was on her mind tonight because of the holiday. She recalled his steadfast commitment to the fast of Yom Kippur, how just before they'd pile into the station wagon for the Kol Nidre services, he would take ten sips of water, counting down from ten. He believed this would fortify him for the day of abstaining. Nicole was sure he remained faithful.

She could also trace her affinity with numbers, her compulsive need for mathematic precision, back to her dad. This served her well in her career as an accountant, a job she found satisfying and meaningful. Now that Jacob was beginning first grade, she would be looking for work, and though she loved her time with the boys, she was looking forward to the transition, for the simple contentment of solving problems, getting an answer. Despite all the multitude of online tools and automated services, Nicole still balanced the family checkbook every month by hand, searching for each lost penny like a stray sheep. She did this not out of cheapness but because it put order to the world. In a strange way, Nicole knew this was why she was doing what she was doing tonight, though she was also certain her father would not approve.

At the Harrisburg Hilton, she paid for the room with the same credit card she used to buy gas and groceries, then took the elevator up five flights. The room had a flat screen TV, a small fridge, and an executive desk. She strolled past the queen size bed without looking at it. At the huge window, she yanked open the drapes to reveal the late day's sun striking the Susquehanna River. Three miles to the north, she knew they were gathering ahead of sundown at Kesher Israel, that even now the parking lot was crowded, with the side streets filling. She hoped Barry remembered to bring Aaron's favorite yarmulke, the one he'd gotten at Eileen's wedding last year. The boy, a budding hypochondriac, hated to use the ones from the lobby bin, calling them "totally gross and unsanitary."

Tonight began with Kol Nidre, the first of the five services of Yom Kippur, the Day of Atonement. As a lawyer, Barry always had a flair for the dramatic, and Nicole wondered if through all their counseling with Rabbi Coleman he'd planned this out, the harmonic convergence of his confession. It seemed too much for coincidence. Before the new Jewish year could begin, true believers were called upon to repent and forgive. At tonight's service, they would beg God to forgive the sins they'd committed against Him. As for those committed against another person, the offender had to seek reconciliation directly. In theory, it was a time of wiping clean the slate and embracing fresh starts.

After three months of coping alone with Barry's cheating, Nicole was pleased to finally be here in the hotel, to take this action to try and rectify such a manmade catastrophe. Above all she was certain of one thing: a divorce would devastate her second child. Aaron was a tender soul, like her father, a boy who would capture spiders and release them outside, who was prone to crying in third grade when other students were disciplined in his presence. All three of her sons would be rattled by a breakup, but Max would recover in time, and Jacob was so young, the brunt of the impact would be diminished. But Aaron, who still woke some nights sweaty and blubbering with what the pediatrician called "night terrors," he would never recover.

So rather than take the path of splitting up, Nicole had resolved, months ago, to simply absorb Barry's indiscretion, to try and forget the conference trip to D.C. from which he returned without his silver dolphin necklace that had belonged to his beloved grandmother. Early in their courtship, during one of their fledgling attempts at making love, the swaying silver dolphin had kept bopping Nicole in the chin, to the point where she burst out laughing. Following this, he always removed it and set it on the nightstand ahead of sex. It was the only time he took it off.

In the aftermath of her discovery, she'd studied her dilemma until she found a resolution of sorts. First she put a great deal of effort into forgetting. For weeks she pretended nothing had happened, but Barry's guilt ruined everything. He was unusually affectionate or distant, smothering her or ignoring her, and this led to protracted silences and midnight fighting, one of them sleeping curled on the basement couch. All this time, they did not make love. Eventually, he convinced her to come see Rabbi Coleman for guidance. Even at that first meeting, she understood where this would lead: Barry would tell her he cheated, and she would have to activate her contingency plan.

To save their family, she would break her vows. That was of course why she was here in the Hilton, to seek out a man—hopefully kind, perhaps even handsome—to invite to the queen size bed behind her, where she would lie with him and balance the scales.

She turned from the window and unzipped the suitcase, from which she pulled the outfit she'd selected weeks ago for the occasion. The strapless black dress was tasteful she thought, and even cute, inviting without being salacious. Nicole hated women who didn't dress their age. At forty-five, thanks to morning workouts before Barry left for the office and a strict diet, Nicole had a fit body, though she hadn't displayed it to anyone other than Barry for twenty years. The idea of all this was scary, like stepping off a cliff, but she couldn't deny a hint of excitement, the thrill of imminent sin.

She glanced at her watch and decided to shower. By Jewish law, it was forbidden now that she should bathe, but given what else she had planned, this seemed insignificant. She pictured Barry in the synagogue with their sons and his family. His mother, bent with age, would have her prayer shawl draped over her grey head. When Rabbi Coleman called on God to allow them to pray with transgressors, could he keep his eyes from floating to Barry? After the opening invocation, the three cantors, like a tribunal, would rise and begin to chant the Kol Nidre. Like all who heard it, Nicole found the song's melody haunting and lovely, though the ancient words confounded her. On this holy night, believers beseech God to release them from vows they might make in the year ahead under duress, or those they never wholly embrace in their heart. "Let our vows not be considered vows," they would pro-claim, "our oaths not oaths." Some scholars said the practice began during the days when Jews were forced to renounce their faith or die; others claim the tradition was even older. Later, the congregants would recite communal confessions—the Ashmanu and Al Chet—and receive God's absolution.

Something about Kol Nidre always troubled Nicole. A deal was a deal; a promise was a promise. One did not simply walk away from a commitment or covenant. But tonight, as the showerhead blasted hot water that scorched her back, as she scrubbed her skin raw with a soapy cloth, she warmed to the notion of being forgiven for a deed she knew to be wrong, even before she did it. And in her heart, she was unequivocally clear that she was making a mistake. It was simply a necessary one.

NICOLE HAD RESOLVED TO BE SOBER when she executed her fail-safe solution. So in the hotel lounge, after she'd mounted a bar stool with a clear view of the entrance, she ordered just a ginger ale. This, she was well aware, was another violation of the fast. But Barry, she noted to herself, was always a more observant Jew than she. His adherence to the old ways was one of the things Nicole's father truly liked about him.

For a long while Nicole sipped on the drink without enjoying it, making occasional small talk with the bartender, Adam. He was a lanky man in his fifties who asked vague questions, listening and nodding when she spoke. Now and then, she feigned interest in the baseball game on the TV suspended above Adam's head. She recognized the teams from earlier, when she'd sat on the hotel bed and flipped channels for over an hour, trying to rally her courage.

Each time the double doors to the bar swung inward, she nervously glanced up, hoping for a suitable candidate. Not surprisingly, most of the patrons seemed like travellers, small gangs of middle-age businessmen. But here and there came a few young couples enjoying a weeknight date on the town. She recalled, with some genuine wistfulness, those carefree days with Barry, back before children. As for single men, only a handful wandered inside. One, handsome with olive skin that suggested the Middle East to Nicole, took his drink to a corner booth and withdrew a laptop from his satchel, never looking her way. Another unaccompanied man ordered two bottles of Corona and left clutching them by their necks with one hand. A third sat a few stools down from Nicole but seemed engrossed in the baseball game, pumping his fist or cursing under his breath. Others came and went.

Nicole was absently crunching on a piece of ice from her soda when Adam asked her, "You need something else in that glass?" and she realized how she must look, anxious and unattractive. So she ordered a glass of red wine and took out her phone, in part to suggest she was waiting for someone in particular. There was a long and rambling text message from Barry, one professing sorrow and begging her to call him. From the time, she guessed he had sent it after he returned from services. She hoped the boys had brushed their teeth before bed and thought how she'd need to make their lunches in the morning. She regretted not saying goodnight to them, especially Aaron, who would have pelted her with questions. She'd had no energy to concoct lies about where she was going, why she wouldn't be joining the family.

Nicole slid the phone back into her purse, where the contract was folded still. The cabernet helped calm her nerves, and she felt the tension in her neck and shoulders replaced by the lightness of wine. She'd just ordered a second when a pale man with doughy skin and red hair slid abruptly alongside her, elbows down on the bar, and said, "Hey there. Who's winning?"

She glanced up and saw the box score displayed in the lower right hand corner. The man, who'd loosened his tie enough that a tuft of hair sprang from his white collar, grinned at her. She set her fingers on the base of her wine glass and told him, "I'm not certain."

He drummed his hands on the bar and asked, "What, so you don't like baseball?"

Without lifting her gaze, she said, "I guess not."

After the dough boy walked off, back to a table of buddies who'd been watching, she saw the Middle Eastern gentleman staring her way over his laptop. He was sitting in a darkened corner, but the shine of the screen illuminated his sympathetic face. His eyes fell again to his work. Nicole was not absolutely sure he had been looking at her, but she wondered why he was here, what work absorbed his attention, what his name was. Taking her time, she finished her second glass, trying to calculate the odds of a positive outcome if she ordered him a drink and sent it over. This cinematic standard seemed too forward, too overt and inelegant. So instead, Nicole decided on an approach she hoped was a little more subtle. Though she didn't need to use the bathroom, she strolled slowly in his direction toward the ladies room. As she passed she cast her glance down, smiling, and his eyes lifted briefly to hers. On his screen, he had a half dozen windows open, each with what Nicole recognized as computer code.

She waited in the bathroom for a minute or two, long enough to make it convincing, taking the chance to reapply her lipstick with slightly trembling fingers. Even this self-adornment was forbidden during the Yom Kippur fast, but what did it matter, given her predicament?

On her return trip, as she came up from behind the man, she saw he was now studying columns of scrolling figures. She couldn't think of any question that didn't sound token, any opening line that wasn't corny, so she merely slowed down and cleared her throat quietly. It was enough to steal his attention, and he turned his face to hers. His smile was friendly and warm, though fleeting. He focused again on his laptop's screen and so she continued on. Apparently, she'd only imagined his interest, and she was convinced everyone had witnessed her clumsy effort. As she made her way back to her stool, defeated, she wondered if she'd simply picked the wrong sort of place. Perhaps she'd have to brave the string of neighborhood bars down the block. From her drive in, she knew these would be louder, with karaoke and perhaps a band, that there would be little opportunity for small talk. In bars like that, she'd need to rely on eye contact to draw someone to her. She imagined a scenario where after such a beginning, she'd simply take a man's hand and, without speaking, lead him out onto the sidewalk, up the block, and back to her room. They need never even exchange names.

But then Nicole got back to her stool and found her wine glass re-filled. She scanned for the bartender, saw him tending to a trio of college-age girls, and then couldn't help but look back to the man with olive skin, still peering at his screen. Nicole decided this meant that he was uncomfortable about this awkward encounter, like her, which made him all the more appealing. Perhaps she'd found a kindred spirit. Holding her full glass, she crossed the room, stopping when she cast a shadow over him. He looked up, wide-eyed, and she raised her wine. "Cheers," she said.

The man's face registered mild confusion mixed with curiosity, and he reached for his liquor glass, half full of some amber liquid.

"Cheers." They clinked, then each took a short drink, and Nicole lowered herself into the seat across from him.

He folded down his laptop and said, "What is it exactly that we are toasting?"

"Do we need a reason?"

"I guess not."

They both laughed pleasantly.

She learned his name was John, and while she was disappointed it wasn't Anwar or Raul, he was a more than likeable man. He was an expert in computer security and had recently left an established firm in Baltimore to break out on his own.

"Sort of like a hired gun?" Nicole asked. "That sounds exciting."

John shook his head. "It's a ton of travelling. I've got to go where the work is. Last week I was in Arkansas. Tomorrow night, I'll go to bed in Vancouver."

Nicole told him how much she hated travelling, though she held back the images of strollers, diaper bags, collapsible cribs. Years ago, when she and Barry did summer trips to her family, it felt like they were moving an army. John talked about the sensation he had sometime that he lived in one massive airport complex, that he'd die if he had to eat one more Subway sandwich at a wobbly table.

When he asked her what she did to fill her days, she fibbed and said she was an accountant. She told a few stories of difficult clients from a decade ago as if they had just happened, and he laughed at the ones that were funny.

"You like your job," he said. "I can tell that about you."

Nicole considered this. "I like problems that can be fixed. I like questions that have a definitive answer."

224

John nodded. "Nothing like a puzzle that needs to be solved. I know what you mean."

When John finished off the last of his drink, he looked at Nicole's empty wine glass. "I should be clear-headed in the morning, so I'm about all done. Would you like another?"

Nicole shook her head, and John continued, "But I'm very much enjoying our conversation. We could keep talking someplace else. Would you like that?"

Nicole stood. "I think I would," she said sheepishly, understanding the weight of her words and the implicit agreement she'd just made. Something about John reminded her of a lover she'd had the summer she graduated from Villanova, a boy who was bashful in public but passionate when they were alone. In a quiet voice, she said, "Listen. I want to be totally honest. Later, when we're finished, I'm not going to stay, alright? I'm not going to—"

John raised a hand. "You'll do what you need to do. Everything will be good. I understand, okay?"

She wondered just what John understood, if somehow his knowledge of those indecipherable scripts of code gave him insight into her situation. They were walking toward the exit together when Nicole saw the bartender following her movement. She said, "Excuse me," to John and went to the bar to settle her bill. Adam pushed a small black folder her way and she quickly flipped it open, slid in a credit card, and looked up to locate John. He was standing at the hotel threshold, facing the lobby. He seemed to Nicole as if he were waiting for someone else to arrive.

The bartender returned and Nicole skimmed her bill, tabulating a tip. As she expected, she saw charges for the soda and first two glasses of wine. When she looked at Adam, he smiled and said, "That last round was on the house. I know when somebody needs a little liquid courage. You have a great night." His eyes slid from her face to John, and he returned to his work.

Heat bloomed across Nicole's neck and ears. She felt a sheen of sweat on her forehead and wiped it clear. Then she finished paying and joined John. Side by side they walked to a waiting elevator. The doors slid shut and they were alone. John reached forward and tapped the button for the seventh floor. As they rose he brought his face close to Nicole's, his gentle gaze aimed at her lips.

With a lurch, she stepped forward and drove a finger into the button for the fifth floor. "Sorry," she explained. "I just need to freshen up first. And I . . . I need to get something. Tell me your room number."

The elevator stopped and the doors split open with a ding. John gave her a number and added, "You know we can take this as slow as you like."

She stepped into the hallway and behind her John said, "Honestly, if you'd like to just talk some more, that would be fine. I'd be okay with that. We could even go back downstairs."

Nicole turned and with effort looked John in the face, where she found an expression of genuine concern. "I'm sorry," she said.

As the doors came together again, John shrugged and said, "Me too."

AFTER CHECKING OUT, NICOLE DROVE in a haze for a couple hours, circling Harrisburg on the interstate highways. Just after midnight, with nowhere else to go, she found herself parked out front of their darkened suburban home. But Nicole couldn't quite bring herself to go inside. For the first time in weeks, the fiery tears returned and she wept violently. What would be the next scene? Now that she'd failed, how could any of this be fixed? The situation seemed unsolvable. For the briefest of time back at the bar, when she was talking with John, everything seemed possible. She was struck by just how easily it came for her to lie. With this thought, Nicole saw a way to rescue the night and save her family.

"Wake up, Barry," she said as she entered their bedroom, flicking on the light. From how he looked, she could tell he hadn't been sleeping.

"I'm so glad to see you, Nicki. You don't know how—"

"Stop," she said, raising a hand. She dropped the countersigned Marriage Contract on his lap and began to get undressed. "I need to say a few things."

Barry lifted the paper. "Of course."

She turned out the light and slid in next to him. "I've just come from the Hilton over in Harrisburg, where I slept with a computer programmer named John. We had drinks in the bar first. You can check the credit card transactions online."

In the darkness, Barry said nothing. Nicole went on. "It was only once. Just the one time. And I know how it hurts you but it's all over now. I know you're sorry for what you did Barry, and I forgive you. But I expect you to forgive me too."

With this, she slid one hand up under his t-shirt and began to kiss his neck. He recoiled and said, "Hold it! This is crazy."

Nicole sighed, convinced of her logic. "If we don't make love now—right now—we might never do it again. That won't work for us. And I know what night it is—I know what's forbidden—but we have no choice. So come on."

She advanced on him again and this time Barry relented. She could tell he was reluctant and uncertain, but after all their years together she understood how her husband's body responded. It didn't take her very long. When the time came she rolled to her back and guided his hips above hers, and by now she was slipping away herself, feeling that urgent rising rush.

Above them just then, past the still ceiling fan, she made out Aaron's soft whimpering, the precursor to the crying that inevitably followed. In minutes, he'd be screaming uncontrollably, plagued by nightmares unknown. Nicole could tell Barry didn't yet hear their son, and she urged him on, hoping they'd just have time to conclude their business before Aaron came charging downstairs. Barry doubled his pace, whispering his love for her, and deep in her private heart, Nicole thought, *Never tell him the truth*. This, she recognized with certainty, was a vow that would go unbroken. And through the ceiling she stared at blankly, she heard her son begin to wail.

Nine Times I Failed My Second Wife
(Selected from an infinitely larger pool)

ONE

At our last visit to Counselor Steve, when the three of us had decided after almost two years of therapy, meditation, and shiny white pills, that my second wife and I could better explore our rich potential as human beings shaped in the divine image of Christ if we in fact stopped being husband and wife, she set her hand on mine in a way she hadn't in a long while and said, "You can't say we didn't try." I looked at the tight open space between us on the two seat couch that Counselor Steve made us sit on. The floral pattern made me dizzy. I thought of what I wanted to say, but instead I shrugged and said, "I guess so."

TWO

On our first date, which technically speaking wasn't a date so much as an encounter, but at a certain point we both realized we'd left behind the groups we'd come to the bar with, had bought each other a drink or two, and were into something interesting and without a proper name. We were past the point where we both knew numbers would be exchanged. We had that warm radiant glow that makes anything, everything, seem not just within reach but inevitable. I'd dropped some casual crack about the bartender that made her throw her head back with laughter. Really, she practically howled, and it felt so good to do that for somebody again. When she stopped laughing, she asked, "Just how crazy are you?"

What I should had said was, "The fact is that yes, I've had a professional assess my mental status and suggest the advisability of a 72 hour in-patient care facility. But this was in the months after my first marriage spontaneously combusted, so there's mitigating circumstances. Of course, in the wake of all that, I'm not at all convinced that I've returned to what we'd think of as 'normal' or 'healthy.' So if you were, for example, my sister, I would urge you to avoid a guy like me as if I had the plague. I would bombard you with clichés like 'There's more than one fish in the sea,' or 'You've got to kiss a lot of frogs to find a prince,' or just go with 'Are you out of your freakin' mind dating a guy who just signed divorce papers?'"

What I said though was, "As crazy as you want me to be."

This was the first in a long series of clever lines. In my defense, the way she smiled, it felt like a small miracle, like a blessing was being bestowed. During those days, nobody much was smiling around me, so that's got a lot to do with why I said what I did. It's understandable, if not excusable.

THREE

On the night we moved into our second home, my back was killing me after carrying boxes and furniture without my lower spine support brace. She'd told me once, as a joke I'm sure, that it made me look like an old guy working at Home Depot. But if you're the kind of husband I am, even if you're absolutely sure it's a joke, you treat such statements as if they were intercepted communications. Anything might hold the secret to why you aren't in the midst of wedded bliss. That night, as I was unpacking kitchenware, trying to find the damn coffeemaker so at least the morning wouldn't be a total disaster, my second wife appeared, grimy from a two-hour assault on the upstairs bathroom, to say she was going to bed. She said she loved me and loved our new house, and yes, she kissed me, but it was only on the cheek. It was not a lips on lips kiss goodnight, something that suggested during that era of our marriage the possibility of nocturnal activity. And sure, of course, I'd been hopeful that after securing a new home for us and coordinating the relocation of all our worldly belongings, I might have a chance at some nookie. We'd reached that point in our relationship where sex only took place on special occasions. There was birthday sex, anniversary sex, just got back from a friend's wedding a little bit drunk sex, sorry your mother died sex, sorry you got fired sex, hurray you got an interview sex. That kind of thing. So my expectations and desires were perfectly in line with our established protocol. That kiss on the cheek ended my hopes, drowned them like mewling kittens, and for the next hour I used a steak knife to rip open boxes and brutally unpack. All the while I was definitely finishing off a couple Heinekens, which did indeed take the edge off the back pain. And then I was in the downstairs shower, getting the day's stink off me, all with a pleasant little buzz and hot water pelting my neck. I found myself thinking about this new life, the possibilities that accompany a fresh start in a new place. Maybe we'd left those persistent ghosts at the old address. Maybe our doubts and insecurities were there now with the ratty stove and the uneven kitchen floor and the stained bathtub. I grew hopeful. That hope manifested in the way many strong emotions do in men of my age. My erection was neither irregular nor unnatural. Nor was what I did with it, another perfectly natural act. There was no guilt following that fleeting euphoria. But ten minutes later, when I slid quietly into bed, turning away from what I was certain was my slumbering second wife, her hand settled on my bicep—and not in a "Hey I'm glad you're here now" or "Okay, just confirming you aren't a total stranger crawling into our bed" way. Its soft grip said, "Roll over and put an exclamation point on this day!" And I couldn't. I knew my body and proceeding would have risked a greater embarrassment than I was ready to face. So in the dark I whispered, "My back is killing me. How about a pain check?" This was a failure for many reasons. First, that little joke was a lie. Secondly, it introduced a glib euphemism that got employed countless times by both parties over the years to come. Third—and surely most damning—even though I was pretty sure that I'd be unable to perform, I could have given it a shot.

FOUR

After we came back from Dr. Ghadari, who clasped one of my second wife's hands between his two when he expressed his condolences and reminded her that she still had years left of optimum child-bearing and we could always try again, we found that the central AC unit had died. The air was stale. This was July in Louisiana, so it was stinking hot. Most of the windows, as is the custom there, were painted shut. I found the fan from the old apartment and set it on the coffee table, blowing the stultified air on her where she lay on the couch. She sipped from ice water and said she was fine, that we'd be okay till the repair guy could come take a look the next day. But I said no, that this was insane, and as her knight in shining armor I'd go out and buy a window unit for the bedroom, which wasn't in the budget but budget be damned. "Just stay," she said. "I don't feel like being alone." I told her I wouldn't be long, that I could also pick up some food. She said she wasn't hungry, but I reminded her that at times like this, it was important to keep up our strength. And when I said these things, they were true. It was my intention to drive at unsafe speeds to Home Depot and through the Wendy's drive thru. But what happened, as I wandered through the vertigo-inducing aisles of pvc piping and light fixtures, was that I became fascinated with projects I could do around our home. First I went back for a basket, which I swung from one hand and filled with the basic supplies any man needs: there was a self-retracting tape measure, some superglue, a stud finder, spackle, duct tape. Then I realized I was aiming too small, and I went back for a cart—and I remember this, it had perfect handling, no gimpy wheel. Into the cart I shoved a ceiling fan, a bucket of primer, a security system, grass seed and a spreader. After an hour, I found myself comparing two gutter cleaning systems when I recalled that we didn't have gutters. I hefted the AC unit from the lower rack and walked away, left behind my cart of projects as if I was walking away from the dreams of my youth. I forgot Wendy's. At home, my second wife had retreated to the bedroom and I woke her installing the window unit. "Almost there," I said. "You'll feel better in a minute." She wiped at her eyes—from sleep? From crying? I didn't ask. She glanced at the nightstand clock and asked what'd taken me so long. "There was an accident," I told her. "A pretty bad one."

FIVE

During my cancer scare, I was awake one particular night scanning the internet for information on the possible prognosis. *Unusually aggressive* one website said. *Largely resistant to most treatments.* After an hour of this, I was feeling like anyone else would be feeling—alone and a bit hopeless. My second wife was sleeping upstairs. Without giving it much thought, I googled my first wife's name, just to see where she was in the world. Not because I had secret hopes of contacting her and rekindling our mutually poisonous relationship, but because I missed her. Or rather, I missed the guy I was when I met her. He was less anxious, more joyful, and not awaiting test results. The only hit was her job at the publishing firm. There was a stamp size photo, too small to make out any detail, but she looked good, and an email address, which I clicked on instantly. Twenty minutes of carpal-tunnel inducing typing later, I'd composed a manifesto of my greatest fears, not just that I would die soon but that, in many ways, I was dying already, had been for quite some time. It detailed the deadness inside me, all the anxieties and frailties and even some downright ugliness. Those words were intimate and private and true. As I finished the letter, I realized I was no longer picturing the audience as my first wife, who had chosen another and sent me packing. I was writing for my second, this woman who had picked me even when she knew I was half a basket case. She deserved full disclosure—an opportunity to hear these things and respond. I deleted the email without sending it and made a simple vow: if I don't die, I'll confess it all, to give us both the chance at the lives we're meant to have.

A couple days later when the doctor's assistant called to say that I didn't have Barrett's Syndrome, my second wife and I celebrated with dinner out at the Olive Garden. Over chicken marsala and grilled shrimp salad, we talked about getting a new coat of paint on the guest room, and how the car probably needed an oil change. At a pregnant pause, my wife said, "So really, how are you?" I took a swig of beer for courage, but found I couldn't look her in the face to begin. Really, who wants to admit that they're damaged goods? I shrugged and said, "It's great to be alive."

Six

At the holiday party for the radio station where my second wife worked after the daycare shut down, my attendance at which proves or at least strongly suggests that I was a supportive, good husband, when Rocking Bobby Walker asked me if she was as hot in the sack as she looked, I didn't punch his lights outs. Worse still, I raised my egg nog (perhaps my third) and we clinked glass cups and I said, "She can be kind of kinky." Then I mentioned a specific sexual act that I had read about in a magazine of questionable literary value. This was an act that held no special fascination for me, and one that I doubt my second wife had ever heard of. Maybe I offered it as a way to show how she was with me, that she and I had secrets far beyond what Bobby, or anyone else, could possibly imagine. I wanted to prove, or at least pretend, that we were intimate in a deeply spiritual and physical way. But as Bobby grinned and leered toward her in the corner by the fake tree, I wished I had that line back.

Seven

On Mother's Day, six weeks after the visit to Dr. Ghadari, after a night when my second wife had two glasses of wine but didn't take a bite to eat, when she shook me off when I cupped the phone and asked her if she wanted to say hey to my mom, when she went to bed early without even a book and then later I woke up to the sound of weeping, I rolled over, propped myself on an elbow, and said, "OK, so what did I do now?"

EIGHT

The morning after we first made love, I woke up in the predawn to that warm but empty space next to me in the bed. We'd slept naked, and when I saw the light under the bathroom door, heard the shush of sink water, I couldn't help but picture her in there, bare-skinned and lovely. My mind filled with the pleasant notion of morning after cuddling, which had the potential to evolve into the legendary morning after encore. The night before, we had tangled ourselves together in awkward but tender embraces—taking a wrong turn or two sure—but don't all life's best journeys involve a detour? I was confident that, while our first effort was undeniably a modest success, our second would quickly build on that fine and firm foundation. Imagine my surprise and disappointment then when she emerged not sleepy-eyed and bare but fully dressed, her long hair pulled up in a tight bun. "Hey," she said. "You're up." I felt suddenly foolish, naked as I was, and pulled the sheet up from my waist to my chest. She leaned in, one knee on the mattress, and kissed me—not just a peck. Then she stood and explained that she had to be at work. A few parents dropped their kids off at six, and she had the early shift. She was going to walk the nine blocks to her apartment and "hop in the shower." I swung my legs off the side of the bed and located my underwear. "Hang on," I said. "I'll walk you home." This was not meant as an act of chivalry or one with overt romantic intention. Simply put, given the choice to be alone or extend my time with her by ten minutes, the decision was a no brainer. But as I dressed, I noticed her strange silence. I was tying my first sneaker, genuflecting by the front door, when she settled a hand on my shoulder. "Last night was great," she told me. "Really. And when I'm done with work later, I'll call. But now, I'm going to walk home by myself, okay?" I let the laces fall limp and looked up at her. She went on. "Because as sweet as this is, I want for us to be here again. I want to spend the night here a lot, and if I do, and you start walking me home, then eventually there will come a day when you don't walk me home. I'll be hurt and I'll be angry. I don't want that. So we're not even going to start, okay? I'll call you later."

As I watched her walk down the sidewalk, I remember wondering just how long she'd been awake. This intricate geometric proof she'd worked out seemed infallible. And though I didn't agree at all with her logic, I decided to honor her clear wishes. Instead of escorting her home, I made coffee, wearing just that one sneaker.

I wish I had another shot at that scene. What she didn't know then, what I'm not sure my second wife really understands after all these years of marriage, is that I would have walked her home forever.

NINE

In the parking lot outside Counselor Steve's office, where we always drove separately because she was coming from work, I walked my second wife to her car and we stood there, composing in silence what would be our goodbye scene. I thought of the many times, because of weakness or desire or human frailty, I had failed this good woman, and the weight of it all made it hard for me to breathe. She took one of my hands in each of hers, and it was weird because she'd already fished her keys from her purse, so the spikey points kind of jabbed me in that palm. But her eyes were warm and she nibbled on her bottom lip a bit like she does when she's afraid she might cry, something she hates. She said, "So you're sure this is what you want?"

"No," I declared. And thus I failed her yet again, this time though by telling the absolute truth. "I say fuck Counselor Steve. The thing is, I know how fundamentally flawed our relationship is, how broken we are, how we hurt each other, how we go through cycles. I know how unlikely it is that we'll ever really get it right. But I want to keep trying. I'd rather keep screwing up with you than get it right with somebody else. That's how crazy I'm in love."

She squeezed my hand tightly and drove one of those keys into my flesh, but I didn't let go. She bit down hard on her lip and her eyes went wet and she nodded.

I knew then that we'd drive home together, where I prayed we'd go on failing each other for all the years we had left.

Still

FOR A WHILE NOW, REBECCA'S been awake in the constant darkness. She'd really like to drive back to her own place across town, except she's afraid that if she moves, she might wake Samuel. He would try to convince her to stay, ask if she was all right. Earlier, when she'd begun to cry as they made love, he'd stopped and held her gently. After she'd calmed, Samuel had whispered, "Just tell me," but Rebecca had held her silence.

When her cell phone hums, she stretches for the nightstand, flips it open, and cups it to her cheek. A man from the agency apologizes for waking her, gives her the specifics, then asks if she's available. Rebecca takes a slow breath to settle her heart. She wants to be sure there's no suggestion of her rising thrill, then she says what she always does when the call comes. "On my way."

Slowly, she slides her legs out from under the covers and stands without making a sound, so she's startled when Samuel speaks. "That's the second one this month."

It's the third late night call, Rebecca thinks. She doesn't sleep at his place more than a couple times a week. Plus there were the ones scheduled ahead of time, during the day. Rebecca doesn't always tell him about those appointments, one of which she has tomorrow afternoon down in Carlisle. "Sorry it woke you."

She steps into her jeans, hitches them up, then gropes for her bra in the dark.

"Can't this wait?" he asks. "Won't they still be dead in a few hours?"

In the blackness, she stiffens. Samuel seems to sense this. He says, "That was a shitty thing to say. I'm just kind of rattled by what happened before. I'm worried about you."

"Go back to sleep," she tells him.

"How about I drive you?" he asks.

On her knees, Rebecca sweeps the carpet with her hands, finally finding both socks.

Samuel says, "We'll get breakfast afterwards. It'd be good to talk."

With a snap, the room illuminates, and she stands and sees Samuel, one hand on the lamp's base. He turns to her with a face so alert, she has to wonder now if he too was wide awake in the darkness before the call.

She sits on the side of the bed and slides on her sneakers. Behind her, Samuel says, "Becky. Look at me."

She stands. "I need to go now. I don't have my gear."

This is a lie. In the trunk of her car out in the parking lot of Samuel's apartment is a black backpack, and inside is one of her many cameras. To placate Samuel, she comes around the bed and plants a kiss on his cheek. "Don't worry about before. That was me, okay?"

"How about I come over for lunch? I'll bring something wonderful."

At the bedroom door, Rebecca bends for her purse. "Fine." She hears the sharpness in her tone and pauses, one hand on the door latch.

240

Behind her Samuel says, "Becky, I just want you to let me in, okay?"

Rebecca looks over her shoulder at her lover. She summons a tight smile, and then she's gone.

The couple have been seeing each other off and on for just over a year. Last month, after dinner at Dockside Willie's, they strolled across the walking bridge that spans the Susquehanna River. Midway, Samuel stopped and asked Rebecca if she ever thought of getting married again. With two hands on the rail, she'd said, "I think that'd be a big change."

Rebecca strides into the maternity ward at St. Joseph's of Hershey, which is not just modern but futuristic. In the delivery rooms, all the medical equipment can be hidden behind paintings. The floor is quiet at this hour, only a few folks shuffling around, and those that notice Rebecca make only fleeting eye contact. Just as she's reaching room 313, she hears the certain sign that she's arrived at the right place— weeping from within.

Rebecca enters the scene she's witnessed dozens of times since becoming a volunteer at the agency. The players are known to her. The cross-armed man at the window is the father. At the bedside (where other times there's a sister/aunt) stands a crying grandmother who would collapse if she weren't leaning into the guardrail. Across from her is the hospital counselor, in this version a nun Rebecca has met before named Sister Helen. On the bed, puffy and bleary-eyed, hair matted to her head, visibly exhausted beyond words, is the mother. And in her arms, swaddled like some typical newborn, is the child.

Sister Helen hands Rebecca a form with some minimal contact information, and then turns. "Gail," she says, startling the mother. "This is Rebecca. Rebecca who we talked about earlier."

The mother doesn't take her eyes off her child, but she nods. The grandmother releases her grip on the guardrail and slips silently from the room. At the window, the father glances Rebecca's way, then turns back to the dark window.

Rebecca sets her backpack down and pulls out the Canon she used for years at weddings. Given the lighting, she'd rather have the Nikon she prefers for portraits, but in this circumstance a tripod would be awkward. Without speaking, without offering condolences of any kind, she positions herself up behind the mother's shoulder, so she can look down on the infant's face. The child is still and its bruised skin is purple-grey. A pink headband stretches across its forehead.

Rebecca is too late for what she needs, but still, this is very good.

She squints her left eye as she brings the camera to her right. Her finger taps twice to zoom in, filling the view with the child's face, then she gauges the light, decides to go without a flash. Adjusting her angle slightly each time, she snaps a dozen shots. Then she pulls back a bit, to bring the swaddled body into the frame. This also provides a nice contrast in textures between the child's skin and the baby blanket, which like the headband is gaudy pink. Rebecca takes another round of pictures, each click like a hammer strike in this silent room. From experience, she's trained herself to get the stock shots first, the ones the parents will see. It's such a temptation to begin with the ones that matter, but she's patient. They come as a reward.

The mother says, "That's enough, okay?" She sniffles.

"Just a few more," Rebecca tells her, these the first words she's spoken. Rebecca lowers the guardrail and kneels, bringing the newborn's face into profile. It's like a lunar landscape now, rolling grey hills, an outcropping by the eyebrow, the nostrils small caves. She's zoomed in on a ruptured vein, forking like lightning from under the headband, and Rebecca imagines how not long ago, it pulsed with blood. She snaps some shots and the mother asks, "Can you please be finished now?"

Rebecca nods but reaches in to peel back the frilly headband. "Almost done."

"Just what the hell are you doing?" the father says. He stands now on the other side of the bed. The mother starts to sob. Sister Helen squeezes Rebecca's shoulder and she stands, holding her camera with both hands.

The nun says, "You should sit, David. It's all right Gail. Rebecca is all finished now." With her hand still on Rebecca's shoulder, Sister Helen guides her to the door, where she turns. Sister Helen's eyes lock onto hers, and without making a sound, she mouths the word, "Go."

Over the nun's shoulder, Rebecca sees the father. He says, "My daughter's name. It's Andrea." He looks not sad but furious, as if he's about to burst into flame, transform into something dangerous and dreadful. Rebecca fights the urge to lift the camera and take his picture.

Later that morning, Rebecca is in the farmhouse she renovated on the outskirts of Mechanicsburg. She sits at her computer, finally able to work on the photos from St. Joe's. The agency's goal is that the photos be emailed within twenty-four hours, one set clearly marked *original* and one marked *modified*. By modified they mean retouched, which means Rebecca uses Photoshop to add gauzy colors, to restore the glow of life with flesh tones and soft peaches. She reddens lips and rouges cheeks. Though she is skilled at this process, she hates doing it. No matter how much she plays with the image, the retouched ones always look like what they are: false.

She's thought about Andrea's pictures all morning, while touring possible venues with Kelly and Randy, a bubbling bride and groom to be who held hands and giggled. They couldn't decide between the sweeping trees along Willow Park, the outlook at Negley, or inside the barn behind Rebecca's farmhouse, which leans at a severe angle but has an uncanny rustic charm. Finally, Rebecca told them they could keep an eye on the weather and make a choice closer to the day of the wedding. And here she imagined Randy in a tux, Kelly in a white gown, and both of them standing in a downpour. That would be a picture worth taking.

At every wedding, Rebecca takes at least ten photos she knows she'll never show to the clients. She'll catch the priest checking his watch, or note the scab on the mother of the bride's neck, or the tiny rip in the veil, and she can't resist snapping a quick shot. Taking all the standard poses, the father/daughter dance, the wedding party picture, the couple gazing lovingly into each other's eyes, all of this Rebecca deplores. She recognizes such things as necessary to her employment but the artist in her knows they are staged and phony. Even some that are unconventional—the sixty-year old woman catching the garter, the barefoot flower girl asleep under the head table—she knows these rely on cuteness and sentimentality, not the artist's eye. With these, she knows she's not capturing the truth.

Sitting now before her computer screen, studying Andrea's unre-touched face in repose, she feels close. Only this subject matter truly calls to her now. She can sense that what she seeks is near.

Her phone rings and Rebecca sees that again, it is Virginia, the agency's director. First thing this morning, she left a message, and later sent a text, asking Rebecca to call her. There was also an email, more insistent. Two months ago, Virginia invited Rebecca to lunch, complimented her efforts. She talked about what challenging volunteer work this was and its unique psychological stress. Virginia reminded Rebecca of the available counselors. There had been a complaint that Rebecca wasn't sensitive to the needs of a particular grieving family. Someone claimed they saw her smiling.

The phone stops ringing, and Rebecca wonders what Sister Helen told Virginia. As she's contemplating this, the front door opens and closes, making the charming bell ding once. She reaches for the mouse to save her work.

In the oversized living room, she finds a man in his late thirties, about her age, staring absently at a wall of her "best" work: giddy bridesmaids crammed in a limousine, a golden-haired ring bearer, a healthy newborn's pudgy fist nestled in its mother's palm. "Can I help you?" she asks.

"Yes," he says. "Or at least, I'm hoping so." Awkwardly he extends a hand and they shake. "I'm Rick Pressler."

"Rebecca Miles."

Rick releases his sweaty grip, looks sheepish. "I know," he tells her. "We've met." Rebecca cocks her head, trying to place his face, and he says, "Last fall. Harrisburg Osteopathic. My daughter's name was Holly."

Rebecca takes a full step backward. Her mind flashes with a black and white overhead shot. Though she didn't make it to full term, Holly had a thick head of dark hair. Rebecca pushes the image away and says, "Mr. Pressler. How can I . . . What brings you here today?"

He rubs his palms together, and she notices a small patch of coarse hair on his throat, a shaving oversight. "I'm sorry," he says. "Could I trouble you for a glass of water?"

When Rebecca returns, carrying a bottled water, she finds Rick sitting on the couch leaning over the coffee table where wedding magazines and photography books are spread. He takes the bottled water and unscrews the top. But then he doesn't drink, instead just setting it on the table. "I'm just wondering, do you keep copies?"

Rebecca eases herself down next to him, one cushion away, crosses her hands on her lap, and shakes her head. "The agency has very clear policies. Everything is deleted. That's all spelled out in the agreement."

"I see," he says. Now he takes a drink. "And you don't have a backup of any kind?"

"I'm sorry," she says.

"You sent us a compact disc. I remember that. But there was an email too, right? One with attachments?"

Rebecca asks, "What happened, Mr. Pressler?"

"Rick," he says. "A lot, actually. Me and Erica—that's my wife— we're not living together right now. Haven't been for a while." Saying this takes some effort, and he tilts the water bottle to his mouth, as if to wash out the taste of the words.

Rebecca can sense the pain of his suffering. Here is a man who went from husband to bachelor, from father to nonparent. She feels herself shifting on the couch and sees her hand floating to Rick's thigh. Beneath the khakis, the muscle is thick. "I went through a divorce about ten years ago," she says. "I know it can be bad."

"A rough one?" Rick asks. He doesn't look at her hand.

"Pretty rough."

Rick nods. "Anyway. Erica was always looking at those photos on the laptop. I'd find her in there late at night, or first thing in the morning, or the middle of a Sunday. She was obsessed with what happened. To be honest, I couldn't bear it. Any of it. But since we split, I've been getting some help. Turns out I didn't deal with my emotions about Holly. And what doesn't get dealt with just gets buried. So says my shrink."

In her own therapy sessions, years ago, Rebecca heard much the same thing.

Rick says, "So lately, I've really been wanting to see Holly's face. And since Erica and I aren't on speaking terms . . . "

"I understand," Rebecca says. "That's where I come in."

Rick manages a smile. "You know, even when you delete an email, a copy is still in your system. You've got to empty out the trash. And then sometimes—"

Rebecca lets go of his thigh and reaches for a drawer in the coffee table, from which she pulls a pen and some post it notes. "Give me your information here, and I'll look around when I have a chance. If I find anything, I'll get back to you."

Rick grins, then scribbles out two phone numbers, his email, his physical address. "You're very kind," he says, rising up and handing her the slip of paper. She stands with him and they face each other, still. They are quiet together, and he lurches forward so suddenly that she barely has time to open her arms and accept the embrace. He hugs her gently, then steps back. For an instant, Rebecca glances at his lips, almost expecting him to kiss her. But then he sets the pen down on the coffee table and walks away without saying anything else.

After Rick has left, Rebecca returns to her computer. She scrolls and clicks, enters a password, then clicks again. The screen fills with the image of Holly Pressler, one of her very best. The shot begins at her waist and she is shirtless, a plump infant with stony grey flesh. Her face is tilted to one side, as if in slumber, and her arms are bent, one fist under her chin, one hand alongside her head. The fingers of that hand are open, in a pose that's always made Rebecca think of benediction. It's like the child is bestowing a blessing.

With noon approaching, Rebecca calls Samuel at his catering business. "Listen," she says. "I can't do that lunch thing. I'm swamped. I could meet you at Pesto's for a drink around eight maybe."

Samuel is silent. She hears chopping in the background. "No good," Samuel says. "I've got that rotary club banquet at six. You knew about that."

"I did," she says. "I forgot. Don't be so tense."

The chopping stops. "I am tense. I thought you might at least call me this morning. I'm sorry but I'd like to know where I stand. I love you and don't understand what's going on."

Rebecca stares at the blank computer screen, then out into her empty studio. "Someone's here," she says. "I need to go."

"I could sneak out now," he says. "We could just talk."

"I have an appointment."

"Then I'll drop off some early dinner," he tells her. "I'll stay for a little bit."

"I don't think I'll be hungry."

"One of those turkey and avocado wraps," he says. "You have to eat."

She raises her voice. "I'll be right with you." Then in a hush she tells Samuel, "I have a client."

"Okay," Samuel says. "If you change your mind about the turkey, just text me. And tonight, if you want, let yourself in. It'd be nice to come home to you."

After she hangs up, she wonders what Samuel would say about Rick

Pressler. Samuel is a good, sweet man, uncomplicated. She first saw him catering a wedding she was shooting, and she watched him at work, carrying out plates for the bride and groom, inspecting individual strawberries dipped in chocolate, spying on the guests enjoying his food.

Rebecca finds him naïve and hopeful, which surprises her considering how his first marriage ended. On the night they first made love, they went to his kitchen afterward and he made Rebecca an ice cream sundae. Very casually, he told her about how his wife had cheated on him with his former business partner, how foolish he felt, how for a year his senses dulled and his world went dead. Rebecca's pulse quickened. Her marriage had also ended in betrayal, a fact she's never told anyone. And in part it's the shame of the betrayal, yes, but more so, Rebecca can't come to terms with the truth of what she failed to see. She's convinced there must have been a moment when her husband's heart had turned, a singular instant when he went from lover to betrayer, from husband to adulterer. After her husband told her about the other woman, Rebecca searched her own feelings and was shocked to find that she too was simply no longer in love. At some unseen turn in their history, she had changed as well. She marveled at how the passion she'd burn with could die down and become this simmering ash.

When people ask her why she volunteers at the agency, as Samuel did on one of their first dates, she tells them she likes to help people in need, and this perhaps is true. But Rebecca can't deny there is something larger at work, something unnamable and profound. Part of it, she thinks, is the purity of the image, the certainty of death, the utter wrongness of a newborn child. There is no ambiguity in such a thing. It is an absolute truth.

It is her search for this that finds her driving down 81 toward Carlisle late in the afternoon. The day filled with other meetings and work, but Rebecca was preoccupied with this appointment. In her earliest months with the agency, these scheduled shoots disturbed her to the point where her hands trembled. The heartbreak of parents deciding that all measures had been taken, that now they would remove the wires and tubes and wait for the inevitable—it's almost too much to contemplate. Yet it makes sense that parents would want a picture of their child free from the machine, but still alive. Those few hours, sometimes just a handful of minutes, seem so sacred and precious. Rebecca is surprised anyone would want to share them with a photographer. But secretly now, she's grateful for these rare opportunities. Because it's here she has the best chance to witness the ultimate truth, the twilight moment when life surrenders to death.

She recognizes it as an obscene hope, this perverse fantasy that she'll be in the room when a child passes. But deep in the recesses of her soul, Rebecca yearns to capture the instant of transformation. How is it even possible, she wonders, for something to change that much—to go from a child to a corpse? These impossible moments of transition, when a soul slides from loyal to unfaithful, when a heart is cherished, then rejected, they haunt Rebecca.

When the elevator doors split open on the fourth floor of Carlisle Medical, Rebecca is surprised to see Virginia. A tall woman with short grey hair, she's standing by the nurses' station, an oversized bag slung over her shoulder. Virginia sees Rebecca at the same moment and walks toward her. They meet at a window that overlooks the parking lot, and Virginia says, "I wish you'd have called me back."

"It's been a crazy busy day. What're you doing here?"

"I'm waiting for the Hendersons. You need to go home and call me later."

"I'm not going to call you later. You're going to tell me what's going on."

Virginia glances back toward the nurses' station, and Rebecca sees two women staring her way. Virginia says, "I spoke with Sister Helen. It's time to take a step back a bit, get some perspective."

"This sounds like we're breaking up. Are we breaking up, Virginia?"

"Be professional, Rebecca. Helen said you touched the child. Something about a headband?"

Rebecca barely hears what's being said. She feels rage at the idea that she won't be allowed into the room. "So cutting me off like this, this is professional? If you knew how close I was, you'd never do this to me."

Virginia rears her head back and her eyebrows bunch together. "How close you are? Close to what?"

There's a rush of activity at the nurses' station, and both women turn. Three figures, heads bent, hustle down the hall. Virginia says, "I need to get focused for the Hendersons. I'm sorry for whatever's going on in your world, but right now, you can't be part of this. Go home."

But Rebecca doesn't want to go home, so for a time she simply drives around country roads, down to Boiling Springs, up through Dillsburg. She passes the cemetery where both her parents are buried, the church where she prayed when she was a child, even the home she owned with her ex. The new owners chopped down the pine tree but left the stump.

When she finally returns to her farmhouse, the moon is out. A cooler bag waits on her stoop. Inside she finds a turkey wrap, along with a bottle of her favorite pinot noir and a note that reads, "Let's share this late tonight?" She carries the bag into her kitchen and uncorks the bottle, but doesn't touch the sandwich.

She locks the front door, pulls the shades, and sits at her desk with a tall glass of wine. On her oversized computer screen, she navigates the mouse, enters the password, and opens the file. In an instant, they are there with her, the dozens of faces closed to this life, still. She clicks on each one individually, scrutinizes the veined and blotchy skin, the closed eyes, the pressed lips, the half moons at the base of the immaculate fingernails. But the thing she searches for eludes her. When she arrives at the photograph of Holly Pressler, she finds herself reaching unexpectedly for a compact disc.

An hour later, mildly intoxicated, she pulls up in front of his apartment building on the West Shore. Rick takes a minute to answer the door, and when he opens it, his eyes go wide with surprise. Behind him the TV is on, and Rebecca hears a sports announcer. "It's late," Rick finally says, stepping back anxiously. "Come in."

Rebecca lets the door close behind her. She lifts her hand, holding the compact disc in a white sleeve. "I'm trusting you Rick. This could make real trouble for me."

He stares for a moment before reaching for it. He takes the disc gently, pinching it, almost like he's afraid it might burn. Then he says, "I don't really understand. But that doesn't matter. Thank you."

Rick hesitates then turns and walks away, and she follows him into the kitchenette, uninvited. A laptop sits on the cheap table covered with paperwork. She takes a seat across from Rick so she can watch his face. Driving over, she imagined the way he would have to compose himself before looking, and the way his expression would disintegrate from calmness to a sorrow beyond measure. The idea of witnessing

252

this stirs something in Rebecca, something not unlike arousal. Sitting here now, her hands take shape as if holding her camera.

But after Rick slides the disc in the side slot, his face remains unchanged. He just stares. Confused, Rebecca comes around the table and sees the box on the screen asking, "Would you like to Open these files?"

"Click yes," she says.

When he doesn't, she reaches for the mouse, setting one hand on his shoulder for balance. He says, "No" and closes the laptop hard.

Rebecca squeezes the tense muscles of his shoulder. She says, "It's important for you to look."

"I'll look later," he tells her. "I'll look when I'm alone."

He gets up and Rebecca moves into him, close enough that their chests are touching. She fixes her eyes on his, wets her lips, and eases one hand onto his hip.

Rick says, "What do you think is going to happen here?"

Rebecca whispers, "We could decide that."

He cups her shoulders and shoves her, hard enough that she bangs into a wall. A framed photo drops to the floor and glass shatters. Rick shakes his head and says, "You'd better leave. Christ Jesus. What kind of woman are you?"

Inside her darkened farmhouse, Rebecca goes back to work on that bottle of wine, now in earnest. Rick's question has burrowed into her, and she's not liking the answers she's coming up with. She's not sure why she did what she did. Sitting in the glow of her computer screen, wine glass at her side, she considers her quest for the absolute truth and what it's led her to become, her own transformation.

Taking a breath, like a diver about to plunge from a cliff, she opens the file and starts with the first image, a child named Nathan from nearly two years ago. She activates the slideshow feature, and each portrait fades away to darkness, then another rises up from the pitch. With each child's closed face, she winces. She does not turn away, trying to honor just what it is she's looking at, the trampled hope of a new life, the extinguished potential, the infinite moments of pain and joy that should have been. As the slideshow loops around and the faces parade past again and again, she does not find the thing she thinks she needs. And she accepts it is not here.

She sees her hand drift on its own up to the mouse. At the main menu, she clicks on the folder and drags it to the trash, and when the computer asks if she's sure she wants to delete the contents, she hits "yes."

Close to midnight, she quietly inserts her key into Samuel's front door. She slips inside his kitchen, slides off her sneakers, and pads down the carpeted hallway in her socks. His bedroom door doesn't squeak. Inside, the ceiling fan churns the air. She stands at the foot of the bed, and as her eyes adjust she makes out his shadowy form. Lifting the camera hung around her neck, she raises it up to her face, then closes her left eye. Rebecca carefully positions her right eye into the viewfinder's slot, then she taps the button to engage the night vision.

Before her is this man, still but alive, curled in a fetal tuck. He is shirtless with the sheet drawn only to his waist, so she can see his chest rise and fall with each breath. She can see his unruly hair and the curve of his neck and his mouth, slightly open. Rebecca knows she could remove her clothes, spoon in beside him and lose herself in the rush of unexpected sex. But Rebecca remains standing at the foot of the bed, poised.

She remembers last night, when she'd felt Samuel tremble in her arms, when he'd whispered his love and she'd opened herself to it, like an aperture trying to let in light. It was then that she felt the metamorphosis, the shift from joy to ecstasy, flesh transforming to bright energy. It had been too much, and she couldn't stop the tears.

Rebecca knows that if Samuel awakens to her, he will be pleased. She does not doubt this man's good heart. She settles the camera a bit deeper into her face, and anticipates what's to come. She will say his name. His eyes will blink and widen, and he'll go from sleeping to awake. His mouth will stretch into a smile as he slides from surprise to delight. And she will capture it, this perfect transmutation, the alchemy of love, and this too might be something true.

About Fomite

A fomite is a medium capable of transmitting infectious organisms from one individual to another.

"The activity of art is based on the capacity of people to be infected by the feelings of others." Tolstoy, *What Is Art?*

Writing a review on Amazon, Good Reads, Shelfari, Library Thing or other social media sites for readers will help the progress of independent publishing. To submit a review, go to the book page on any of the sites and follow the links for reviews. Books from independent presses rely on reader to reader communications.

For more information or to order any of our books, visit
http://www.fomitepress.com/FOMITE/Our_Books.html

More Titles from Fomite...

Novels

Joshua Amses — *During This, Our Nadir*
Joshua Amses — *Raven or Crow*
Joshua Amses — *The Moment Before an Injury*
Jaysinh Birjepatel — *The Good Muslim of Jackson Heights*
Jaysinh Birjepatel — *Nothing Beside Remains*
David Brizer — *Victor Rand*
Paula Closson Buck — *Summer on the Cold War Planet*
Marc Estrin — *Hyde*
Marc Estrin — *Speckled Vanitie*
Zdravka Evtimova — *Sinfonia Bulgarica*
Daniel Forbes — *Derail This Train Wreck*
Greg Guma — *Dons of Time*
Richard Hawley — *The Three Lives of Jonathan Force*
Lamar Herrin — *Father Figure*
Ron Jacobs — *All the Sinners Saints*

Fomite

Ron Jacobs — *Short Order Frame Up*
Ron Jacobs — *The Co-conspirator's Tale*
Scott Archer Jones — *A Rising Tide of People Swept Away*
Maggie Kast — *A Free Unsullied Land*
Darrell Kastin — *Shadowboxing with Bukowski*
Coleen Kearon — *Feminist on Fire*
Jan Englis Leary — *Thicker Than Blood*
Diane Lefer — *Confessions of a Carnivore*
Rob Lenihan — *Born Speaking Lies*
Ilan Mochari — *Zinsky the Obscure*
Andy Potok — *My Father's Keeper*
Robert Rosenberg — *Isles of the Blind*
Fred Skolnik — *Rafi's World*
Lynn Sloan — *Principles of Navigation*
L.E. Smith — *The Consequence of Gesture*
L.E. Smith — *Travers' Inferno*
Bob Sommer — *A Great Fullness*
Tom Walker — *A Day in the Life*
Susan V. Weiss —*My God, What Have We Done?*
Peter M. Wheelwright — *As It Is On Earth*
Suzie Wizowaty — *The Return of Jason Green*

Poetry

Antonello Borra — *Alfabestiario*
Antonello Borra — *AlphaBetaBestiaro*
James Connolly — *Picking Up the Bodies*
Greg Delanty — *Loosestrife*
Mason Drukman — *Drawing on Life*
J. C. Ellefson — *Foreign Tales of Exemplum and Woe*
Anna Faktorovich — *Improvisational Arguments*
Barry Goldensohn — *Snake in the Spine, Wolf in the Heart*
Barry Goldensohn — *The Hundred Yard Dash Man*
Barry Goldensohn — *The Listener Aspires to the Condition of Music*
R. L. Green When — *You Remember Deir Yassin*
Kate Magill — *Roadworthy Creature, Roadworthy Craft*
Tony Magistrale — *Entanglements*

Fomite

Stories

Fomite

40105573R00163

Made in the USA
Middletown, DE
03 February 2017